"You're crying."

Blinking, Ediva lifted one small hand to her cheek.

Adrien sat down beside her. He took up her hand and held it quietly. "I have seen you on the parapet. You'd mentioned that you dreamed of running away."

"I thought about escaping to the forest. I wondered how long I could survive there."

"Why didn't you try?"

She looked at him, her eyes softened by tears. "If I left, my husband would have turned his rage on my people."

"Ganute is gone, Ediva." Adrien squeezed her hand firmly. "He can't hurt you anymore."

"And you, Adrien? You're a soldier, with violence in your blood."

'Twas true. In the past, he'd justified his nature and work well enough and not given it another thought.

Until now, sitting beside Ediva with her questioning eyes and her pain so deep he feared no one could heal her.

At a loss, all he could do was lift her hand to his lips and kiss it.

Books by Barbara Phinney

Love Inspired Historical

Bound to the Warrior

Love Inspired Suspense

Desperate Rescue
Keeping Her Safe
Deadly Homecoming
Fatal Secrets
Silent Protector

BARBARA PHINNEY

was born in England and raised in Canada. She has traveled throughout her life, loving to explore the various countries and cultures of the world. After she retired from the Canadian Armed Forces, Barbara turned her hand to romance writing. The thrill of adventure and the love of happy endings, coupled with a too-active imagination, have merged to help her create this and other wonderful stories. Barbara spends her days writing, building her dream home with her husband and enjoying their fast-growing children.

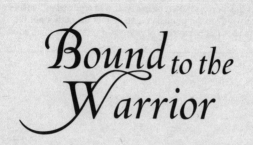

Bound to the Warrior

BARBARA PHINNEY

⬥ **HARLEQUIN**® LOVE INSPIRED® HISTORICAL

If you purchased this book without a cover you should be aware
that this book is stolen property. It was reported as "unsold and
destroyed" to the publisher, and neither the author nor the
publisher has received any payment for this "stripped book."

Recycling programs
for this product may
not exist in your area.

™ LOVE INSPIRED BOOKS

ISBN-13: 978-0-373-82958-3

BOUND TO THE WARRIOR

Copyright © 2013 by Barbara Phinney

All rights reserved. Except for use in any review, the reproduction
or utilization of this work in whole or in part in any form by any
electronic, mechanical or other means, now known or hereafter
invented, including xerography, photocopying and recording, or in
any information storage or retrieval system, is forbidden without
the written permission of the editorial office, Love Inspired Books,
233 Broadway, New York, NY 10279 U.S.A.

This is a work of fiction. Names, characters, places and incidents are
either the product of the author's imagination or are used fictitiously, and
any resemblance to actual persons, living or dead, business establishments,
events or locales is entirely coincidental.

This edition published by arrangement with Love Inspired Books.

® and TM are trademarks of Love Inspired Books, used under license.
Trademarks indicated with ® are registered in the United States Patent
and Trademark Office, the Canadian Trade Marks Office and in other
countries.

www.LoveInspiredBooks.com

Printed in U.S.A.

Whoever does not love does not know God,
because God is love.
—*1 John* 4:8

To my writer friends, the Domino Divas, and all the Love Inspired authors. Thank you for your support and encouragement. This book is for you.

Prologue

November 1066 A.D.

Ediva Dunmow had been told she was blessed to have her husband's body returned. For at Duke William's order, the English who'd died at Hastings were to remain on Senlac Hill.

But the only reason she had sent Geoffrey, her steward, for the body was to prove the vile man had actually died.

Now, as she stood over her husband's grave, the wind turned raw and rain threatened. The villagers and tenants had just paid their last respects to their fallen lord and then gathered to hear her speak. Anxious for security, they needed to know that Duke William's army wouldn't ride into Essex to kill them all, a punishment perhaps for Ediva retrieving Ganute's body.

And perhaps they, too, needed to know that Ganute was truly dead and gone. He may have reserved a special brutality for Ediva, but he'd been cruel to all. And his cousin Olin, now standing beside her, showed hints of the same temper.

Enough was enough.

Stiff-shouldered, Ediva lifted her hand and the mur-

murings fell silent. Her veil and long, blond braids billowed in the strong breeze, as did her cloak. But she stood
resolute, refusing the wind its due. "*I* will protect you. I
will allow no one—not even Duke William himself—to
plunder this land."

Cold, chapped faces showed disbelief like the trees
showed bare branches.

"*I will!*" She pulled in a breath, and then, finding her
cloak cumbersome, threw it off. It sailed off like a crispy
leaf, and with a cry, Margaret, her maid, rushed to retrieve it.

"How can *you* keep us safe?" a male voice from deep
in the crowd called out.

"Have I not survived all these years?" She shot the
chaplain a biting glance, but from where he stood within
the keep's shadow this short, raw day, his expression was
hidden from view.

He'd often said 'twas her penance to endure a harsh husband, for she was a sinful woman. Well, that ability would
prove to be her strength. She knew how to survive. She'd
kept herself alive through all the abuses of her husband and
had protected the maids from similar attacks in her stead.
And now that Ganute was gone? *She'd cower no longer.*

Ediva faced her people. They dared not believe her yet.
But that would change. "I promise that I *will* protect you.
You won't be hurt in any way, even if it costs me my life!"

Some of the more superstitious gasped, but Ediva ignored them. She may be tempting God, but frankly, what
could He do to her that was more horrible than all she'd
endured these past five years?

Nay, she refused to temper her words. She *would* protect her people. "Think of what I had done when your lord
was alive!"

When several women began to cheer, her decision, like her newborn will, was mortared in place.

Aye, she would always protect her people.

Chapter One

March, 1067 A.D.

Adrien de Ries paced in front of the closed door that led to his liege's Great Hall. He did not like waiting, even for the king, but if William was conferring with his advisors on matters of this new kingdom of England, then Adrien must wait. He was a soldier, not a statesman—there was naught he could do to aid the discussion or hurry it along.

"'Tis too fine a floor to wear a path through, *Prado*. Sit or you'll be buying the king a new one."

At the sound of his childhood name, Adrien spun to face his younger brother. Eudo, William's personal steward, usually had the king's ear, but not today. Yet having more of a talent for diplomacy than Adrien, the younger sibling wisely patted the low bench beside him and ignored his brother's foul expression.

Adrien refused the offer of a seat. "Why should the king ask for me? Have I not served him well, here in London as well as in battle?"

Eudo shrugged. "Mayhap he wishes to reward you, brother. The king wants to secure this land. He has won it with bloodshed, but trust me, William wants peace. He might offer you a share of that peace in the form of lands or titles."

"I need only to serve as a soldier. William understands such. He's a warrior—"

Beyond the heavy door, they heard a woman's muted cry, not one of fear, but something akin to mockery. Immediately, the king's voice boomed, harsh and angry. Adrien glanced at his brother, who shrugged again.

"Is that a woman in there?" Adrien demanded, pointing to the door.

"Aye, but have no fear, *Prado,* she'll not be harmed."

Disgruntled, Adrien turned from his youngest sibling. Eudes, or Eudo as he preferred to be called, was not the guileless simpleton he was pretending to be. He'd deflected the king's murderous punch once, holding the royal fist at bay and whispering in the royal ear long enough and well enough to save a man's life and secure the post of steward for himself. And in that post, he was always certain to know everything occurring at court. Aye, Eudo would know who was receiving the king's fury but obviously cared little for it.

The doors flew open and Adrien turned. Aubrey de Veres, one of the king's most trusted advisors, motioned for Adrien to enter.

With a wary eye, he stepped forward to peer beyond the threshold. Within the richly decorated inner chamber, William sat in a large, comfortable chair, his embroidered surcoat draped over one side. His meaty fists gripped the ends of the chair's arms. A dark expression burned on his face.

To Adrien's right stood a young woman, face flaming, eyes burning a hole in the carpet below the king's dais. Weak, winter light from the high windows washed her light-colored cyrtel in a pale gold. Her cloak was thrown back and he was surprised to see she had allowed her pale yellow wimple to fall away from her braided hair.

Thanks to fashion and good Norman propriety, Adrien rarely saw women's hair and found himself staring hard at her golden locks. All of his family had dark brown hair, the color of walnuts after they'd been hit by frost. This woman's blond tresses were truly her crowning glory. Several other men in the room stared also, yet she appeared to ignore her hair's beauty and its effect on those around her.

"Adrien, my faithful servant," William barked after allowing him to bow his respect at the open doorway. "Enter. You, too, Eudo. I want you both."

Cautiously, Adrien stepped closer. William chuckled. "You have served me well, Adrien."

"I've tried, my liege."

"True. Especially at Hastings." William waved Eudo closer. "Eudo, my steward, come to my side."

Adrien watched his younger brother move to stand at William's left, as was his place. Adrien noticed that his brother shot the woman in front of the king a curious, furtive look with more than idle interest in his eyes.

Immediately, Adrien's suspicion swelled. His younger brother *did* know the reason for this audience. He was sure of it.

"England is a good land, Adrien. Don't you agree?"

"'Tis pleasant here, sire." *But 'twould be more pleasant to leave the place behind.* Since Hastings, Adrien had spent the winter in London, continuing his service in Westminster out of loyalty to the king, but little affection had blossomed in his heart for the conquered land. He had no desire to enjoy the green countryside and certainly not another raw winter like they'd just endured. His life was to protect the king. Rumor had it that William planned to return to Normandy, and Adrien hoped that he'd be chosen to accompany him and leave this land for good.

"And whilst England is pleasant to look upon, there is little peace," William continued.

Adrien straightened. "Nay, sire." Surely the king did not ask him here for idle talk? As everyone knew, there was little peace indeed, except in London, where the troops forced it upon the locals.

"The land is rife with those foolish enough to oppose me."

Beside him, Adrien watched the young woman stiffen. From the corner of his eye, he saw her shoulders pull back, her chin jut out. The torch above the king glowed upon her flushed cheeks.

"Peace will be had, Adrien," William carried on with a fast glance to her. "But I would prefer it not by further bloodshed. I've proved my right to the crown and will subdue this lawless land through direct measures with every lord and lady. I will raze the holdings of those who oppose me and leave the land of those who don't. But to kill everyone would be a fruitless endeavor."

Adrien silently agreed. Though a soldier and loyal to the king, Adrien knew their Lord and Savior wanted peace in *all* lands. Respecting the lands of those willing to pledge loyalty to the king would do much to smooth the path to peace. Saxons who would battle against pillagers might give way to a king who honored their holdings.

For himself, Adrien had no taste for pillage. The spoils of war belonged to the king, and the men under Adrien's command knew they'd have to face him first if they decided to steal from the conquered.

William was a God-fearing man, but feared *only* God, many whispered. "So, I must secure my hold with my most loyal subjects in strategic places," William continued, "with soldiers to keep the peace."

Adrien beamed. He would go wherever his liege sent him, but William wanted him out on the front lines. Aye. 'Twas far better than the fate Eudo would probably receive. Many men were being ordered to marry Saxon noblewomen, whereas he, Adrien noted to himself, would be sent to where soldiers, not husbands, were needed.

Thanks be that that was not his fate. Nay, marriage made no sense to Adrien. The Good Lord had given him a fighting heart, not a family one and he did not mourn its absence. All a family heart was good for was to create loyal followers. A man should not be required to marry himself to some fool woman whose emotions were as scattered as the old king's army when Harold had died...

William waved to him. "Come closer. I have a gift for you."

Beside Adrien, the young woman's head shot up, her shocked expression bouncing off the well-pleased king to hit Adrien. When he locked gazes with her, she tore her sky blue eyes free to look to the distant end of the Great Hall. Yet even with her face averted, he could see that fury billowed from her like smoke from a soggy campfire.

What did this mean? Was this woman some captured rebel? Many a widow or daughter of a dead soldier kept up the fool fight against William, and Adrien had heard they lost their lands and more as punishment.

"You are a loyal soldier, Adrien."

He tore his attention away from the furious beauty. "Thank you, sire."

A smug look grew on the king's fleshy face. "My reward to you, then." He held out his arm toward the woman.

"Are you giving me her lands?" He was a soldier, not some guardian to lord over her property because she refused to hand it over to her rightful king. What was he to do with it? He was no farmer.

The king laughed heartily, as did Eudo. Adrien shot a filthy look toward his brother. But the younger sibling grinned back with cheek.

"More than land, Adrien. *Baron* Adrien," the king offered, his voice booming as his arm slashed across the cool air of the hall. To his left, one of the torches flickered with the breeze. "I'm giving *her* to you. Marry her, take her back to her keep and give me strong babes that look like you. All the whilst controlling her lands and servants."

Horror drained Adrien's being of all but shock. "Sire, I have no experience running a town or a keep."

"But you have experience training soldiers. You can start training this woman, for she has defied me more than once in the short time she's stood before me. I will see her, her lands *and* her men subdued. And you, my loyal servant, are the soldier to see them conquered."

Adrien tossed a glare at the woman, who met it squarely with a glower of her own. With a spine made no doubt of fine steel, the woman warned him of one definite proclamation.

The battle forthcoming would not be an easy victory.

Ediva turned and shut her eyes. All was lost. When a young messenger had delivered the news of Ganute's death, she'd thought nothing could spoil her happiness. The cruelty called a marriage was finally over. The daily insults, the nightly brutality so awful that she battled constantly with the temptation to flee, staying only out of concern for her maids and other innocents. How she praised the day when King Harold gathered his troops and Ganute's duty drove him to fight against the Norman duke!

Ediva had cared little for the royal household. She

barely survived her own. It was always a relief when her husband left for Westminster to serve his military duty. And his leaving for war did not take her to the keep's chapel to pray for his safety, despite the chaplain's strong suggestion that it should.

God hadn't listened to her prayers for deliverance during her first year of marriage, and Ediva would certainly not offer them for her husband's safety after that. Mayhap 'twas best, she thought wryly. Any prayers she might have offered in the keep's small chapel would have been for the first arrow of the battle to pierce her husband's vile heart.

How odd that now she'd been practically dragged here and ordered to serve *her* time, not as a soldier herself, but as a wife to yet another one. This one chosen for her by the new king himself.

This new king had terrified her the moment she'd first laid eyes on him. Big and strong, he looked like he could break her like a twig. Then he'd spouted off something about God expecting each woman to serve Him as a good wife and, despite her fear, she'd laughed in his face.

And incited his anger.

He then revealed his ultimatum.

Marry or lose your lands.

Never! she'd wanted to cry. Never did she want to marry again, and yet never would she give up the lands that were legally hers. With no issue from her marriage, *thankfully,* and no male heirs in either family, Ediva considered it her right to keep Dunmow. A fair trade for the cruel marriage she'd endured. But the king had ignored her protests.

Still, she shot a furtive look to the man beside her.

He was as tall as, if not taller than, the king. And whilst William had a paunch from too much fine food, this man was thick-shouldered and slim-waisted, his tunic a dark brown, with only the most basic embroidery at the neck and of good enough quality to hang well on his torso. His hose was wrapped so tightly with fresh thongs, she could see warrior-hewn muscles defining strong legs.

His thick leather belt kept his outer tunic snug to his torso, and Ediva knew enough that the empty scabbard indicated respect for his king. Somewhere beyond this chamber, his weapon waited for him.

The man, whose name appeared to be Adrien, was handsome enough to gaze upon. But Ediva was not a simple maid. She was nearly twenty years along, and had been married for the last five. She had learned early that a finely chiseled face meant nothing. Ganute had one when they'd first been wed. 'Twas the heart that defined a man, and none she'd met yet had a good one.

"Adrien, my chaplain is waiting," the king snapped.

Adrien looked at her, his gaze drilling into her so fiercely she felt it press against her cheek. "Sire," he said, moving to face his king. "I don't even know this woman's name. Where is her keep? Is she a maid or widow?"

William dismissed the questions with a wave. "She is Ediva Dunmow, widow of one of Harold's unfortunate knights. You'll learn the rest on your journey to her keep. Women can talk a hound off its quarry." He flicked his hand at his steward. "Eudo, go witness your brother's nuptials."

That was it? Ediva fumed. She had no say? This foreign king was just dismissing her without discussion, without giving her a chance to make a different offer? If the king required a pledge from her that she would ensure the loyalty of her people toward the new reign, then she would willingly comply. Or was it restitution he required, after her husband's allegiance to his enemy? She'd heard of some powerful families purchasing back their forfeited lands.

She had the coinage to do that, but the king had not even offered the choice. How was she to protect her people now?

A firm hand caught her elbow and she looked up to find Adrien, her newly betrothed, prepared to direct her out to their nuptials. His grip was firm but not unkind. He masked all but the calmest expression, a look as bland as milk, with the exception of tightness in his jaw. At the moment, his expression showed no depravity, as she'd seen in Ganute's on their wedding night. But who knew what expression he would show when they were alone and the masks fell away?

Nay! A carefully hooded evil was still evil. Ediva yanked back her arm and marched out as quickly as she could for her body still ached from the horrid ride into London. And with no deference to the king who'd ordered this marriage.

Expecting to be hauled back for her insolence, Ediva found herself stomping from the Great Hall to the sound of William's hearty and satisfied laughter. He cared naught of her impudence. He had her lands.

She skidded to a stop when she spied a military chaplain holding a small prayer book. The nearby soldiers kept one hand on their weapons. She muffled a sarcastic snicker. Were they so afraid of one small woman that they needed weapons? She could scarcely lift a sword, let alone stab it into one of them. She was hardly a danger to them.

But then it hit her, fully, with the force of a terrible storm.

Her freedom was gone. She was facing another marriage, this time to a man as obscure to her as the sun on this late winter's day.

Another example of how God had turned his back on her.

Chapter Two

"Are these guards necessary, Poitiers?" Adrien snapped at the chaplain as his squire returned his sword. He saw no need for soldiers.

"*My* men brought your betrothed down here. They needed to drag her here with great force."

Adrien couldn't help but laugh. "Obviously your men require more exercise if two are needed for such a weak task. Have them report to me, and I will train them properly."

Behind them, Eudo snickered. The red-faced Poitiers growled, "I'll handle my men. You'll soon have your hands full with this Saxon wench. She's lived a strong life in some castle in Essex not far from your brother's holdings. Farm stock, no doubt. She's no timid maid."

Eudo slapped his brother's back, his grin merry as he strolled past. "William wants me to build a keep in Colchester with the rubble left from some pagan temple. I won't be far. You'll be able to come next winter, Prado," he said, using that annoying childhood name. "Mayhap we can celebrate Christmas together, with wives heavy with child?"

'Twould do no good for Adrien to rise to his brother's

goad, for the man had no wife yet and was simply mock-
ing him. Adrien took his newly betrothed's arm again.

She yanked herself free. "I can walk of my own accord,
sir," she answered in French.

Irritated by his brother, his king and this woman who
apparently knew his mother tongue, Adrien swept his arm
sarcastically toward the chapel. "As you wish, my lady. Let
us get this unpleasantness over."

She pulled up her wimple and followed the chaplain
down the corridor. Adrien watched her take her leave,
her soft sashay not enough to disguise a slight limp. Had
Poitiers's men caused that? His jaw tightened. For better
or for worse, this woman would be his wife and was therefore under his protection.

At least she was pleasing to the eye. And he was more
than a little surprised by her ability to speak French, albeit with a sharp, Saxon accent that seemed in contrast to
the smooth, gentle features. But her accent was nowhere
near as sharp as her obvious displeasure over their match.

Give me strong babes that look like you.

William's words echoed in his head. But he doubted that
this woman, Ediva Dunmow, would open her bedchamber
to him, and Adrien refused to bend his pride and insist.
He watched the woman walk stiffly behind the chaplain
as if she was walking to her death.

To her death? Insult bristled through him. And despite
the interest in her beauty, he had no desire to marry any
more than she did. She needn't act as if all the disadvan-
tage lay on her side. But 'twas far better to obey than to
incur the king's wrath. So he hastened his own steps toward the chapel.

This would preserve her lands, at least. 'Twould be hard
enough for England to accept a Norman king, but if this
woman remained on her land, married and settled, there

may be some measure of peace for her people. Surely even she would see the logic in that.

He followed Ediva into the chapel, all the time aware of the soldiers at his heels. But wisely, the armed men kept to the back, propping open the heavy oak door and allowing the wind from the river to dilute the potent odor of burning wax. The old chaplain stopped at the front, offering respect to the altar before turning. He cleared his throat as he opened his small leather-bound book.

The ceremony was short and in Latin, and Adrien was again surprised to find Ediva completely fluent in yet another language.

When Poitiers ordered them to seal the nuptials with a kiss, Adrien turned to face his new wife.

His wife! He'd never considered this day, always expecting to live out his lifespan as a bachelor and a soldier. Now he'd pledged to God that he would devote himself solely to this woman, a stranger not even of his own country.

And judging by her regal bearing, this woman was in a class far above his. Poitiers's insult of farm stock was foolish. She was obviously higher in status. Aye, his family had influence with William, but Adrien was happy being only in the king's service. Would his wife despise him more for his Norman heritage or for his low upbringing?

Ediva blinked up at him, her arrogance gone and now revealing smoldering, stubborn fear that was, oddly enough, tempered with a slow swallow.

'Twas just a kiss ordered by the king through Poitiers. Yet her pale eyes were awash with tears and her lips clenched so tightly together they must have hurt.

He pulled back his shoulders. He wasn't in the habit of forcing himself on women.

"Seal this union, Adrien," Poitiers growled. "It has the king's license."

Behind him he heard the chink of half-drawn swords hitting mail. Ediva tilted up her chin and that fine, steel backbone stiffened as if prepared for an accursed death.

He lowered his head and deftly leaned to one side. He would kiss this woman and quite possibly save both their lives. A brief kiss, barely a brushing of lips, a touch light enough to feel the breath of her gasp as she realized what he had also realized.

They were now husband and wife.

Ediva could no longer control the emotions roiling within her. There was hatred for her situation, yet no revulsion, certainly not like during her marriage to Ganute. When Adrien gave her the barest kiss, she'd shuddered with an expectancy of more.

But no more came and her nerves danced like the traveling acrobats who'd entertained last year.

"'Tis over, madam," Adrien's low voice whispered close to her parted lips. "You may open your eyes now."

Heat scorched her cheeks, and her eyes flew open. "I was expecting more, 'tis all. My first wedding was a more extravagant affair."

"Alas, we have no fanfare."

"Not unless you consider the chink of weaponry in case I fussed. Much different than the sound of trumpets."

Adrien lifted his eyebrows. "Trumpets?"

"A chorus of them from the battlement of Dunmow Keep. My mother wanted my wedding heard a league away. My ears ached for a week, but she was as deaf as a stone and cared little for me. Much like those here in London."

She stepped back. She hadn't thought of her mother in years. Like Ganute's mother, her own mother hadn't seen the end of that year due to an outbreak of fever. They had been peas of the same pod, and neither cared enough for Ediva to notice that Ganute abused his position of husband. They wanted only that the monies of the two families stay within the county.

Ediva tried to relax. 'Twould do no good to stew upon her selfish mother's actions or on the memory of her kinder father, who had been the first to succumb to the fever weeks before the wedding. What a bitter year that had been.

Adrien lifted her hand to his lips, but paused before kissing it, to whisper, "'Tis unwise to complain here. The king has ears even in the chapel." His gaze flickered to Poitiers as he brought her hand to his lips.

The warmth seeped into her cold skin. And his rough fingers brushed her palm, evoking a shiver deep within. She wanted to snatch away her hand, but Adrien kept his grip firm as he led her from the altar. He stalled by the door, turning to speak to the old chaplain. "My thanks to you, Poitiers, and you, dear brother, for being available for such a grand event. You both may report to the king his will has been done. May I depart for this woman's keep to inspect my new acquisition?"

Ediva heard the steward—now her brother-in-law—laugh. Peeking over her own shoulder, she watched the chaplain scowl at her new husband's impudence.

"Go, but be mindful of the king's orders." Poitiers then added, "May God bless your marriage."

Ediva glanced at Adrien. His mockery turned to a scowl. Once out of earshot, he turned to her. "Have you a maid to prepare you for the journey home?"

"A maid! You jest, sir. I have no one with me. I have naught but the clothes I wear. When the guards arrived at the keep, they insisted that I travel immediately. They wanted only fresh horses, so I had just enough time to be given my cloak and throw my steward some duties over my shoulder before being dragged down here." She glared at Adrien. "I spent this past night with other women who were as bewildered as I was, none of whom were any better supplied."

Adrien frowned. "How did the king know of you?"

She shrugged. "My husband wanted to be well-known in King Edward's court, and then in King Harold's short time in court early last year. Mayhap he left a spy who saw fit to inform the new king of my status as widow."

Aye, probably so, Ediva thought with disgust. And if that was the case, then she knew who it must have been. Olin, Ganute's second cousin, had been in the thick of royal intrigue, sending many a missive on the machinations of the court back to the keep. Ediva had intercepted several. 'Twas simple enough to pry off Olin's hasty seal and reset it again. But after she'd read a few, Ediva saw the messages as foolish gossip. Olin was wasting good parchment to earn a stipend from Ganute—and likely, he'd earned another stipend from the king for reporting back on Ganute's replies.

Now there was a new king, but Olin was apt to swear allegiance to the new seat of power as quickly as a hawk turned toward its prey. Mayhap he'd thought that by courting the king's pleasure with jots of information he would be given her keep and lands. But, she reminded herself, all that she owned now belonged to the tall, silent Norman beside her.

"How is it that you know French and Latin, milady?" Adrien asked, wanting to break the awkward silence. "What other tongues do you speak?"

"Just those. My mother wanted to secure my sisters and me good marriages, so she brought in a tutor who'd lived in Normandy." She tossed him a hard look. "But do not believe that because I've learned your language, I support this invasion. Especially now that you have stolen what is rightfully mine."

As much as he desired to keep their relationship cordial, he could not let her remark go unanswered. "The king decides what belongs to you, woman. He fought for that right."

"The only good thing that happened at Hastings was *not* William's victory!" she spat out.

Her words made no sense to him. Adrien looked curiously at her, but when she refused to expand on her cryptic explanation, he continued his walk outside.

She followed him until they reached the king's stables. Adrien barked out a stream of orders to several young men. One immediately departed on a small horse, while another disappeared into the stable.

"Nay," she whispered, as she drew her cloak tightly around her and shook her head as if she had trouble believing where they'd ended up.

Adrien turned. His long outer tunic swirled in the breeze from the Thames. "Milady?"

"My lord," she answered with a horrified shake of her head. "I rode in yesterday from Essex with only one stop for the night. I was up before the sun that morning, back on a horse, and rode all day."

"You had last night to soothe your muscles."

She scoffed out a noise. "I spent the night with other women, sharing one inept maid who brought us only one pitcher of water to share. We slept on the floor and were given only cold broth to break our fast. I cannot ride again so soon." She offered him a pleading look. "For I do not ride."

"You cannot ride a horse? You just said you rode in here."

She bit her lower lip. "On the horse's bare rump behind one of the soldiers, clinging to his mail 'til my hands were too cramped to hang on. Once I slipped off!"

What had Poitiers claimed? That she'd been difficult? The chaplain had reddened at Adrien's sharp reply. Had the man of God been duped by his own inept men? Ediva was sharp-tongued, but judging from her look, she was also very scared.

Adrien glanced at the horses being led from the stables. He'd ordered his stallion and a small mare. The stable boy had obeyed him with his mount, a courser as fine as a knight was allowed. But the mare the boy also walked out was the same size. A grand dam she was, fit for a queen.

But not for a young bride with no experience.

He looked back at her. "You cannot ride at all? How did you expect to return home?"

"Since coming here was not by my choice, I had no time to consider it." She looked annoyed. "As for riding, I had no need to learn. I was taught only the duties of running a keep, managing its expenses and staff. I do not prance around the countryside with nary a worry in my head!"

"What do you do whenever you travel?"

"Before coming here, I had only left my home once to attend my nuptials at my husband's keep. I was taken there in a covered cart."

How was that so? She was a lady of rank and privilege. Surely she'd have traveled somewhere? Her nobleman husband must have taken her with him on his journeys. How could he not have? Adrien would have been as proud as his faith would allow to take a beautiful wife such as Ediva with him on his travels.

Perhaps there was no love in her first marriage. Nobility often married only to secure fortunes and alliances.

He shook off his thoughts. The past mattered little when there were the trials of here and now to face. Such as getting his new wife out of London. He would not spend his wedding night here where privacy only existed for the king. With her sore and aching body, Ediva deserved more than the crowded, uncomfortable accommodations he would be able to secure. The sooner they arrived at her keep, *his* keep now, the better.

"I'm afraid you'll have to endure the saddle one more time, Ediva. We must leave for the keep at once."

"But the day is almost over, Adrien." His name on her Saxon lips sounded strong, yet it quivered like a leaf in autumn.

"There are several inns along the north of the river outside of London. I've sent a boy up to the first one to prepare a room for us."

"Us?" she echoed softly.

"We are husband and wife now."

With eyes widening, she wet her lips and swallowed. He took a step toward her but was rewarded by a fearful step back.

He frowned. "You heard the king's orders."

She looked away.

With a sigh, he grimaced. He didn't have time for this. Daylight was dwindling, and he wanted to reach the inn before dark. If she was some fearful maid, he'd deal with it when they arrived at the keep.

"Don't fret, Ediva. 'Tis not my intent to incite fear. If you like, I will give you your privacy. You may take the room at the inn for yourself. But we will need to discuss this when we arrive at our home. Now, allow me to help you mount the mare."

The stable boy led the horse over and stilled the huge dam beside Ediva. She tilted her head up to look from the huge mare's legs to the saddle. She gathered her cloak tight about her neck and dropped her jaw.

He shook his head. "We don't have to take this mount if you don't want to." He turned to the boy holding the reins. "Get her something smaller."

"Sir, she's a gift from the king. This mare was meant for the new queen's stables."

And a good gift she was, too, but Adrien shook his head. "If my wife cannot ride her, I must decline."

A small hand touched his arm and he looked down at Ediva. "Nay, my lord. William may be a brutal king with blood on his hands, but his gift is of good value. Though I fear I cannot ride her home, we should bring her with us all the same."

Adrien turned to the boy, thankful for Ediva's logic. "Tie her lead to my mount, then." He swiftly mounted his own horse and leaned down to the unsure Ediva, extending his arm.

She took it, and after he'd secured a good grip on her, he swung her up onto his lap. When she'd settled as best she could atop him, he spoke to the stable boy, ordering him to tell his squire to deliver his mail to Dunmow Keep immediately.

Then he rode out of the stable. After they traveled along the street that lined the river and invited the cool wind on their faces, he spoke.

"My thanks, Ediva, for accepting the horse. The mare is too fine a gift to be ignored. It is a mark of favor from our king, and 'twould be considered ungracious to refuse."

Her answer was as cold as the dying day. "I care nothing for that."

"Then why accept his gift?"

"As you say, she's a fine horse. And the king does have a claim on my gratitude, though it has nothing to do with the horse."

Her sideways fealty to William made no sense, but he felt it related back to her other cryptic remark. "How has King William earned your gratitude?"

Ediva didn't answer, and as Adrien held her tight about her waist and the horses trotted along through the ever-thinning sprawl of huts, he pondered her puzzling words but refused to ask the question again.

They said nothing more until they reached the inn at the edge of London town, barely seen in the dwindling light of day.

Chapter Three

They arrived at Dunmow Keep late in the afternoon. Two quiet days had passed since they'd left London. Although they'd ridden only a few hours each day and stopped for more than adequate rests, Ediva's body throbbed with pain. She'd barely been able to stand at the last stop they'd made.

But at least Adrien had not forced her to keep the same punishing pace she'd endured to London. Nay, he had not shown himself to be cruel…yet.

She'd never considered the sight of Dunmow to be welcoming. Ganute had been proud of it, for the large, round tower was a rare stone keep. Imposing. A scar on the landscape, really, but today Ediva was glad to see it again after all she'd endured. Too much time on a horse…discovering she'd lost her land…forced into marriage. Aye, seeing Dunmow felt almost comforting.

The bailey below had been enclosed with a thick battlement just after she'd married, and as they rode toward it, she caught sight of the rising motte and its early spring garden.

"Your new property, my lord," she said close to his face. Gone was all embarrassment. They'd spent too long on one horse.

"This is it?" Adrien asked with awe in his voice.

"Aye. 'Tis Dunmow Keep. The village is Little Dunmow. There used to be a timber wall surrounding the huts, but one winter was deep and many stole the posts for firewood. Ganute refused to rebuild it."

Adrien's gaze swept across the village, but soon it returned to the huge keep. "'Tis made of stone! When was it built?"

"Ganute's father built it when King Edward was crowned."

"In commemoration?"

She shrugged. "Most likely to curry favor."

"But we passed no quarries. There are mostly fens and swamps here."

"The stone came from the west." She studied the keep with a critical eye. "They call it limestone and say 'tis easy to cut but hardens over time. I like the color. 'Twas the one thing I liked about it when I first arrived. Only when I was widowed did it begin to feel like home."

Adrien shot her a questioning frown, but she refused to explain herself. Someone from the sheep-filled village ran toward the main gate and heaved it open, allowing Adrien to ride into the bailey with the big mare in tow. There, Ediva slipped free of his arms and dropped into a young squire's grip. Oh, but she ached! And her legs could barely hold her. How was she ever going to climb the steps to her solar?

She looked around. Geoffrey, the steward, had ordered the yard cleaned. Mayhap that boy who Adrien had constantly sent ahead had warned the man that his new lord was on the way and her steward thought it wise to put forth a good first impression.

She mentally shook her head. Shortly after Hastings, Geoffrey had voiced his dislike of Norman rule, as had the chaplain. Tidying up wouldn't have been done to impress a man who, in Geoffrey's eyes, should not even be here at all.

"My lady! You're home!" her steward called as he exited the keep and trotted down the stone steps. "We've just heard the news of your marri—"

He stopped as Adrien dismounted.

Her new husband had come without the fanfare of troops, yet didn't appear to miss them, either. He'd ridden with great confidence, as if daring any thief to ambush them.

None had taken the offer.

Standing akimbo, he faced the young steward. "I am your new lord. You will address me, not Lady Ediva."

A crowd had begun to gather. And with Geoffrey looking stubbornly at Adrien, Ediva sighed. "I will handle my staff, Adrien." All she wanted was a bath and a rest, but she should nip in the bud any conflict that might arise with Adrien's arrival.

He glared at her. "They are my staff now and are subjects of the new king."

Should she allow him to prove his worth? He was hardly a nobleman—merely a knight lucky enough to fight on the winning side. He may be unfit to lead these people, despite the strength that flowed from him so easily. But how would Adrien respond if he received disrespect? He'd treated her far better than she'd expected thus far. These two nights since their wedding he had ordered her a private room and slept outside her door, a far cry from what Ganute would have done.

Yet he was still Norman, and his punishment might be as cruel as the rumors about them suggested. If that were so, her people would suffer.

She could not allow that. Now, as always, it was her

place to stand between her husband and the people under her protection he might see fit to harm.

She set her hand against his hard chest only to remove it quickly, remembering with embarrassment its firmness on her cheek when she'd dozed late yesterday. "My lord, allow me. 'Tis all I have ever trained for. We both need rest and food and a change of clothes. Allow me to arrange that."

He looked down at her coolly. "And you have clothes for me?"

She thought a moment. A big part of her was fighting the whole idea of being the dutiful wife. He was a Norman stealing her land, after all.

But she had no desire to incite his or the king's anger. Who knew what would happen then? 'Twas rumored that ten Saxon men would be killed should one Norman be injured. Nay, 'twas best to keep the peace. "I have some clothes from Ganute's younger days, when he was far slimmer. They are hardly your style, nor do they have your length, but with a few stitches they will do until yours arrive."

Adrien handed the reins of his horse to the shy, young man, Rypan—who, Ediva noted, watched with huge eyes. "Treat these mounts well, or you'll be treated as you've done to them," he told him in heavily accented English. The boy nodded, most likely understanding only the fierce tone.

Adrien glanced suspiciously around, and his mere size caused several maids and men to step back. Geoffrey stood his ground.

Ediva leaned close to Adrien and spoke tightly in quiet French. "These people have lost family at Hastings. I doubt any have seen a Norman before, except the troops that marched through to inform us of our new king. Some of those men were very brutal. Be wise, lest you find yourself wondering if your next meal has been poisoned."

She tempered her words with weariness. She'd already buried one husband and after this frightful trip, was reluctant to bury another. Even if she could escape the fury of the king should Adrien die, new widowhood would risk Ganute's cousin, Olin, descending upon her with foolish airs of his wrongful claim on Dunmow Keep.

Adrien drilled her with a penetrating look. "Mayhap I will have you taste my food first. You don't want me here any more than they do."

She answered him with a heavily burdened sigh. Of course, he would show his control over the keep she'd vowed to protect. But at this moment, she couldn't care less. "Such a delightful way to start a marriage," she muttered. "I'm sure you will want to inspect your new holdings. Go ahead. I plan to have a bath and a meal and a sleep. And if you feel the need for me to taste your food, wake me. For I really do not care." She lumbered stiff-kneed up the motte and into the keep.

Adrien confirmed to himself his horses were being cared for before ordering a young, brash-looking boy to take him to Ediva. He, too, wanted food and a bath and a good sleep before he inspected his new home, but those must wait. He would not have his wife ordering him around in front of his new staff and he planned to tell her so.

The boy took him up the stairs to the top floor, then down a corridor that was rounded like the tower's outer wall. The door at the end led to Ediva's solar, and when Adrien threw it open, he found Ediva sitting with her steward by her side while a maid dug through a nearby trunk of clothes. The curtains that usually closed off the bed were pulled back and a light breeze rolled through the room by way of two narrow windows. The private solar was bright.

A whitewash lightened the curved walls, and pushed to one side was a large, round brazier with an ornate cover.

Ediva was tossing clothes into Geoffrey's open arms. Another young woman sat at a table, sewing feverishly. His new wife didn't look up from her task, even when his gaze finally lit on her. "I've found some things for you," she said.

Geoffrey held a mix of fine linens and sturdy wools. As best as Adrien could tell, all items were old-fashioned and of Saxon design. The leather thongs looked stiff and useless, but he'd find replacements for them easily enough.

"Thank you."

She said no more. The girl on her knees pulled out a piece of cloth, one that snagged Ediva's attention enough for her to fall to her own knees and grab it. The girl started back in surprise. Immediately, Ediva stuffed the linen back deep into the trunk again. A burgeoning silence swelled in the room.

No one moved.

Curious, Adrien strode up to peer into the chest. A tail of the material stuck out a moment before she shoved it deeper in. The cloth was pale blue in color, as lovely as Ediva's brilliant eyes. Her hand lay on the other clothes, shaking ever so slightly. Adrien crouched and looked into her face. Her eyes were closed.

"Ediva?"

She swiped her hand over her cheek and opened her eyes. Glaring at the brash boy who'd accompanied Adrien, she snapped, "Harry, why are you still here?"

Harry looked down at his feet. "I came in with my new lord."

"Well, you can leave now." She twisted to speak to the woman sewing. "Margaret, I don't need half of Dunmow Keep traipsing through my solar."

"Ediva?"

She turned her attention to Adrien, her expression cool as the late winter rain that had fallen that morning.

"Harry will be your squire," she carried on in English, still on her knees. "If you need me, he will know where to find me."

"I have my own squire."

"Harry has some knowledge of French and a good ear for learning. Use him as much as possible." Her voice was steady, but her hands still trembled and though she looked toward his face she would not meet his eye.

Irritated, he stood and folded his arms. "I will decide the staff, Ediva."

"You know nothing of the staff here. This is *my* keep, Lord Adrien, and as its lady, I make such decisions."

With that, she slammed the lid of the trunk down. All the servants jumped.

Enough, Adrien decided as he threw open the trunk lid. Whatever was in this thing had shaken Ediva more than anything he'd seen her encounter, including the king's command to wed. Retrieving the blue garment she'd hidden, he discovered it was a woman's shift.

Holding it up with both hands, he drew in a sharp breath. There were long, violent slashes in it, and splattered about them were brownish stains.

Blood. He'd been a soldier long enough to recognize the unwashed stains. 'Twas a sleeping shirt of good quality, and most likely hers. What had happened? "Is this yours, Ediva?"

She snatched it back and thrust it into the arms of the girl beside her. "Never mind. Turn this into rags, girl." Immediately after, she ordered the servants to leave.

After the servants had filed out and the door shut firmly behind them, Adrien said, "That's blood. What happened?"

Her chin had wrinkled. Just as he thought she wouldn't answer, she said, "Ganute's departure gift to himself."

Adrien fought for words, but nothing decent surfaced. Her cheeks pink, Ediva returned to her seat. "He… surprised me, 'tis all."

Was that all it was? Nay. From her expression, there was more. He paused, also hating how he couldn't seem to form a sentence or even find the right words to say. "You… had been married for some time, surely. You are…old."

Silence followed, with a sudden tension Adrien had felt only before battle. All he'd meant to say was she was old enough to know what some men want. Obviously, his English needed work.

Unless the departure gift was…

His blood ran cold.

Slowly standing, Ediva turned to him. "Old? *Old!*" The word bounced around the quiet room like an angry bee in a clay pot. "Am I a battered pan into which you slop bones and broth for your sup?"

She wiped her eyes furiously. "I am many things, my lord, but I can tell you with much certainty, *that I am not old!*"

Snatching up her hem, she limped past him and threw open the heavy oak door with the ease of a man twice her size. As it slammed against the wall, she did her best to stalk from her solar with as much dignity as her bruised and aching body would allow.

Standing there, Adrien felt a pair of eyes lingering on him. He found Harry, the young whelp Ediva had assigned as his squire, peeking into the solar. The boy barely reached his elbow and was as clumsy as a half-grown pup, but he lifted his brows and shook his head like a wise old man.

"What's your problem, boy?"

The boy's French was horrible, but he understood. "Milady don't like to be called old. Even m'maw and my sisters don't like being called old."

Adrien scowled at him. The boy colored, appropriately so, in Adrien's mind. Harry quickly turned away, but as he did, Adrien caught his arm. "What kind of man was her ladyship's first husband?"

The boy looked around him, as if to confirm they were alone. "I didn't know him well, sir. But I remember seeing her ladyship in the kitchen garden after he left, tending herbs. All covered up."

"Of course she'd cover herself. She's a modest woman. And what do you mean, tending herbs? The lady of the keep does not garden, boy." Did this child think he could lie to his master?

"She likes to tend the herbs, she says. M'maw says she needs the peace."

"She needs— Why?"

"M'maw said his lordship had his way before he left. She said that his lordship didn't deserve her."

Adrien's stomach turned as his suspicions deepened. Why hadn't he seen the signs before? She'd practically told him that the only good that came out of Hastings was her husband's death. And the bloodstains told their own tale of a brutal man.

And here he had been, bullying her further.

Father in Heaven, I have sinned against You and against Ediva. My ways are of a soldier, not of a husband. Help her to understand me. And for me to understand her.

He strode out to find Ediva and confirm the truth from her. But, as he trotted down the curved stairwell, he reminded himself that she had her right to privacy.

Nay, he argued back, he needed to know the truth behind her first marriage. He could help her. He could—

Finding her in the herb garden that rolled down the short motte, Adrien paused at the open kitchen door. Behind him, water for her bath was being warmed over the hearth. Any words he'd formed in his mind dissolved instantly. She was seated at a wooden bench, staring at a patch of herbs barely out of the ground. The air still bore a crisp feel but promised spring. 'Twas the time of year that pledged new life, new growth—a new beginning. A new master for the keep who would not repeat the cruelties of the previous one.

Ediva needed to know that she was safe in her own home. He'd made a silent promise to God during his nuptials that he would honor his wife as God would want him to. Ediva deserved that much. And she should not have to leave her own solar just to find a moment's peace.

She looked up at that moment, eyes hurt and hollow. He'd called her old, and he was wrong. She was broken, hurt by Ganute so much that Adrien actually regretted the man's death. If Ganute was still alive, then Adrien would be able to teach him a lesson he would not soon forget.

With a stilling breath, Adrien forced out the violent thoughts. The Good Lord wanted him to show mercy and love. His new wife needed such. He walked toward her and wasn't surprised when she turned her attention back to the garden. Sighing, he sat and took her hand.

"Ediva, I meant no insult when I called you old. 'Twas not a slight against your youth or beauty."

She didn't move. He pressed on. "I'm a soldier, Ediva, not a fine prince who knows the ways of courtship. And we both know you're not a maid."

She looked at him, blinking. "You don't know that."

He frowned. "I do. You were married to Ganute for five years."

"I could still be a maid."

Adrien shook his head gently. "We both know that's not so. Were you ever with child?"

"Nay, I gave him no children." Her gaze darted about. "Some said God made me barren to punish me."

"For what?"

She bit her lip. "For not giving my all to Him. For not rejoicing in the marriage consecrated in His eyes. For turning my back on Him when I was—" She cleared her throat. "The chaplain would tell me to pray for Ganute's safety in battle." She glanced up at him and he saw a fierceness there as her voice dropped. "If I had prayed, 'twould have been for his death, not his life."

Ahh. 'Twas the reason for the backward fealty to William. She owed the king because one of his soldiers had ended her misery.

His breath drew in sharply. He'd fought at Hastings, following the king who'd led the battle. Adrien had slashed his way through several Saxon knights that day.

Had Ganute been one of them?

Still, her words about God… Was she not a Christian woman? The tutor his family had employed had said once that some hearts were closed to the Lord.

Was she hard of heart?

Ediva blinked rapidly again, offering the real answer. She was as hard-hearted as a kitten. She was simply afraid to trust—in man or in God. Life had scarred her.

He lifted her hand, smooth and cold and shaking. He tightened his grip to warm it and prevent it from slipping free. "Ediva, God doesn't punish those who are already hurting. He has mercy."

"Mercy?" Her brows shot up. "There was no mercy for five years. Not even from my own family. I was told to endure my marriage because 'twas my duty to my family."

Glancing around, his gaze fell on a bare vine clinging to the sunniest wall of the bailey. Buds were swelling on it. He dug through his memories for something to say. As third son, he'd been expected to serve the church and had studied with monks for much of his childhood. Surely there was some Bible story… "Ediva, God prunes the vine so it will produce good fruit. You must have produced good fruit, for God does not prune that which produces no fruit at all."

She shook her head. "I told you I am barren."

"Fruit isn't babes only, Ediva. The respect you have here and the care you show for your staff that leads them to care for you are all good fruit. Even for the short time I have been here, I can see you all care for each other."

Her eyes narrowed. "You're a soldier. How do you know these things?"

"I'm not the firstborn son, so I was expected to serve God instead of lead the family." He pulled her slightly closer but not so close as to scare her. "Enough of me. Ganute was cruel to you, wasn't he?"

She nodded. Shaking his head, he leaned forward. Immediately, she drew back, too quickly for the cause to be anything but instinct.

His stomach tightened. "Don't be frightened. Never will I force myself upon you. There is no honor in hurting a woman, Ediva."

Her short, wobbly laugh brushed his cheeks. "We are married and the king has ordered children."

"I will handle the king. He won't expect babes overnight." He shook his head. "We may be married, but until you find it in your heart to accept me as husband in every sense, I will demand nothing from you. Nor will you be bruised and beaten at my hand or anyone else's. I promise you that."

And along with his vow came the urge to press his lips

against hers, to warm her very soul. He began to lower his head…

Abruptly, she pulled back her shoulders and steeled her spine. "Adrien, you say that God has been pruning me. But I fear He's not done yet. Look around. All I own has been given away by a king as brutal as Ganute."

"William is not brutal!"

"Ha! Did he not herd me to London like a sheep for slaughter, then not feed me so I would be weak and compliant? He has no care for me—no more than Ganute cared for me. No more than God cares for me. Don't say that God allows me to suffer to make me a better person. I have no desire to hear anymore of how good God is."

She pulled free her hand and held it up as she flew to her feet. "Nay! Keep your peace and your God because I don't want either. But remember this. You promised me you'll not touch me 'til I am ready. I will hold you to that."

She spun and stomped up the stone steps into the kitchen, leaving him alone among the herbs only just budding from the cold, damp earth.

Chapter Four

Ediva sank into her chair, pretending to prepare for her bath, but she wanted only to ease her temper, lest she bark at her servants.

Her hand rose to her mouth, as if she could draw back in the harsh words she had spoken. Adrien had done nothing to warrant her anger, except injure her pride by calling her old.

Rubbing her pounding forehead with a shaky hand, she stood. She ached all over and needed to bathe away the smell of horseflesh and sweat of travel.

Mayhap you should first apologize to Adrien?

The nagging voice thumped between her temples, but grouchily, she ignored it. Husband or not, he had no right to know the details of her humiliating marriage to Ganute.

Her maid appeared in the doorway, spotted her and turned to depart immediately. "Margaret," Ediva called. "Where is my bath water?"

"'Tis ready, milady. I will see that it's brought up immediately."

The girl hurried off. Discarding any soft thoughts of an apology, Ediva slowly removed her wimple. With the filth of travel on her and very little sleep these past few days, she needed to bathe and rest more than seek out her husband. How many times had she begged Ganute's forgiveness for some imaginary folly only to keep the brittle peace that was as delicate as an eggshell? No, she would not apologize again.

Shortly, Margaret led in three servants with buckets of steaming water and the wooden tub. The young girl deftly prepared Ediva's bath, helped her with it and then left her to her nap, with cloth-dried hair spread over the furs.

Sometime later, Ediva awoke. Immediately she turned to the window. Even through the vellum shutters, she saw the sun setting. The shutters were a marvel, for they blocked the wind yet filtered light into her solar. Ganute was proud of them, the vellum being the finest and thinnest, stretched upon dovetailed wood frames. He'd claimed it to be his invention, but Ediva secretly suspected he'd seen them in London.

Movement caught the corner of her eye and she flipped around. Adrien was sitting in her chair by the other window, reading the keep's ledger whilst her maid was busy folding clothes into the trunk.

He looked up, and in the briefest of heartbeats, their eyes locked.

"Why are you here?"

He closed the book and locked the long hasp wrapped around it. Where had he acquired the key? From Geoffrey or from her belt whilst she slept? She would ask later. "I have spent the afternoon with your steward, inspecting the keep and the coffers. I wanted to check on you."

She sat up, and then, realizing she wore only her inner tunic, she pulled up the fur bedclothes. The heavy pelts were suddenly a great comfort to her. She glared at Margaret, who didn't seem concerned that Adrien was patiently waiting.

"You inspected the coffers? And the records, too, I see? Were they satisfactory?" She tugged the pelts closer, even though her maid had piled coals into the brazier and closed the shutters to keep the warmth inside. Still, Ediva felt need to cover herself further. "And you have sat by my brazier since, awaiting me?"

"I have only just sat down, milady. I fear I awoke you when I entered."

"I must ask you to leave. Margaret will assist me now."

Adrien lifted a finely curved brow, one as dark as her brows were pale.

"I will see to our supper, then. We shall dine in the hall."

Ediva's stomach growled. She'd missed the noon meal and was grateful that Adrien had delayed supper for her. Since Ganute died, she'd moved the castle routine away from two heavy meals. Their breakfasts were small and fresh, enough to keep them going 'til noon. Supper had become a reflection of breakfast, with broth that had simmered all day, something only to warm the belly. It suited her better than Ganute's heavy meals, and with the change, Ediva had been able to cut spending, thus adding to the coins in her coffers.

Another cold thought washed over her. No doubt those coins will soon be off to London as taxes to the king. Ediva had not increased the rent, thus easing the burden on her tenants, and had instead practiced good, sensible thriftiness to allow her to save enough to keep the castle going all winter. She'd hate to see it all leave now.

But Adrien has already counted it. Geoffrey had opened the strongbox for him.

She would deal with Geoffrey later.

"I'd appreciate it greatly, sir, that you wait for me to escort you about the rest of the keep."

Adrien had already reached the door. "'Tis all done,

Ediva. I have seen all I need to see, counted the silver and secured the strongbox. I do, however, have some changes to make."

She felt her ire rising and tamped it down, for she couldn't exactly stomp away this time. "The king may own this keep, but the coffers are full because of my careful management. There will be no changes."

Adrien smiled. The warm curling up of his mouth took her so completely aback, she wondered what foolish thing she'd said.

"You are quite right about your good management, milady, but know this, the coffers now belong to the king."

She straightened her spine. "*My lord, know this.* My people have no one save me." She tried to maintain her determination, but her current position offered little help.

Her husband tilted his head and she knew he was recalling how she'd flashed fear at him before. "Your words do not match your eyes, Ediva."

She drew back in her bed but lifted her chin. "When I buried Ganute, I told my people I would do my best to keep them from harm. I'll do so even if it costs me my life."

He walked over, barely taking two strides to reach her. The ropes and wooden braces upon which the overstuffed pallet sat now strained as he pressed his knuckles onto them to lean close. His voice was soft, yet filled with warning. "Let us pray such a high price shall never be demanded."

Straightening, he left her alone. Alone and wondering if her new husband would really extract the high price she'd inadvertently suggested.

Adrien strode into the kitchen and ordered some food for them. Several maids scurried in obedience, leaving him alone in the smoky room. The day was nearly gone, but the door out to the small garden where he and Ediva spoke earlier remained open. He watched the youth he'd handed his reins to dump kitchen scraps near where Ediva had been sitting. From the shadows bolted several cats that grabbed the refuse before darting away. One small dog, mange-filled and bone thin, chased them for their prizes.

Spying him, the youth jumped, turned tail and dashed away. Perturbed, Adrien jammed his fists into his hips and glowered. Aye, he was tall and well-muscled—he was a soldier, after all—but he was hardly an ogre.

"That's Rypan, milord. He's not good with folks," a fresh voice called out. "He's not too smart and often can't speak."

Adrien turned to find young Harry sitting by the hearth. A cook hurried past, snapping at him to move out of the way as she tended to the meal. Harry jumped up. The complete opposite of the boy who'd dashed away, Harry had bright, bold eyes and a saucy expression. His most annoying, yet beneficial, trait was his ability to speak French.

"Where did you learn French, boy?"

Harry grinned proudly. "I listened. M'maw worked for Lady Ediva's family. Milady learned it, so I learned it, too."

"Did Ediva bring you when she was married?"

He shrugged. "M'maw came with Lady Ediva, and I guess I was too young to leave her."

"Who's your mother?"

"One of the cooks. But not *the* cook."

Adrien tossed a look over his shoulder to *the* cook bustling around behind him. The woman shot Harry a sharp glare.

"She's Rypan's aunt. He's got no folks besides her."

"Your French is horrible, boy. I'll have to teach you proper grammar."

An even bigger smile split the cheeky boy's face. "I'd

like that. Milady speaks to me in French, for her lord could not understand it."

Adrien frowned. "Ha! I doubt very much you were her *confidant*."

Harry shrugged. "I do not know what that means, sir. She'd just ask me to get her things."

"What kinds of things?"

"Sweets, mint from the garden, herbs for teas. She don't drink strong ales."

Again, Adrien rolled his eyes at his substandard French. "That wouldn't require subterfuge."

"Nay, 'twas not subberfuge I got for her."

Adrien sighed. The boy had no idea what the word meant. "I meant that it would hardly require secrecy. What kind of herbs?"

Harry shrugged again.

"Harry!" A voice rang out from the depths of the kitchen. An older woman appeared with a lantern. "Find your sister. She needs to take food to the hall."

As Harry dashed out of the dim kitchen, the woman shot Adrien a fast glance before setting down the lamp and stoking the fire.

"What kind of herbs would Lady Ediva need, woman?" he barked at her, feeling unreasonably annoyed by Harry.

"Milady doesn't drink any ales or wines, sir. Herbal teas, juices and broth are all she wants." She bustled about the trays of food, doing her best to ignore him.

He refused to take the slight personally. She was none too happy to have a Norman lord, Adrien guessed. As a soldier, he was used to ill-tempered people, even many of the knights who were better educated than anyone here were surly and ill-spoken. 'Twas part and parcel of the work.

When the yelps and growls of that scruffy dog penetrated his thoughts, his attention snapped away from the cook.

When he looked back, she was gone. His thoughts returned to Ediva's earlier words, how she'd subtly suggested Adrien could be in danger of being poisoned. And with that boy suggesting Ediva knew her herbs made him wonder…

Had she considered such an end for her first husband? An uneasiness wobbled through Adrien. He'd threatened to have her taste the food first. Had Ganute ever thought to do the same? Poisons were often effective. With a cruel lord of a manor lounging through the long winter nights, 'twould be easy to plan a murder. And yet that had not been Ganute's death. 'Twas on the battlefield that he saw his end. Adrien pursed his lips in frustration. Would life at the keep prove too great a test for him?

For now, he had little fear of attack. The keep was subdued, watchful. Waiting to see what sort of lord he would prove to be. He pondered the same question himself as he climbed the stairs to Ediva's solar to retrieve her for the evening meal.

Hours later, as he lay on a pallet in his private room off the great hall, listening to the servants settling for the night, he still found himself pondering the issue of herbs.

Wondering if he should force Ediva to taste his food first.

And hating that he'd even need to.

Chapter Five

Ediva awoke early. The eastern sky was barely tinged with morning when she freed the vellum from the window. A hint of spring eased into the room, and she heard her maid roll over on her pallet. Margaret hated to rise early, and because there was no reason to today, Ediva let her sleep. Quietly, she grabbed her cloak and slipped from her solar to walk the parapet above.

Outside, she drew in cool air. She much preferred the warmth of summer or the insect-free autumns, but early mornings were wonderful any time of the year.

Ganute often had slept in, and after the nights she had wanted to forget, Ediva would slip down to the kitchens for a small bite of bread and some broth. She'd order her bath water and return to the parapet to wait for a servant to announce its arrival, reveling in the brief span of time that she had to herself and dreading her husband's awakening.

Nay! That part of her life was over, she told herself sternly. Ganute was gone and her new husband had vowed not to touch her, a promise she meant for him to keep.

She had to remain strong and detached. Her husband did not need her—her people did. Dunmow lost too many men at Hastings, and when she'd surveyed the mourners the day she'd buried Ganute, far too many widows stared back at her, all needing strong leadership. And there were worries anew, with the uprisings to the north and Norman soldiers gathering in the town of Colchester ten leagues to their south.

"Let us pray such a high price shall never be demanded."

Adrien's words from last night rang unbidden through her head. She'd seen a heat in his gentle smile, like a fire whose coals looked deceptively cold but whose inner warmth could burn skin.

A flush rose in her, and she determinedly turned her thoughts away from the memory. The sun peeked over the ridge beyond to paint the battlement pink. Ediva could hear several roosters crowing in competition and a shepherd calling his sheep from their night pen to search out the tender grasses of early spring.

Another set of noises caught her attention. She leaned forward to peer down into the bailey but the thickness of the walls refused her curiosity.

She heard Geoffrey's complaining voice, followed by Adrien's sharp retort. Both voices rose like the mist on the distant hills.

Adrien sounded fully awake, unlike Geoffrey, whose sleepy petulance echoed in his tone. Adrien spoke of stakes, ropes and something she couldn't catch.

Her husband's voice rippled over her and her breath stalled in her throat. The wind rising did nothing to cleanse her of the warmth. Foolish, it was, to have a Norman's voice command such a reaction from her. She was far from a slave to her body's whims, having learned long ago to control herself. Even a shudder of revulsion could bring about a beating.

She heard a maid on the stairs. Mayhap the morning

ablutions will set her mind on more important matters. Let Adrien wander around the bailey. 'Twould teach him real life, not the one of a nomadic soldier whose only task was to sit upon a high horse and direct soldiers.

She spent much of the next few days slipping out to visit the new mothers. Her only contact was with Margaret or her steward. Of that morning, Geoffrey would only say that Adrien had ordered a cleaning of the bailey and a meeting with the villagers.

When she'd asked about the coffers, Geoffrey said that after counting the coins within, Adrien had studied the ledgers but had removed nothing nor sent word to London. The only other act that had stood out in her steward's mind was the fact that Adrien attended chapel each morning, something Ediva had long given up.

She had eyed Geoffrey for any hint that he might have joined his new lord in prayer, but the man gave nothing away and she refused to outright ask. With Geoffrey loyal to Ganute, and then to her, and with his dislike of Norman rule, she doubted the steward would switch allegiances, but rather do the minimum to placate his new lord. It wasn't Geoffrey's habit to go to the morning services because Ganute barely tolerated the chaplain in his keep, and Geoffrey believed he was better off favoring Ganute. Or mayhap the steward didn't like being told what to do by the old priest.

The next Sabbath dawned much the same as the days before. Up early, and this time with a stool to help her, Ediva peered out over the parapet at the bailey below. Her brows lifted sharply at the sight below.

The bailey nearly sparkled with cleanliness and Ediva noted the extra freshness in the air. Young Rypan was dumping kitchen refuse into an enclosed pen instead of into the garden. Ediva hoped the soil in the garden would not lose its strength this summer.

"Do you approve, milady?"

She spun, wobbling on the stool. Adrien stood several feet away, having climbed the stairs on silent feet. He walked closer and peered down at the handiwork. "Be careful when you lean forward. You may fall, though I suppose the landing would be soft in the garden waste. I ordered all kitchen scraps to be put in there and not scattered."

She stiffened. "My bailey was not filthy."

Even as she said that, she knew what a long winter could do to a keep. But still, her servants were hardly lazy on that matter.

"Nay, this place is well-kept. But I want the kitchen and garden to remain clean. 'Twould do us little good if we became sick from all matter of rot scattered about."

True enough. Regardless, she frowned. "How do you know of such things?"

"I have lived in camps with men and seen what makes even a strong man sick. In hot weather, 'tis worse. Do you not check a brook for dead animals before pulling water from it?"

"Aye. The midwife said a carcass fouls the water and makes one sick."

"'Tis the same with all waste." He paused, then with a frown, he added, "Ediva, I did not come up here to discuss the work I'd ordered. 'Tis the Sabbath, and you will come with me to worship."

Ediva wanted to decline, but his tone made it clear 'twas not a question. Her appearance at the chapel on the Sabbath had been erratic, and when she did participate in the services, it was by rote. Why worship a God who had turned against her?

But her husband thought otherwise and expected her to kneel by his side in the chapel. She looked up into Adrien's face, with its subtle challenge. And in that moment, she re-membered Geoffrey's report about Adrien and the coffers.

Oh, aye, she'd be wise to go through the act of wor-ship again. King William would be looking for monies and taxes, and Adrien would make the decision as to what went to him. He would also decide who needed taxing. She needed to have Adrien, who the king seemed to like, on her side.

So she dipped her head in agreement, albeit reluctantly. "Allow me to change my tunic, my lord."

She slipped past him and down to her solar. A few min-utes later she found Adrien outside her door. He offered his arm as they climbed down the narrow stairs that led to the main corridor.

Many of the tenants and villagers had already arrived and stepped back to allow Adrien to lead Ediva into the chapel.

"G'morning, milord."

"Morning, sir."

"'Tis a fine day to worship the Lord, sir!"

The salutations given to Adrien from various tenants filled the quiet morning. Adrien answered each person, a smile here and there, a ruffling of some small child's hair occasionally.

"'Twould seem you have impressed the villagers, Adrien," she murmured with a sniff, feeling piqued that he'd man-aged to win over so many of her people so quickly. "The king would be proud of you, I'm sure."

"'Twas not done for his benefit, Ediva. These people deserved to meet their new lord. There are many changes afoot, and they need to know who I am, first."

"Aren't you the good overlord, then?" she noted, her tone seasoned with sarcasm. "But a fine manner before plunder is still plunder nonetheless and these people can ne'er afford it."

"I have seen your coinage. There is no reason to show yourself righteous when you have collected so much."

She bristled all the way into the chapel. More than half the benches were filled, though the chaplain was nowhere to be seen. Geoffrey was already seated closer to the front than the maids and cook, along with his mother, the midwife. Everyone rose when she and Adrien entered.

"I noticed your pews are not sold," Adrien said quietly.

"I did away with it. I see no reason to add to the church's wealth by selling the benches on which people sit," she hissed back. "Our chaplain speaks of poverty and yet charges for all manner of blessings. The grain in the tithe barn in Cogshale rots because there's too much of it whilst my people go hungry. I refuse to sell parts of the church, as well."

Ediva threw a sharp glance at Geoffrey. He'd been charged with such sales before Ganute had died, and she could tell he was straining to hear her private words.

"'Tis an acceptable practice," Adrien answered softly as they walked toward the front. They reached the front pew and Adrien stepped back to allow Ediva to enter first. "Still, I understand. After you, my guardian wife who watches over our people so diligently."

She huffed at his humor before sitting down. Behind the pulpit, the mural glowed with rich colors. Men with long beards, gentle eyes and adoring expressions centered Jesus, and ornate calligraphy invited the weary to come for rest. She looked away. She remembered Ganute had seen murals in bigger churches and ordered this painting. It had more to do with his snobbery than any piety.

Candles flickered. On her wedding day, the chapel had

been strewn with scented herbs, saved since the fall, and the finest beeswax candles offered heat and light.

Ediva shut her eyes to the horrid memory. Ganute's generosity on that occasion had a high price.

The service droned on, and the only pleasure Ediva took from it was a chance to watch her new husband. His handsome, dark profile caught the candlelight. The last time she was here, weeks ago, they'd gone through the entire service in nearly complete darkness, no candles at all because she'd refused to donate any.

But today warmth glowed across her husband's face, a gentle light, flickering when the chaplain moved.

Curious, Ediva watched Adrien bow his head. He closed his eyes, and she focused on his mouth during a silent prayer. She felt her own lips part and a quiet voice within her mouthed the words with him.

His very handsomeness seemed to draw her closer. She found herself wanting to reach up and lay her hand upon his cheek, then drag it down if only to prove such good looks were real.

When he opened his eyes again, Adrien turned immediately to her.

Heat flooded into her face and she snapped away her attention. How did he know she'd spent the entire final prayer gawking at him? Aye, he was fair of face, but it meant nothing, she told herself. The moment of quiet solemnity had stirred her female heart, 'twas all. She drew in a restorative breath, hoping it would return her good sense.

But Adrien's scent rolled into her. Mint and orris root, heady over the odor of beeswax, an incongruous mix.

She was too close, she decided, but she would not retreat further along the length of bench. 'Twas her chapel, her keep, her spine that kept her so close to her new husband. The chaplain offered a benediction and filed past to bless the people. But still, neither she nor Adrien moved.

Indeed, after a few breaths, those still waiting for Adrien to stand and file out simply gave up and left, starting with Geoffrey.

Adrien did not move until finally Ediva leaned forward. "My lord, 'tis time to leave."

He continued to watch her. "Why are you in such a hurry to leave God's house?"

She folded her arms. "The service has ended. Our meal awaits."

"Jesus said He is the Bread of life."

She gaped at him, having not heard such words since her youth. She looked away. "I would prefer my cook's bread today, Adrien. 'Twill be fresh and will fill my belly."

Adrien lifted a hand and slipped his fingers into the loose part of her wimple to touch her jaw. The veil on top, secured with a simple diadem, brushed his arm.

"Sir, remember where you are!"

His attention stayed focused on her. "I'm in church with my wife. And from the quiet around us, I'd say we are alone."

Blood surged into her neck and she was sure he could feel her skin warm. "Adrien, you promised you would not touch me."

"I promised you I would not expect my rights as husband until you accept me." He leaned closer. "I'm only holding your attention."

"For what purpose?"

He leaned dangerously close. Despite her rigid spine, she could barely keep herself still. She found herself struggling between the urge to pull away to protect herself and wanting to ease closer.

A mere hint of space lingered between their lips, but

she refused to lean toward him. "I am not like your first husband, Ediva."

Holding her breath to crush the instinctive wash of fear, she found she could do nothing to escape. His eyes held hers and his lips had begun a slow descent onto hers, sending her emotions swirling like snow in a winter storm.

She couldn't endure much more. She could either give in to the kiss and be done with it, or pull back. But if she allowed the kiss, she would be allowing him power over her, something that she had promised she would never allow again. If she backed away, she risked the dangers she'd faced the first and only time she'd stood up against Ganute and his harsh demands for her wifely duties.

Nay, Adrien had given her his word, and despite the churning indecision, she knew deep down he wouldn't retract it. They may be married and she may be willing to show courtesy due to his new rank and give the king his taxes, but she wouldn't give of herself as she'd been forced to do many times before.

Testing the air that weighed heavy with expectation, she eased slowly back and felt with relief Adrien lowering his hand. A flicker of disappointment danced in his gaze but he gave her no word of reproach.

"'Tis time for our meal, Adrien," she whispered shakily. "'Twill only be hot for a short time, and the day is cool for me."

"You are quite warm, Ediva. A lie in the house of God isn't good for one's soul," he answered blandly.

"I have no hope for my soul."

Unexpected tears stung her eyes and she shifted away to blink at the mural. The Biblical offer of rest reached her watery gaze.

Beside her, Adrien sighed. He gathered her hands in his and held them gently. "There is always hope, Ediva."

A moment later, he drew her hand up to his warm lips. She fought the tears filling her eyes. She didn't want this foolishness between them. She didn't want him to be patient and kind and to love God.

Pulling free her hand, she stood. "Our meal awaits us."

He moved away. Thankfully, the tightness in her chest eased. Oh, 'twould be far easier to deal with Adrien if he was difficult and demanding. She'd learned years ago how to tuck her heart away from all her body could endure.

But right now, it felt as though her heart was out on a battlefield, ready for the final death blow.

She hated it.

Adrien pulled on the reins, bringing his mount to a stop. He'd risen early this mid-week morning, several weeks since his first chapel service with Ediva. Since then, he'd spent much of his time dealing with minor disputes, overseeing the cataloguing of all Dunmow Keep owned and other items of minutiae. Today, he decided to forgo morning chapel in order to inspect the estate's potential, especially at the perimeter of the keep's control. The king expected a full report, not only on the coffers, but also the viability of the land.

Atop the rise west of Dunmow Keep, he could see the River Colne, and to the north, the fens of East Anglia. Adrien's new home would surely be the point where the upstarts against William and the king's forces would meet. The land here was rich and fertile, worth fighting for.

He itched to return to battle. To do anything but what he'd come to Dunmow to do. Like an aging mare put to pasture, he found himself staring ahead at endless days dawdling about the keep. Aye, he'd met the villagers, inspected the coffers and viewed the records. His ancient *grand-mère* could have managed those things.

Under him, his courser stirred, sensing his edginess. Or mayhap the horse was bored of simply loping around a field without the disciplines of battle that, like Adrien, had been bred into him.

Adrien leaned forward to pat the stallion's massive neck. "Aye, 'twould be good to fight again."

Better than the dance he was doing with Ediva. He'd kept his distance the whole full moon cycle he'd been here, but she still seemed uncertain and skittish in his presence, as if she expected a blow at any moment. Only those few moments in the chapel weeks ago was he given the opportunity to close that yawning gap between them. Reaching her heart seemed almost within his grasp then, but she pulled away. And since that time, there had been nothing but politeness and distance between them.

Of what good would anything he tried be? He'd practically ordered her to the Sabbath services and, even then, he knew her heart was leagues away. So much good would come if she let God into her heart. He wanted that more than earning her trust.

But it would be nice to have both. Very nice.

After he sighed, Adrien urged the stallion forward toward the keep. He'd seen enough this morning, and with nothing in his belly, he was anxious to return for the noon meal.

And to see Ediva. Though the distance she enforced between them was a trial, he could not deny himself the joy he took in spending time with her. Even in the chapel where they kept the politeness to a fault, he valued their time together. The only mark on such time was the tension he'd felt between her and the chaplain. Entering the bailey, he spied Ediva. His wife. And yet, not his wife, save on some record kept by Poitiers.

She turned then, and her cyrtel, a pale pink like the

roses that climbed the wall near the door, swirled with the movement. Her hair had been coaxed free of her simple veil by a warm breeze. Her wimple was gone, and he was glad to see her long, flaxen braids dropping down below her veil to rest upon her cyrtel.

She met his gaze, and then turned from it far too quickly. Unexpectedly, his heart sank. She still did not trust him even with her own shy looks.

Adrien walked his horse up to her. Thankful that she had the good manners to wait upon him, he nodded to her. "Good day, milady."

"Good day, sir. You chose an early ride this morning."

He dismounted. He towered over her as it was and certainly didn't need the horse to add to it. When Harry ran up, he handed the boy the reins. With cheek enough to last his lifetime, the young squire threw them both a bold grin before leading the horse away.

"I chose this morning to view the fields. They're good for livestock."

"Aye, our beef and mutton are the best in the county."

He agreed. But such was not on his mind. "Ediva, I want to ask you something."

A guarded look shot across her features. "I may not know the answer."

"You do know the answer, for it concerns only you. You don't talk much to our chaplain. May I ask why?"

Her spine stiffened. "He often told me to obey my husband. When I discovered the nightmare I'd married into, I went to him for help for I had no family save some sisters I do not wish to trouble, as they are married and busy with their own lives. But the chaplain said 'twas my duty to obey Ganute for I was a temptress needing to be leashed."

The flatness in her voice didn't match the fire in her

eyes. Stunned, Adrien reeled. "Leashed? You are not an animal, Ediva."

"You called me a guardian in the chapel, as if I were a sheep dog."

He felt his neck heat. "'Twas just a jest because of your desire to protect your people. I meant nothing that the chaplain might have meant."

She feigned indifference as she shrugged. "Why should I obey a man who felt I needed to be hurt each night?"

He led her to a narrow bench, chasing away a pair of children playing on it. When they sat down, he could see the sun sparkling in her tear-filled eyes. His story of pruning the vine now sounded cruel. Why had he even mentioned it?

And why would the God who had blessed him so much turn His back on Ediva? His heart denied such an accusation, but the pain she'd suffered was clear, and God certainly had not blessed her with Ganute.

Why would a loving God allow her to suffer so? He shifted away from Ediva, who stared into the distance beyond the open gate, lips parted slightly, her upturned nose something he found himself wanting to kiss.

Mayhap her chaplain was right. Mayhap she was a temptress and needed a short rein. With her watering eyes and soft, pained words, was she coaxing him from his God? Was that even possible? After all, 'twas not her fault she was so beautiful.

He grimaced. He had devoted his life to fighting, not wooing women. He knew nothing of them, and his inexperience mocked him.

She looked down at her hands, then up to him, again with those watery eyes. He felt as though he'd kicked the timid dog that chased the cats for scraps. He should say something, anything.

Her face aflame, she stood. "I see you agree with the good chaplain. Your words may have been in jest, Adrien, but from the heart does the mouth speak. I see I have no one, not even God to help me." She lifted her cyrtel to step away.

Snapping from his selfishness, Adrien leapt to his feet and caught Ediva's wrist. "I have sanctioned nothing of the sort. My thoughts were not of that."

When she yanked her arm back, he let her go. "What were they of, then? You looked at me as if I were something horrible."

He scrubbed his face, hating that her intuition had led her to such an assumption. He simply didn't know women well enough, and aye, he *was* suddenly afraid that she could so easily tempt him from everything he held dear. "You are not horrible, Ediva."

"Ahh, your honeyed words. They do my heart good."

He groaned at her sarcasm. He was not made for court, with fancy words and charm enough to choke a person.

A commotion rose by the gate, and both of them turned. Ediva, though, spun in the other direction where high upon the battlement, a man pointed to the south, past the village of Little Dunmow. He shouted something Adrien couldn't understand.

"Soldiers and a wagon are coming," Ediva translated. "The guard can see the royal standard." She hurried toward the wall and its narrow stairs to the vantage point. A few feet into her march, she stopped and spun. "Mayhap the foolish king is looking for one of those babes he demanded. An impatient man, indeed!"

Adrien set his jaw. Her sarcasm scraped on his nerves like a blade on a grindstone. He barked out to Harry to fetch his weapon.

Thankfully, his sword arrived long before the soldiers.

'Twas the royal standard, but not the king who bore it. Adrien soon recognized his brother, Eudo, trotting merrily up on a horse as black as Adrien's mood.

"Prado! I'm happy to see you!"

Adrien groaned inwardly at the baby name. Eudo, whose name was a derivative of Eudes, had taken a liking to Adrien's middle name of Prades, giving it a childish spin like his own name. Adrien hated it, but his mother had said it meant rich fields, so he'd tolerated it. Until now.

"'Tis Adrien, brother, not Prado. Not even Prades, in case you prefer that," Adrien said, sheathing his sword and catching the horse's foamy bridle as his younger brother pulled to a stop just inside the gate. Eudo had ridden ahead. The cart and soldiers were still lumbering through the village. "Why the king's standard? Do you have him hidden in the cart?"

Eudo swung off his mount and dusted himself off. "Nay, stealing the king away is yours and our brothers' work, not mine." Eudo smiled brightly. "I'm just a steward on his majesty's orders, having been loaned his standard to ease my travels."

Remembering the day, years ago, that he and his brothers had saved William's life, Adrien growled back, "I am proud to have saved the king's life that day in Falaise. I'd do it again in a heartbeat." He patted the horse's sweaty neck. "What brings you here in such haste? Surely the king's standard would not ease your passage with rebels hiding in the woods?"

"When I learned your wardrobe was being dispatched, I decided your honeymoon was over and I wanted to visit you." He glanced around. "Where is your lovely bride?"

Coming for just a visit? Adrien didn't believe that for a moment. This was no social call. Eudo merely enjoyed the element of surprise too much to reveal his true purpose as yet. Adrien pointed to the battlement. "My sweet bride is up there, wondering if she needs to pierce your heart with an arrow to defend her keep. Or is it *my* heart she wishes to pierce? 'Tis more likely the case, so I suggest you move away from me. I don't know how well she handles a bow."

Eudo's brows shot up. Ediva was leaning hard on the stone wall, which was lower than the parapet she frequented at the top of the keep. Her hands gripped the merlons, and she bore a harsh expression. Beside him, Adrien could hear Eudo's indrawn breath. Ediva pivoted and hurried down the stairs and across the bailey to them.

"My lady, and now my sister," Eudo bowed to her. "Forgive the unexpected visit. I'm here on the king's order."

Ediva shot Adrien a blackened glare.

Dread washed over him. All he could think of at that moment was his promise to her that he would decide what went to the king and when.

Eudo straightened. "Time to pay the taxes to the king."

Chapter Six

Ediva thrust herself forward, only to be blocked by Adrien. She tried to push him away, but his frame refused her.

"He has come to steal our money, he means!" she spat out.

"We will always have taxes, my lady," Adrien growled. "You paid them before without a fuss."

"To an English king, not some Norman Duke from across the channel!"

Adrien shoved his face closer to hers. "Go to your solar, Ediva! I will handle my brother."

"This is my keep also, Adrien," she snapped. "Should I not have a say in what monies are stolen from it?"

"You knew this day was coming." Abruptly, he hauled her close, his face a mere breath from hers. She stilled and looked hard into his eyes. But as she was learning, there was no harshness reflected there.

But that brought no comfort. Aye, she knew this day would come. She knew she'd lost her position as the keep's full owner. But neither tempered her anger.

Adrien loosened his hold. "Allow me to handle this, or you risk losing far more coins. I will not allow one mite more than necessary to be taken. But you must not challenge the king's authority." He dropped his voice. "Go. And trust me."

She stepped back. Did she dare trust him? Rather, did she dare refuse? If King William learned of her defiance, what punishment would be in store for her and her tenants? Perhaps she could trust her husband—with this, for now. She tossed a scathing look at the surprised Eudo before pivoting on her heel and returning to the keep.

In her solar, she fumed to Margaret, the only available ear, about the king from across the channel.

"What's a channel?" Margaret asked.

Ediva sighed. The young girl had no education save the one she'd learned from her mother—to sew and care for her lady, to braid hair and tidy rooms and do her lady's bidding. She knew nothing of the lands beyond her county.

Ediva waved her hand. "The waters between England and Normandy. William was born there and 'twas there he says the throne of England was promised him. Now he has stolen our lands and demands the taxes."

"If the king is here to take the money, Lord Adrien will surely give it, won't he?"

"That's not the king down there, girl!" Ediva was usually patient with her, but not today. She stopped her pacing, knowing there was no one in this keep with whom she could properly vent. "That man is Eudo, the king's steward, younger brother to your Lord Adrien."

"Then as brothers they will settle this, milady. Blood is thicker than water."

"Aye." Ediva sank into her chair, hating that she could not be downstairs but unwilling to risk trouble. Or did she actually trust Adrien? "They will settle this, but to Dunmow's benefit?"

Her maid began to tidy the mess Ediva had caused with

her rant. "I have four brothers, and they're as thick as thieves." As soon as she spoke, the girl cringed. "'Twas just an expression, milady! Lord Adrien will do what's right. He's only seen a few Sabbaths here, but even my father says he's a good man. He'll keep us safe."

Ediva jumped up. "That's *my* task, not his. *I* should give the taxes to the king." She brushed down her cyrtel and fixed her veil, even setting her skewed braids back into place, as her ire rose again. "And I will know just how many coins my husband hands over. Every last one."

She threw open her door.

Adrien had set a guard by her door, but the man shrank away when she shot him a deadly look. "I will see my husband, and no one will stop me."

The man backed off as she stormed past. She found Adrien and Eudo with several other men, including Geoffrey, in the main hall. They were swarming over the strongbox, while Geoffrey held a quill above the ledger.

Each man glanced up as she entered. With her back so stiff it hurt, she marched over. "I will know what is planned for the contents of Dunmow's coffers," she told Adrien bluntly. "It cannot be construed as an insult to the king for me to know how much is being taken."

"His majesty has the right to take as much as he pleases. The keep belongs to him," Adrien answered.

"'Tis my home, though, and I have run it well since Ganute's death. The king can have no complaint, as it is my good management that filled the coffers he now seeks to empty."

"The king has no complaint against you, woman," Eudo announced, folding his arms. "He merely expects you to pay your taxes."

After a sharp glance at the coins stacked on the table, she leaned forward to press her knuckles into the battered wood. She eyed Eudo darkly. "But must my people and I be forced into poverty?"

She could hardly believe her ears. She'd never sounded so defiant, but this was about her keep.

She could feel her husband's heavy gaze upon her skin. If necessary, she would justify her words to him later in private. Lifting her chin, she met Eudo's eyes as regally as she could. "I demand to know how much the king chooses to take. And I deserve to know exactly where 'twill be used."

Eudo stiffened. "How the king uses his money is his own business."

"How strange then that he needs to send the very brother of his servant here, a man whose duty is only to fill the king's cup and serve his food. Aye, you may be capable of handling the monies, but I suspect the king sent you because of your good rapport with my husband, and—" she lifted her brows "—because he has also ordered you to build a castle in Colchester, not far away. And so thus, you need the money."

Slowly, the steward smiled until a short chuckle escaped from his widening lips, proving to Ediva he was merely testing her, something that irked her further. "I can see why you fear for your life, Pra—Adrien," he said in a surprisingly merry tone. "I'm thankful she had no bow up on the parapet when I entered. I might not be standing here right now."

That remark's meaning was lost on Ediva, so she ignored it. She spun the record book around as Geoffrey jumped back. The last line had not yet been completed, but a note above it stated that some men and tools were also leaving.

She gasped, hardly believing what was written. "He will take our men, as well?"

"Aye," Adrien answered coolly. "And if you'd stayed in your solar, I would have told you all this."

She smacked the table, actually making the two guards jump. "We cannot spare the men! 'Twill soon be time to plant! And with the threat of revolt in Anglia, they will need to be available to defend this keep!"

"I will leave one soldier for every three men I take," Eudo promised. "And the tradesmen in the village are hardly farmers, Ediva, so do not tell me of their need to plant."

"You know nothing of our ways. All farm here, Lord Eudo—tenants, tradesmen and even the chaplain if they expect to eat next winter," she snapped. "But one man for three! The number is far too small. Even if you left a soldier for every man you took, do you expect your soldiers will know the work to be done here? Do they know how to farm, or shoe horses or sheer sheep? Those skills are needed here."

"The soldiers will defend your keep, and with two-thirds fewer mouths to feed, I would say you'd be glad to see the trade."

Immediately, Adrien set his hand upon hers to stop her from smacking the table again. His palm was warm, rough, *strong* and was successful in stilling any movement that was aimed to insult Eudo. "Ediva, arguing will do no good. Eudo is borrowing some of the men to move rubble, 'tis all."

"He can use the king's soldiers."

"The soldiers must stay here. The king considers this keep too important to leave its guard to your men. 'Twill only be for the spring and summer."

She could hardly believe her ears. "The work will fall back on the women, and some will give birth soon. Many are still nursing babes!"

"Have faith."

"In what? Faith and an empty cup won't fill a belly. We need our men." She turned to Eudo earnestly. "Three to one is an unacceptable ratio. Two men for one soldier."

Eudo lost his smile. "I will be taking twenty men and leaving six."

She rolled her eyes. "Do you think I'm a foolish maid who doesn't know her numbers? 'Tis even less than the three to one trade you promised!" She paused, her eyes narrowing. "Leave me ten and take eighteen."

Eudo glanced at his brother. Adrien remained smugly silent to his brother's plight.

With a lifted brow, the steward said, "Hardly a two to one exchange, either. Do you think that I don't know *my* numbers? I will leave you seven."

"Leave me ten, and I promise you that they will be returned to you fitter and stronger than when you left them." Ediva lifted the corners of her mouth slightly. "Adrien will ensure they continue their training. A more than fair exchange, sir, to receive back finer soldiers than you left us. You will do the king proud, I can assure you."

Eudo leaned across the table. Ediva did the same. They very nearly touched noses. She'd listened to Ganute barter many times for the things he wanted. She knew her numbers well, and more important, she knew the skill of persuasion. When the steward began to frown, she offered him her most charming smile. "I will take very good care of them, sir. 'Twould hardly be in my interest not to do so."

Abruptly, Eudo laughed as he straightened. "Ah, the head of an exchequer and the wiles of a siren. You have your hands full here, my brother. Very well, woman, I will leave you ten men."

"And two runners, should we need to send for you." She

smiled sweetly. "You'll want to know if we're attacked and the king's holdings are in danger, will you not?"

Eudo grimaced. "Very well. But the two runners will be squires. I won't leave one more man here."

She straightened and shut the record book with a slam, causing Geoffrey to pull back his quill lest it be jammed inside. Adrien chuckled and shook his head.

But Ediva saw no humor in the situation. "There is nothing funny here, my lord." She thrust the record book at Geoffrey. "Lock it and the coffers before we lose it all. We must see about feeding these men as I have promised, so I want a full inventory of the foodstuffs."

With a deep bow, Geoffrey took the book and the box and exited. She lifted her chin. "Excuse me, my lords, whilst I see to the noon meal."

She lifted the hem of her cyrtel and left the brothers alone, hoping desperately that there were enough provisions to fulfill the bargain she'd just negotiated.

Adrien watched her leave. For all that had just happened, he could only think of one thing. They were terribly mismatched. His wife was a clever woman, wedding a sharp mind and a fierce determination to protect her people to astonishing ends. She had actually outmaneuvered his brother—a feat of which few could boast. He had little experience in such negotiations himself but knew for a certainty that he could not have handled them as well. Did she think him a fool, fit only for following orders?

Lord in Heaven, help me understand her.

Eudo slapped his shoulder. "Prado, I have never seen a woman negotiate so well. I'm at a loss to speak."

"Ha! If I could only be so fortunate to see you so stricken. And the name is Adrien. Remember that."

Laughing, Eudo answered, "Come, we need to unload

your things and see about the men I will choose. And I'm hungry. Surely by the time we've done our tasks, that magnificent wife of yours will have some fine fare for us."

Magnificent? Aye, she could be, without even realizing it, but they were still a poor match. She considered him nothing more than an illegal king's representative and refused to give him the opportunity to protect their people. She didn't trust him.

Adrien spent the rest of the day unpacking his things brought by Eudo, as few as they were. His battle gear meant the most to him, and he saw it oiled and hung in his room. Thankfully, Eudo was seeing to the horses and didn't reappear until suppertime.

Supper irked Adrien. Ediva chose not to sit with them, but rather spent the time ordering Geoffrey and the other servants around so the men could be fed. He cared not to sup alone with Eudo and his sharp eyes. His brother missed nothing, even the fact that Ediva kept her distance from them.

So Adrien found himself watching her intently. She looked lovely, although harried. The heat from the kitchen set her cheeks aglow and a sheen of moisture beaded on her nose. She had abandoned her veil for a simple scarf. Even the gilded diadem had been set aside. Her braids had been tied back by a thick ribbon. The chain belt she often favored about her slim waist was replaced by an apron. Her sleeves were rolled up as she set about the task of ordering the food platters around.

'Twas a good meal of young fowl, roasted vegetables and thick slices of warm bread with cheeses melting on the tops of them, but Adrien would rather have had a simple sup with his new wife at his side. And that surprised him.

Then, in the midst of such busyness, she looked up and across the room to him. His heart leapt. As swiftly as their eyes met, she tore her gaze away, and Adrien felt the disappointment ice his heart.

"Seems your wife has found good fare for us, Adrien," his brother said companionably. "'Tis just simple food but well cooked. And the ale is fine, too."

Adrien had no idea where the ale had been hidden these past few weeks. He'd not tasted it nor been offered it since his arrival. But, he noticed, Geoffrey served it in small doses, so it must be in short supply. Regardless, he preferred his wits to remain with him, so he took only juice.

Did Ediva not want a company of drunken soldiers and so doled out the ale in drams? 'Twas likely so, Adrien thought, noting also that the only servants allowed in the hall were males, with the exception of an ancient woman dropping vegetables onto the trenchers.

Indeed, she did protect her people. Her maidservants, especially.

"Why does your wife avoid us?"

"You want to eat, don't you? She promised you'd get your men back healthier and stronger. She cannot do that without providing some supervision." Irritated by his brother's sharpness, Adrien added, "Do not concern yourself with her. I can take care of my own. Was I not doing so whilst you were still in swaddlings?"

Eudo laughed. "You're only three years my senior. You can't remember me in swaddlings."

"You refused to be trained."

The king's steward laughed hard, enjoying the banter. "Tell me, how is married life?" he asked when he stopped. "Or is it so nasty that you have to take it out on your poor brother?"

"'Tis fine," Adrien snapped back. *All he'd ever dreamed of,* he added sarcastically to himself. But by far, the marriage was safer for both of them the way it was, in name only. For they would never see eye to eye on any matter, and any intimacy would only muddy the waters.

He swallowed his bite of food. "Tell me about your new home in Colchester."

"There's little to tell. King William has given me several estates, and I plan to visit them all, but first he wants a castle in Colchester. It's an old Roman town, so there's plenty of good stonework to use. But as for a wife, I have no news."

Adrien watched Eudo study Ediva. As though feeling Adrien's heavy stare, the younger brother dropped his gaze. A surge of satisfaction rushed through him. "The king will no doubt order you married before long," he goaded Eudo. "In fact, I'm surprised that he didn't give you a wife the same day I was given one."

Eudo swallowed down his ale. After he'd set down the tankard, he dried his lips. "He very nearly did, Prado. He'd wanted to give me Ediva." Eudo faced him with a smug expression. "I was to be here, not you."

Adrien sat back. "What stopped him?"

"The king changed his mind when De Veres reminded him that Colchester needed a castle, which would require much supervision to build, while this shire merely needed a good soldier to manage it. Of course, I had not laid eyes on Lady Ediva at that time. Had I, things might have been different."

Adrien tightened his grip on his mug.

"I could have done both, I think, now that I see your wife," Eudo carried on. "Indeed, I may just do both. For I need only the poorest eyesight to see that all is not well for you and Ediva. 'Twould not be difficult to annul this marriage, and we both know I'm better suited to have Ediva as a wife than an old soldier like you. I think the king would agree. He wants babes to come. 'Tis clear to me such won't happen here."

With a small, self-satisfied smile, Eudo took another drink. "This keep is good and strong and not far from Colchester. And its mistress is quite comely. I could do the king proud here."

Adrien had heard enough. He stood quickly. His hands flew out to grab his brother's tunic. Knees banged harshly on the underside of the table as he plucked Eudo from his chair. Mugs and bowls rattled and tipped in the commotion.

Kicking aside his chair when it got in the way, Adrien leaned close to his brother's shocked face. "You will take the king's taxes, and my tenants and all the tools you need, but that's all you will take," he growled. "Do you hear me, brother? For if you say one word to the king about my marriage, save that all is well, I will find you in whatever estate you may be and throttle you with my bare hands!"

Eudo's eyes gaped wide. The dumb nod he offered would have been laughable at another time, but not today.

Satisfied that Eudo had learned his place, Adrien dropped his brother onto the wood floor, uncaring that Eudo struck his face on the edge of the table as he fell. Then, as a horrified silence reigned in the hall, Adrien set his chair aright, then sat and finished his meal with a black glower.

All the while feeling Ediva's surprise from across the lengths of tables.

Eudo was right—the marriage was false and Ediva would not ponder but a moment to have it annulled.

So mayhap 'twas time to change that.

Chapter Seven

With her maid's help, Ediva prepared to retire, though she was hardly tired. Rather, edginess nipped at her, like a cat tiptoeing past a line of sleeping dogs.

The commotion at the head table earlier this evening continued to linger in her mind. She'd restricted the ale in the cups, not only because of its short supply, but also because she hadn't wanted a company of drunkards in her hall. Adrien and his combative brother may think they could handle the men, but considering their own foolhardy brawl, she had her doubts. She'd expected foot soldiers to come to blows, not those two.

Siblings fought, 'twas a fact of families, but 'twas mostly children. Adrien and his brother were men. Surely Adrien wouldn't rise to Eudo's provocation? Surely he was mature enough to settle problems with words, not fights?

So mismatched she and Adrien were, she decided. A brawling soldier for a husband. Her mother would have cringed in horror. Ediva had been trained to marry into English royalty, not into Norman military.

Regardless, 'twas easy to see who had won that skirmish. Adrien had had his brother by the scruff, leaning over the younger man threateningly.

She shook her head in disgust, only to catch her maid's hand as the woman unwound her hair. Margaret cringed. "Oh, milady, I'm sorry!"

"Nay, 'tis my fault. My mind is elsewhere."

"Down with those men, methinks." Then, catching the cold glare from her mistress, the girl hastily added, "I mean your home is overrun with soldiers who demand our taxes and our men! My mind would be there also!"

"Keep your mind on your own business. They leave on the morrow. And until then, you stay up here, girl."

"Aye, milady, I heard that command from the kitchen. Too many men about for any decent maid's liking. Why, I can smell them all the way up here!"

True, some of them *were* in need of bathing, but Ediva could tolerate such slovenliness as long as they hastened their departure. Her thoughts returned to Adrien. With the shock of seeing him battle his brother came the indignation of knowing that he would not stop the man from taking her men *and* her coins, razing her keep bare in the name of the king.

She gestured for her maid to cease. "I'm fine for now. Go to bed. We'll need to be alert in the morning. I expect they'll leave for Colchester early."

Margaret stepped back. "Will you also retire, milady?"

"Nay." She took her cloak from the hook and threw it over her shoulders. "I need air."

"Should I come?"

Ediva shook her head. "Nay. I'll stay on the parapet." She fastened her cloak's brooches. As she prepared to draw up the hood, her maid held out the kerchief she'd worn at supper.

She declined. "I need cool air on my head. It's pounding."

Margaret brightened. "Shall I get you some herb tea?

The midwife left some willow bark in the kitchen for aches and pains."

Ediva considered it and nodded. "Add some chamomile also. But mind you only go to the kitchen and come straight back."

Clearly glad to be doing something after spending her evening cloistered in the solar, her maid hurried off. Ediva rubbed her forehead. Her head was indeed pounding and she hoped that the willow bark tea would taste better than it usually did. Perhaps the chamomile would sweeten it and help her to sleep.

She thought of all the pain she'd endured with Ganute—nearly every pain a woman could feel, short of childbirth. She was grateful to have been spared that. She would never have wanted to have a baby with him.

What kind of life would her children have had with Ganute as their father? He was brutal to all unfortunate enough to cross his path.

You were deemed barren and deserve to be called so for being so stubborn, a nasty voice whispered in her head as she closed her solar door. She hadn't cared what people had called her, but once, when the chaplain had suggested that God had made her barren because of her bitter nature, she'd very nearly cried.

Enough of those memories, she told herself sternly. 'Twas just the old chaplain's opinion and he would dare not voice it again. Adrien—Ediva paused. What would Adrien do if the chaplain spoke to him of those matters? She straightened. There was no way to know—and pondering it only worsened the ache in her head.

She padded quietly up the spiral stairs to the parapet. The night was quiet and she eased against the merlons that rose between slots archers might use. Surprised by the chill, she drew her cloak close. With the clear sky and full March moon, the night felt colder than she'd expected.

But she would not retire yet. The peace this vantage point offered was too tempting. Peace after the confusion in her heart. Adrien had promised he'd protect her tenants, a vow he'd tossed off like an old bone. And seeing him fight his brother cut her to the quick. She'd feared for his life, with Eudo's guards so close. Her marriage may be mismatched, but where would her tenants be if Adrien had been sliced in two by his brother's men? They'd have no protection then.

A footstep onto the parapet forced her to turn. Adrien stood beside the small alcove that held the door to the stairwell. She knew her husband's finely toned body, though the moon didn't cast its glow upon his face.

She straightened. "If you have come for peace and quiet, I shall take my leave."

"Nay. I met your maid in the kitchen. She told me where you were."

Margaret was far too chatty. "I ordered her not to speak to anyone."

"I am her master, not a soldier from whom you kept the women tonight."

"Do you blame me?" She arched her brows. "I have no desire to see these maids have their hearts plundered by your *charming soldiers* like your brother has done to my strongbox. He's not only helped himself to that, but to my tenants, too."

Adrien stepped closer to her. "Ediva, I had no knowledge of his plans for that when he first arrived. I expected a courier to bring my wardrobe and word on when to send in the taxes. I didn't think my brother would come and demand more than coinage besides. 'Tis not his responsibility. The king has other men for that task. Nor could I know that he intended to start the castle in Colchester so soon."

She believed him. *But, oh, the betrayal.* Whether he'd known Eudo planned to take the men or not, he'd done nothing to stop it. The contradiction churned within her. "So why the brawl? Because of his plans?"

"Nay." After a pause, he added, "My brother said something I didn't like. I know, 'twas wrong to fight. I acted before I thought."

Horror swept over her. All that anger just over ill-chosen words? She drew her cloak closer as she eased further down the parapet. She'd never considered that Adrien had a bad temper, but 'twas evident tonight. Ganute often took out his anger on the closest person, which was nearly always her. Was God giving her yet another man like that?

Oh, please don't be like Ganute.

"What did he say?"

"'Tis a matter between brothers. Eudo has always provoked me. I merely corrected him."

Quite the correction, she thought with a swallow. "And if I say the wrong word some day, will that be my correction also?"

He stiffened. "Nay! I would never hit a woman!"

She could only blink at him. Adrien ran his hand down his face. "Ediva, the brawl was a private matter. I've promised you I would never use force against you in any way. I keep my promises. And Eudo can handle a bit of brawling from me. He's earned it before."

Such strength in his words. Her heart lurched with the urge to give in to his reassurances. Still disquieted, though, she searched her mind for an excuse to leave. Of course, her headache. Though the cool wind had cured her of the worst of the pain, she still needed the chamomile to ease the edginess. The morrow would start before sunrise.

"I'll bid you good night, then. 'Twill be an early morn for me."

"Ediva?" There was a pause as expectant as a ewe in springtime as he stepped between her and the stairs. "You have sent Harry to get herbs. What were they for?"

She brushed past him. "Mostly for headaches."

In the moonlight, Adrien turned and frowned. He tilted his head. "Just headaches?"

"And other aches. 'Tis a delicate subject, my lord." *Not to mention humiliating,* she added to herself.

"I am your husband. There should be nothing we cannot discuss."

"Then tell me what happened between you and Eudo. And why you didn't argue about Eudo taking our men!"

He'd moved into the glow of moonlight, showing battle-hardened features frowning in concern. Deep concern that seemed to steal her breath. "Ediva, don't worry yourself with that or with Eudo. Your people will be treated well in Colchester."

"They're needed here!" She shook her head, and daring to raise her husband's ire, she stepped forward to press her point. "Adrien, they work hard on the land, for the king and for the church. To give them more work is unthinkable!"

"Trust me, Ediva. We will have the fields planted and sheep cared for. You secured more men for that task."

"While you didn't!"

He folded his arms as the moonlight glinted on an expression now stony. "I would have, had you not spoken. Once you entered into the negotiation, your skills and wiles interested Eudo more than they should have. I had no idea that Eudo would be so—" He cut off his sentence. "I know why you fought for more men. 'Tis obvious that you plan to use them in the fields rather than practicing their skills in the bailey."

"Is that wrong?"

"Nay." He sighed. "The Word of God tells how men built the walls of Jerusalem—"

"The Word of God! Finally something sensible from it!"

"Ediva! How can you say that? God's Word is His gift for us."

As she stepped away, closer to the merlons, she folded her arms. "I don't know that. I have not read it. My chaplain says I could never understand it, and indeed, I fear he's correct. It says I am evil whilst still an innocent maid. Such makes no sense to me."

As Adrien moved closer, Ediva jammed herself between the merlons, where the crenel gaped open against her back. But Adrien's face showed nothing but compassion.

When he reached out to finger her chin and raise it up, she held her breath. "God does not want to see you hurt, Ediva."

"'Tis too late for that," she whispered.

His words stayed soft. "He loves you."

She turned her head. "Don't do this."

"Do what?"

"Tell me such things. My chaplain would disagree."

"Then he's wrong."

She turned her head and stared into his eyes. The moon was to his right, reaching only half his face. But she easily saw his expression, and her heart lurched. "Please, Adrien. 'Tis very confusing."

"It doesn't have to be so. Trust in Him."

She ached to believe him and to still the disquiet within her. It was so tempting to trust in his faith, his strength, his offer of comfort. The urge to brush the burr of his short beard with her palm and trace the arches that were his eyebrows, all washed over her.

Nay. 'Twould do no good to be beguiled by this man.

She stepped back. "You said that God is pruning me. Oh, how He must love me to slice into my heart!"

Adrien caught her then, pulled her up to him and for a flash she was sure that he'd show the ferocity he'd shown his brother earlier. She gasped, and immediately he set her down on her feet again.

She stumbled against the merlon, her hand finding its corner edge as a sudden wave of regret swept over her. Was it wrong to blame God? Adrien had said man's sins were not God's fault. But hadn't God created them all?

Mixed emotions roiled within. She should ask Adrien to explain and yet, she didn't want to hear his words.

As she opened her mouth, he stepped back. "'Twas wrong of King William to force us to wed, Ediva. I find myself doubting my faith when I think of what God has allowed to happen to you." His voice wobbled. "'Tis not proper to have a marriage do this. One cannot mix oil and water, and I wonder if the King is trying to do that."

He shifted, and the waxing moon captured his expression, burning it into her mind's eye. 'Twas like looking at a man torn apart. What had she done? She took a step closer, but still the mere feet between them felt like leagues.

He held up his hand. "Nay, Ediva. I cannot be a good husband to you. We are too different, not only in faith but in the lives that we lead. My life is devoted to soldiering. You need a husband whose words are not full of folly. You are the lady of the keep, and I am a simple soldier."

"You're a knight," she found herself correcting him *and surprising herself.* "And a baron."

"Such fine words are for the chronicler when he records our marriage, but I cannot be a good husband to you if I cannot even guide you from your bitterness without coming to question my own faith. All I know is that you did not deserve the life you had with Ganute, no matter what the chaplain said."

Her eyes stung with tears. "I wonder if the chaplain sided against me to curry favor with Ganute, lest he be sent to someplace less comfortable."

"Would Ganute have done that?"

She shrugged. Ganute was generally careful who he angered, but there had been times when he'd cut off his own nose to spite his face.

Adrien turned. With a swirl of his long tunic, he walked toward the stairwell. Then he returned. "Those herbs you ordered. Were any of them meant for Ganute?"

She laughed, but the sound reminded her of the crush of thin ice underfoot, brittle and sad.

He shook his head. "You say they're for pain, and I'm certain the ones you requested tonight are, but I can't help but wonder if you had others with the intention of poisoning Ganute."

She felt her jaw drop, realizing how Adrien had misinterpreted her character. No, she had not loved Ganute. Yes, she had rejoiced at being free from him. But could she have brought herself to poison him? No. The herbs had only been to ease the aches he had inflicted on her. "'Twas not to poison Ganute. Nay, the only way I considered ending my suffering was to leave the keep and hide in the forest. But I feared my staff would bear the brunt of my cowardice. I could never stand to see them hurt, especially ones like Margaret, who might have suffered as I had." Ediva bit her lip and looked far off beyond the parapet to where the moon soaked the sloping field in a soft, pale light.

"Ediva? I'm sorry. I should not have even entertained the thought. You're more the protector than the aggressor."

She gripped the merlons. He turned her and with the barest brush of his fingertips, he caressed her cheek. Such a simple movement following such sweet words tightened her heart like a band of steel around a strongbox. All she wanted that moment was to fall into his arms and let him hold her there, snugly, securely.

But she'd only be putting her heart on a platter to be sliced open, for Adrien loved the very things that would surely hurt her.

"Ganute was harsh in claiming his rights as husband. The herbs eased the pain, and the poultices Margaret made from the leftover tea helped the bruises."

"I hope you will never think I'm like that. I have promised you that I will not demand anything of you." His voice dropped, the tone deepening, shaking almost. "'Twould be enough if all I take into battle with me is the memory of your fair looks. If it would be my last thought, recalling how you look tonight, I would die quite satisfied."

Was she really hearing this? Would he truly be satisfied with just that? This made so little sense to her. But then her mind turned to the rest of his statement—the mention of battle. "Would you have to go?"

"I'm a soldier, Ediva. I fight for my king."

She sighed in frustration. "Must there be another fight? Have not enough lives been sacrificed?" Could her people handle further loss? The village held too many widows already. And what would become of them if Ediva herself were to be widowed again?

"'Tis not for me to say," Adrien replied gently. "But should the battle come, I will be ready to fight for my king—and you. To defend our keep." He stepped back and dropped his hand, leaving her cheek feeling the loss keenly. "And mayhap it would be better that I *do* go, for I am also just a man."

She blinked. What did he mean?

Before she could give her question a voice, he straightened. "Nay, I must go with my brother to Colchester to see the work planned for our tenants. I'll return when I am satisfied that they're cared for. We will leave early on the morrow, so there is no need to rise with me."

He spun on his heel and melted again into the shadows. She heard the door beyond click shut. And after that sound, she sagged.

Only when she reached out for the cold stonework beside her did she realize that her hands were shaking like a dry leaf holding to its branch in a harsh November wind.

Then, when she was sure he was no longer in the corridor or stairs, she returned to her solar.

Her disquiet returned with her.

Ediva yanked off her kerchief and wiped her moist face with it. The warm spring breezes felt good on her bare head. In the three weeks since Adrien had left, she'd organized the soldiers in her care into small groups and assigned them to various tasks about the village.

One young sergeant, an obvious leader, had balked at her suggestions that his men drive sheep or guide a plow or sow seed, but she'd remained adamant. And with that, she went to work herself, checking on the women, new and expectant mothers alike, as was expected of her position.

"Milady!" Margaret called out. "Your kerchief!"

She sighed and shoved it back on her head. 'Twas proper form to cover her hair, but Ediva was sure she'd melt like tallow. "I'm done in."

"Milady, please return to the keep. 'Twould do no good for you to get sick. You've worked too hard since Lord Adrien left."

Agreeing, Ediva returned to the keep, though she walked slowly through the village, taking in all she could see. She was too tired to speak with her people directly, but she could watch them as she walked and observe how they were doing with so many of their men away, the soldiers toiling by their sides instead. Life was hard here, and unless the crops were planted, most would starve before Michaelmas, when the first frosts killed the grass.

Were the men who'd been taken to Colchester faring well, she wondered? What about Adrien? There had been no word of them in the time they'd been gone.

An ache grew in her chest. The conversation they'd shared the night before he'd left had etched out a hole in her. He seemed to act as if she'd hurt him, and each time she recalled it, the hole within her grew.

Nay. He was a Norman, a conqueror like his king. She shouldn't be caring if she hurt him. 'Twas because of the emotion of the moment. 'Twas as soft as a minstrel's song, one that would have Margaret sighing with the very romance of it.

But had he not admitted that he was only a soldier and could not be anything else, like a good husband? She should be tossing out all silly daydreams. Letting herself care for Adrien when she couldn't rely on him was hardly good for her heart.

She quickened her step as much as her tired frame would allow.

"Good day, milady!"

Ediva turned to see the midwife in her garden. As she raised her hand to return the greeting, she wondered if the aging woman would follow her, ask her if she needed more herbs? The midwife was far too curious, no doubt knowing why Ediva needed the herbs, as if 'twere her business. If Ediva said she had no need for pain relief, would she ask if Ediva needed a draught to strengthen the babe she might think was growing within her?

She hurried on her way. Rypan, the addled boy, opened the bailey gate for her. "Thank you," she said to him.

He nodded to her shyly. He spoke so infrequently that she expected no answer as she made her way into the keep. The soldiers would return soon for the noon meal, and Ediva could smell her cook's thick pottages and fresh breads. Her own stomach grumbled, but 'twould have to wait.

She needed to attend to something else first. One tenant, who'd been ill when taxes were collected, was better now. His wife had paid the levy owed. Ediva needed to put it into the strongbox and record the amount remitted.

As she untied her money pouch, she sank heavily into the chair in the room off the hall that Adrien had claimed as his own. It was small, orderly—more so, she thought, by Adrien's own sense of tidiness than by Harry's, whose cleaning and organizational skills were sorely lacking.

For a moment she allowed fatigue to conquer her. Her feet tingled from too much walking and her throat burned from too little water.

Finally, she rose. Adrien's trunk sat secure beside the strongbox, and out of curiosity, she opened it. He hadn't taken many clothes with him. Most of his tunics lay neatly folded one upon another, with sprigs of cedar deftly layered to ensure a fresh smell.

Ediva reached for the top tunic, with its sleek, embroidered trim. She let her hand slide along the silken stitches before closing the trunk once more.

But before she lowered the lid, she adjusted one large sprig of cedar, forcing the scents up to her nose. Adrien's own unique scent mingled with the cedar. He preferred mint and orris root in his bath waters. There were fewer satchels of those herbs in the kitchen, she'd noted the other day.

She cleared her throat, reminding herself why she was here and that she had no time for idle thoughts. Dragging the strongbox across and up to the table and pulling up her key from her belt, she set about her task.

It took but a moment to unlock the box and throw open the lid.

She gasped.

The coffers were empty. A wave of cold washed over her as she stared down at the box. Then, her composure restored, she hefted up the record book and opened it.

Geoffrey had recorded the last entry, as she'd seen him do the day Eudo had arrived for the taxes. The last figure was a naught. Nothing. Ediva could only stare at Geoffrey's messy inscription, no doubt caused by her yanking the book away to slam it shut.

Eudo had taken it all. Her last mite *and* her men.

She wanted rage to burn through her, but fatigue from days of supervising the planting, feeding of soldiers and watching constantly from the corner of her eye for a certain knight on horseback to return had drained her of all anger and fury.

She dropped her head onto her arms as the sting of tears threatened. Unless her husband returned with provisions to feed the men, plus the extra soldiers she'd negotiated with Eudo, the keep faced a long, hungry summer. She had to manage more men and see to it that they not only stayed healthy but became fitter than before, as she'd promised. Before promising, she should have ensured there was the coinage to do that! She was paying for her foolishness, for the foodstuffs that had vanished too quickly this spring.

With a slap of her hand on the record book, she straightened. Enough complaining. She had a cook who could stretch a hock of ham over several meals, and the spring greens were reaching their peaks. The hens would be taken off their clutches earlier than usual and the eggs eaten. She would manage. She *had* to manage.

The door to Adrien's chamber flew open. Her maid, face flushed, stumbled in. "Milady! Come quick! There's trouble in the village!"

"What kind of trouble?"

"It's at the smithy's house! You must come quick!" Margaret's eyes were bright with fear as she gripped the chamber's door. "I fear a murder will happen soon!"

Chapter Eight

"Get the soldiers! Hurry!"

Her maid dashed away. Ediva glanced for Adrien's sword but saw that he had taken it. She could barely lift the long, heavy weapon, anyway, so instead she raced for a knife from the kitchen. Outside, the brilliant sunshine struck her hard as she charged out the bailey gate. The blacksmith's house was at the end of the row, the last on the road that led into the woods toward Colchester and first seen when you entered the village.

With the smithy gone with Eudo, his young wife had struggled to do the rudimentary work but 'twas too much with two small babes. Ediva hurried down the hillock toward the house, hoping that the children had not been harmed.

A scream from a woman cut the air, followed by a harsh shout and the whinny of a horse. Ediva hiked up her cyrtel and broke into a full gallop, prepared to stop the murder with her bare hands if necessary.

She ripped around the daubed corner of the hut and skidded to a stop.

Adrien stood there, his horse prancing excitedly behind him. He'd drawn his long sword, the tip of which was pressed against the throat of a man. Beyond them stood the smithy's young wife, Wynnth, her cyrtel ripped at the sleeve and her kerchief gone. A babe squirmed on the ground, crying until the woman released her sleeve and scooped the child up.

Ediva snapped her attention to Adrien. He stood looking as if he considered skewering the other man.

She glanced at his quarry. "Olin!" Ganute's second cousin hadn't been seen since the funeral, after which she'd sent him packing when he'd not-so-subtly suggested he was the rightful heir of Dunmow Keep. She'd forgotten how much he resembled Ganute, and seeing him now turned her stomach.

Adrien gaped to her. "You know this man?"

"'Tis Ganute's second cousin." She glanced back and forth between all those staring at her. "What has happened?"

As if sensing the fear in the air, the babe wailed louder, and barely holding back her tears, Wynnth struggled to comfort him.

"This man was attempting to take from this woman what doesn't belong to him," Adrien announced, all the while remaining as still as a stone.

Olin stared cross-eyed at the blade. "Not true! Ediva, who is the Norman? Order him off of me at once!"

Ediva folded her arms. He even sounded like Ganute. Olin and Ganute may have shared only some distant ancestors, but the apples didn't fall far from the tree.

In addition to arrogance and brutish cruelty, she now added foolishness to their attributes. Surely Olin knew that a Saxon woman could no more order a Norman knight any more than she could order the moon to fall from the sky. "This man is my husband. 'Tis his keep as well as mine, so if you have returned to claim it under some addled pretense, you've journeyed in vain."

Adrien lowered his sword. In a move as fast as lightning, he grabbed the smaller man's neck and pressed him up against the hut. Flakes of daub from the wall showered down around them. "I saw this man accost the smithy's wife. I will run him through, for he deserves no less." For a moment, her breath caught in her throat, but she soon realized he'd uttered the threat for Olin's sake, to frighten him into moderating his behavior. Her husband was a warrior, to be sure, but she also knew him to be a man of faith. He would not kill if there were other options available.

"I would not mourn his loss, and I do not believe many others would either, Adrien, but I fear he will bleed out onto the wall and 'twill cost too much to repair the daub." She met her husband's gaze as evenly as she could manage, which was none too evenly at all. His appearance here was as much a shock to her as Olin's appearance was, but her heart did not dance about in her chest for her cousin-in-law as it did when she looked upon her husband's fine form.

She ignored her silly reaction. 'Twas far too serious an accusation he made. "We'll take him into the keep."

"He deserves to be chased from the village."

A series of pounding feet behind Ediva made her turn. Several of the soldiers raced around the hut to skid to a stop. Adrien released Olin's neck, and the man slumped to the ground with hoarse gasps.

"Lock this man in the cellar." He ordered as he sheathed his sword. "Keep a guard on him."

After the soldiers left, Ediva hurried to the smithy's wife. She was a comely young woman whose only faults were that her house faced the woods and her husband was gone.

"If Lord Adrien is back, milady, would the men be returning also?" Wynnth asked as Ediva led her around the house.

A fast glance at her husband as they turned the corner told her 'twas not so, but she dared not dash the woman's hopes. "Come, let's go into your house and settle the babe."

Sunset had arrived by the time Ediva returned to the keep. She and Margaret had helped Wynnth repair her cyrtel and calm the children. Ediva then ordered milk, herb broth and a quarter of cheese be brought to the house. She'd stayed until bread was rising by the hearth and both babes were fast asleep.

"'Tis not good for a woman to live here alone at the edge of the woods," her maid warned as they walked home. "She cannot defend herself."

"I will send a soldier to guard her house tonight."

"Why is Lord Olin here?"

Ediva shook her head, the knot of unwanted memories rising too fast for her to handle them. "I know nothing, girl. Now, go, help in the kitchen whilst I see to my husband."

Ediva found Adrien in his room. The door stood open and she hovered at the threshold for a moment. He was behind his table, staring down at the record book she'd left open.

"What is this?" he asked, indicating the mess she'd abandoned.

"I was given some coins for taxes and had brought them in to record them, but Margaret interrupted me." She fought down the guilt that chose that moment to rise in her. She hadn't been snooping about his room, yet she felt like a child caught stealing sweetmeats.

"Where are the coins, then?"

She gasped and rushed forward. "They were—" She spied them and blew out a heavy sigh before scooping up the pouch from the floor. "Here they are. I had not yet entered them."

Adrien frowned at the strongbox that still sat open, and empty. "There is no money in here," he said.

Ediva tossed the pouch down. "Of course not! Eudo took it all!"

With widening eyes, Adrien scanned the record ledger. "Nay! Eudo took some but not all!"

"Read the last entry. He took it all. We have nothing but these few coins, my lord, and since you returned alone, we have no men, either. Your brother, under the guise of *obeying your good king,* has stolen it all!"

Adrien shook his head slowly. Eudo did not take all the monies, he was sure of it.

Nay, he wasn't so sure. Ediva had interrupted the exchange. And when she'd learned that her tenants were going, too, she'd distracted the whole group.

What had happened after? Eudo had made a sly comment about Ediva's wiles. She'd ordered the strongbox and record book put away but not without practically snatching the ledger from under her steward's nose. Adrien could see the line of ink where Geoffrey's quill had been dragged along the page.

He rubbed his forehead. In his mind, he was still outside facing that cur, Olin. Even now, his heart pounded with the righteous anger at what could have happened.

Nay! This needed his attention more. Olin was locked up down below. "Eudo couldn't have done this."

She thrust out her arm. "Read the ledger. The coffers were empty when I unlocked the box. And Eudo had graciously reminded us that *all* the money belonged to the king."

Adrien frowned as he pulled up his chair and sat in it.

Who had closed the box? Geoffrey had. And after Adrien locked it, what had happened? Adrien could not recall hearing the jangle of coins in it when it was set down, for his mind was elsewhere. And looking disapproving, Geoffrey had finished the entry and closed and locked the ledger. Disapproving that Eudo had taken it all?

Hating that he'd been so easily distracted by his wife, Adrien couldn't remember exactly how many coins were on the table, either, only that his brother had scooped them up.

Eudo had been doing what during that time? Admiring Ediva?

He refused to speculate. Eudo would never cross *that* line.

Adrien grimaced. But Eudo *had* provoked him with the idea that Ediva could have belonged to him. Could he have taken all of the money to teach them a lesson? Or to provoke his brother, as he was wont to do? Ediva had claimed she would return the men stronger and healthier than before. Did Eudo deliberately take away her means to do so?

He looked up at her, keeping his expression guarded and his mouth a thin line.

"And now," Ediva finished with folded arms, "all I have to feed us is this pittance from one of the tenants. You know the crops aren't ready yet, and I must purchase other foodstuffs. More so now, as your soldiers eat like horses."

Adrien shut the record book. He would confirm this with his brother later. His mind was too distracted now to remember all the details of what had occurred the day Eudo had collected the taxes. Indeed, his mind was so full of the sight of Ediva after the long weeks away from her that he could barely think at all.

After their talk on the parapet, he'd wondered if he should stay away from Ediva permanently. However, a month in Colchester had taught him that, regardless of their vast differences, he much preferred his wife's company to that of his brother's. Indeed, he preferred his wife's company to that of anyone else he could bring to mind. And that was why he needed to ease her immediate fears as quickly as he could.

"While you tended to the smithy's wife, some of the men returned," he said tersely. "We brought with us food-stuffs and several barrels of ale and cider. If Eudo took all the money, he did it knowing that he'd need to send provisions back for his men. Which is what he did."

Ediva blinked at him. "You brought food? Meat?"

"Aye. Plus a dozen geese, sacks of grains and flour and a fresh deer, taken down this morning."

He watched relief wash over her face. In the month he'd been gone, she'd worked hard. The faintest of violet circles arced under her eyes showed as much, and she'd lost some weight. Her cyrtel, the pale gold one she'd worn that day in King William's hall, fit her less snugly, he noticed. 'Twas good he had returned now, instead of later in the summer.

"I ordered supper." He found himself anxious to see her sit beside him for a decent meal. "Join me."

"I'm too busy—"

He stood. "Nay, not for your husband. When was the last time you sat for a meal?"

She looked away. "I broke my fast this morning, as always."

"Cold broth was not meant to last a person all day." He walked around the table and took her arm. But when they reached for the door, he stopped and turned her to face him.

"I'm glad to be home, Ediva," he said softly, taking in her own cautious glance up to his face. His month in Colchester had felt more like a year. The rubble that had been some Roman temple centuries ago was more of a mess than expected, and more had been scavenged over the many years for building materials. The work was taking longer than expected and the men were anxious to return to their families.

She asked, "Who did you bring home with you? I saw no one while you'd pinned Olin to the wall."

"I'd ridden ahead, and while you were with the young wife, three tenants, two of my men plus our provisions arrived."

"Why just three?"

"They were older, and one has hurt himself. Not seriously, but I told Eudo they needed to return. *I* needed to return also, and 'twas best for us to travel together. The forest can be dangerous."

Something flared in her eyes briefly, then fluttered away when she blinked. What was it? Fear? Shock? 'Twas gone too quickly for him to decide. "Then we're still in the same situation, aren't we? I thank you for the food, but now there are six more mouths to feed, so I had best see to the meal."

She tried to slip away, but he caught her elbow. "Nay, you may inspect the provisions after our meal. I have stared at my brother for a month and not at my comely wife. You far outdo Eudo's plain face, which I may add has healed from when I'd shoved him down."

The look on her face had him adding, "And yes, I apologized for my brutish behavior. 'Tis one thing to act that way whilst camping before battle but another to do so in my own keep. Now, we will eat, and after, you may retire to your larder whilst I deal with Olin."

"Olin!" She looked as if she'd forgotten him. "Is he in the cellar with all that good cider?"

"Your cider and your ale are now stored in your larder."
He paused. "I was surprised you had no jail down there."

"There hasn't been a need for one. Anyone who has
broken the law has been punished immediately and sent
home. Often it meant a fine, that's all."

"Then Olin will christen the new jail, such as it is. And
I will see a part of the cellar made into a permanent one."

He led her from his room, releasing her only to lock the
door. The smells of cooking greens and fresh bread filled
the hall as they entered. He could also smell what he hoped
was part of the foodstuffs he brought, such as a fine goose
breast grilling in the hearth. "I brought honey also. I hope
the cook will create some sweet pastries for us."

Ediva entwined her fingers, her attention on the corridor to the kitchen. "She's well-known for her fine desserts.
But the beekeeper had a poor crop last year. 'Twas too wet
for most flowers, and the winter before had been harsh and
killed many bees. We keep the honey for medicine only."

"This spring has been good. There'll be more this fall."
Adrien led her to a pair of chairs inside the hall and held
one for her to sit. A maid brought them a bowl to wash
their hands, then a long bread trencher to share, something
he had not yet done with Ediva. He looked forward to the
meal more so now.

He watched her finger the bread, wondering if honey
would be the only sweetness he'd find this coming fall.

Fresh bread and cooked greens with thick slices of a
large goose breast. Goose! She'd not had such fine fare
since Ganute's last meal here, where he'd ordered all the
best the keep could offer before leaving for Hastings.
Ediva's mouth watered at the sights and scents swirling
around her.

"I ordered the cook to take one of the birds and prepare it immediately," Adrien said. "Enjoy."

He offered the empty mug for the maid to fill with fresh juice. Ediva sliced the cheese that had been laid before them. Her stomach fairly ached with the anticipation of being filled. Furtively, she wet her lips. When Adrien handed her the mug, she took it, not inclined to pull away as his fingertips brushed past hers. How odd that she should not feel any aversion to the delicate touch. Indeed, the slightest brush of his fingers stirred her heart.

The drink was cool and tangy, not at all like the watered ale she'd been serving the soldiers. She set the mug down when her thirst was quenched.

"How is the smithy's wife?" Adrien asked as they began to eat.

"Well, my maid and I repaired her gown and calmed her children. I had some food and milk brought to her."

Adrien nodded. "Good. I fear that if you'd come a moment later, I would have killed Olin."

"Was he really trying to…"

"Aye. I saw it with my own eyes. She was struggling to get away."

Her appetite gone, Ediva sat back. Adrien probably had not met Wynnth before but had seen enough to know that Wynnth's life was at risk, not to mention her honor. He'd acted on his own good sense of right and wrong.

She felt a frown crease her forehead. Adrien made no sense. He'd shown loyalty to her people but had allowed the coffers to be emptied and the men removed. Did she really believe he'd not known about all the money being taken? Aye. He was as surprised as she'd been. But that did not help the keep.

"Olin needs to be punished."

Ediva pulled her thoughts back to the conversation. Now

Adrien was ready to see her cousin-in-law held accountable for the crime of accosting a woman. A rare man, indeed, to believe such a thing was a crime worthy of heavy
punishment.

Stealing a swift look at him, she added, "Be careful
of Olin."

He lifted his brows. "Why? Is he someone of import?"

"Nay. He's only Ganute's distant cousin, but I do not
trust him one jot."

"Tell me what he's like. Had you seen him often after
Ganute died?"

"He had arrived with Geoffrey and Ganute's body,
though I was not told how he learned of the death. He
stayed for the funeral and then went to London, only to
return before Christmas. By then, he'd decided to set himself up as lord here." She could hear the spite in her own
voice and tried to swallow it down with another sip of juice.

"He was unsuccessful, I see."

"He had no rights to my estate. He's only a second
cousin."

"Geoffrey told me that there are no immediate male
heirs on either side of the family. So this estate *should*
have gone to Olin."

"'Tis a Norman law, Adrien, not a Saxon one. I had
rights as the widow." She let out a small laugh. "Olin said
he had the authority to claim Dunmow Keep by order of
the king, but I knew differently."

"How would you know?" He took a piece of meat. Beside him, she inhaled the rich scent.

"Because he came with no writ. I asked him for one,
and he said that King William was busy and would be
sending one on later."

"How do you know all this? Even educated Saxon men
could not know Norman law."

"Remember I said my mother brought a man from Normandy to teach us French and Latin because she'd hoped for good marriages for her daughters? Our tutor taught us Norman laws, too, though 'twas not of interest to us. Our heads were filled with fun and love and future babes. Still, we learned and learned well."

She picked at her meat. "Olin is crafty, but I know him. King William is Norman and prefers the feudal system. I was certain he would not allow this keep to be held by a Saxon lord—certainly not one such as Olin. Though he has allowed several influential Saxon families to remain in their castles and keep their titles, it was at a considerable cost. Olin is a spendthrift. He has no money."

"You could have negotiated such an agreement. You had enough coinage."

"I had no foreknowledge, and the king ordered me to London before I could assemble an offer. But even I could see that he'd want only his most trusted barons in places like Dunmow Keep. 'Tis a well-placed estate. And Ganute ensured a record of it remained in London when King Edward was alive."

"'Twas still a gamble, Ediva. Olin could have come into money."

She set down her knife. "My gamble surprises you? Did I not gamble to keep more men here?"

"And you've done well."

His tone had softened, and she felt her heart hitch disgracefully. She took a moment to nibble her meat to hide her fool reaction and then, setting down her knife, said, "What punishment do you intend for Olin?"

He chose a thick slice of bread. "I haven't decided. I can have him tried and my word as witness will bear much weight."

"He'll be issued only a fine and pay Wynnth a portion of it."

"He wasn't successful in his attack on her."

"Nay, but the fine will be split just the same. My only fear now is that he has no money, and Wynnth will be left with only her shame."

Adrien looked thoughtful for a moment and then nodded. "I'll see him whipped and fined."

She gasped. "Neither your law nor mine requires that."

"Nay, but 'tis wrong what he did. He had no right to that woman, nor to anything at the keep." He paused. "Aren't you curious as to why he's here?"

No, she didn't care. With Adrien here, her position as Lady of Dunmow remained secure. Olin could be tossed out of the village at the drop of her kerchief. But she reminded herself not to be too certain that Olin could do no harm. She knew him to be crafty and ambitious—for all that her position seemed secure, she had no way of knowing what steps he had taken to undermine it.

She finally said, "He's spent a lot of time in London. He can turn his allegiances quickly, and 'tis possible he may have acquired some Norman friends. Hence my warning to be careful."

Adrien studied her for a moment. "I will. Enough talk of Olin. He'll ruin our appetites." He ripped some bread and plucked a piece of cheese from the platter before them. She did the same, allowing her attention to wander about the hall. With very little formality, others had entered. Many of the soldiers were surprised to see Adrien here. He'd acknowledged them with only a short nod.

No one had told them of a special meal and all the pomp and order that went with one, so despite the fine food, the atmosphere was relaxed. Frankly, Ediva was glad. She'd had her fill of such nonsense. Along with Ganute's overconsumption of ales, the ceremonies of a formal supper had a hollow feel. Ediva preferred to simply eat the meal and be done with it.

Finally, Adrien spoke again. "The man will get what he deserves and more. And he will compensate Wynnth, too. I have sent word to Colchester to her man about what has happened and ordered him back. She needs him more than Eudo does."

The words filled her with warmth, but the sensation faded quickly. Adrien was protecting his tenants, but his true allegiance would be to the king. He'd been bothered by the lack of coins in the strongbox, but not overly, she thought. He'd simply handed the funds over without as much as a batted eye.

All her hard work, all her rights as widow and Dowager Lady of Dunmow, all now drifted down the river that fed the nearby Colne. Tears sprang foolishly into her eyes, and she blinked them back.

"There's word from the north that they plan to march south to fight King William," he said softly, unaware of the turmoil within her.

Her head shot up. "When? How do you know this?"

"The king sent spies north, who returned through Colchester. Eudo may have to put his plans for a castle aside and meet the rebels at Ely."

"Ely!" She'd been diligent in her studies of maps and knew well the land there. "'Tis an island surrounded by fens. Hardly worth a battle."

"But good for rebels to secure, is it not?"

She bit her lip. She knew nothing of battles, save the ones within her keep. Still, this talk concerned her. "Will you also fight?"

He straightened. "I live only to fight for my king."

A cold draft shivered through her, and she wished she

had her outer cloak to wrap around her. Adrien's words should hardly be a surprise. He was a soldier, a knight now made baron who'd not taken a wife before. Of course he lived to fight.

And he would die for his king, too. For all his kindness, his promises of justice, all the confusing sides to him, she knew he was just a soldier at heart. A man who would fight for William, pray to the Lord with a faith she could only imagine and be willing to die for both.

And what would King William do then? Would he be so kind in his gift of a husband the next time?

Nay, he wouldn't. She'd heard of Norman ruthlessness, and the next man William would choose for her may make Ganute look as tame as a newborn kitten.

Horror washed like ice through her. She was being selfish. Here Adrien was speaking of dying for his king, and she was concerned only for herself.

Should Adrien die…

Her throat tightened and her eyes watered. She didn't want him to die. 'Twas a simple fact that she could not deny.

"Do you really think another battle will come?" she whispered, barely trusting her voice.

He stared down at his food as his mouth tightened. "'Tis inevitable. East Anglia is fighting King William to the bitter end and he will not tolerate it at all." He covered her cold hand with his warm, rough palm. "I will do my duty. I was never meant to be a baron of a fine English keep anyway."

She found her breath stalled within her as he finished, "Will you return my body to my home in Normandy should I die in battle?"

Ediva gasped. She'd not considered anything such as a war or death. Not for him. "Don't speak of that, Adrien."

"I'm a soldier. It should be discussed."

She busied herself with her food. "Consider it discussed. Let's not speak of it anymore."

Chapter Nine

Two days later, Adrien frowned to himself. He'd not seen Ediva since yesterday morning. Her maid said she'd gone to help the midwife birth another babe for Harry's older sister who was delivering early. Such was the busy life of a lady of a keep. She'd had some tiny clothes sewn and, with a gift of a polished rattle, she'd left early. The birth must have become difficult for her to be away from home still.

Adrien had spent yesterday prosecuting Olin, and with the few landowners remaining sitting as jurors, they found him guilty.

Now, just after sunrise, as he led Olin outside, he looked up to the parapet. It was as empty as he felt at that moment. And as grey as the cloudy day outside.

Olin called over his shoulder as he was led away, "Beware, Lord Adrien. You think you rule here, but this is *my* keep! Fight, people," he yelled to those around him. "Fight for your proper lord! Fight for me!"

Adrien ordered another five lashes for the man's attempt to incite a riot. 'Twas dangerous to inflame the people. They were but poor serfs who did not understand Norman law as well as his clever wife and might be misled by Olin's foolish talk. Should William learn of this man's provocation, there would be unnecessary bloodshed. As distasteful as it was, to whip one man would be better than to take many lives.

Adrien was glad when the punishment ended, though it did not bring him the feeling that justice had been meted out. Wanting a moment's escape afterward, Adrien ordered his horse and left to survey the planted fields. Later, he'd confront Geoffrey to find out what exactly had happened to the missing money. Had Eudo taken it all? He kicked himself for not paying closer attention to that task. Instead, he'd stood there and admired his wife like a fool.

The wiles of a woman had lured away his good sense.

But for now, Adrien thought as he mounted his stallion, he needed to ride. He simply needed to—

His gaze had already begun its journey up the keep's wall and stopped at the top.

Ediva leaned over the merlon, her flaxen braids flicking about in the rising wind and her wimple nowhere in sight. She wore a light blue cyrtel today. When he'd first seen her, her pale hair had enthralled him, but this time, there was the lightness, relief, to her expression to draw him in. The birthing business she and the midwife had been about must have been successful.

His mount stamped its feet anxiously, but instead of giving in to the horse, Adrien slipped off it, handed the reins to the bewildered Harry and strode into the keep.

He found Ediva on the stairs heading back to her solar. The torch above her was nearly out, but he could easily make out her fine form.

"Milady."

She nodded to him, her hand pressed against the rounded stone stairwell. The day was grim, with heavy clouds hiding the sun. He could barely see her in the darkness and waited a moment for his eyes to adjust.

Then he held out his hand. "Come for a ride with me."

She didn't move. "You know I cannot ride."

"You will not be riding alone—you will join me on my horse. You've recovered well enough from the last time. Come. We need this time away."

"We do?"

"Aye. 'Twas distasteful to punish Olin. He's at the chaplain's house recuperating. On the morrow, as long as he's healing, he'll be escorted off the estate."

"So why do we need to get away?" Ediva asked quietly.

"The keep is dismal today. I want to see the brook that feeds the Colne. That river travels right through Colchester. There's a meadow at the junction and a stone large enough to sit on. I want to take you there."

"I've been there."

"How often?"

"Once was enough. I'm hardly so feeble that I cannot remember things."

"Have you ever sat and looked out across the river?"

He couldn't see her eyes, but the air about them chilled. Her answer was cold. "I do not need to do so again."

After he'd fought with Eudo, she'd mentioned to him how she'd considered running away from Ganute. Did the stone bench hold bitter memories for her? Was a longing to escape associated with it?

"*I* need to see it." He reached out and took her hand and added gently, "And I need you to be with me." He wanted them both away from the keep, away from the dreary pall that lingered.

Without allowing additional protest, Adrien led her down the stairs, stopping only to order Harry to bring a meal to them when the sun reached its zenith. He swung up onto the horse and bent down to whisk Ediva up. She let out a squeal of fright, but he settled her down onto his lap.

"Comfortable?"

"Nay, but will that stop you?"

He laughed, feeling the pall finally lift. "Of course not, but be assured, we won't travel any faster than a trot."

She screeched when the horse obeyed and she was thrust back against him, making him laugh again.

Today was for naught but to spend with his wife. There were concerns of missing money, a disapproving chaplain and skirmishes to the north that should have him training with his men, but Adrien wanted none of those problems today. He wanted only to spend time with Ediva.

They trotted onto the road that skirted the village. He urged his horse to follow a sheep path that led to the pasture with the rock.

The wind tossed one of Ediva's braids up across his face, and blushing, she pulled it down quickly, obviously not wanting to lose the death grip she had on him. He took both reins in one hand and wrapped his free arm around her waist before pulling her close. They trotted along in silence for a while, and he was glad to feel her finally relax in his arms.

The place where the brook met the river would be a perfect balm for the ache inside him, he decided. It pastured sheep that cared little for the goings-on of men. Likely a shaggy dog would be watching nearby.

The rock appeared over the rolling ridge. In the distance, Adrien could hear the sheepdog barking out a warning but ignored it. The sheep nearest to them trotted off, lambs following their dams as were their custom.

He slowed his mount to a stop and eased Ediva down before dismounting himself. "'Twas not so bad, aye?"

"Nay, not too bad. But 'tis a short distance. I can still see the keep."

He turned, catching a glimpse of the keep's parapet rising above the hillock. Clouds burgeoned, but to the west blue sky was peeking through. The day would improve, he was sure.

Ediva shrugged back her shoulders and inhaled deeply. "I love the smell of spring."

"Let's sit. I want to do nothing for a while."

Ediva brushed off the stone before easing down onto it. As one large piece, the rock had been hewn into a simple bench. Some long dead carver had cut a series of symbols on the side. Adrien assumed they were Danish. Much of the east coast of England had battled Danes over the centuries.

He flicked the reins off the horse and unbridled it, removing the bit so the animal could graze. After a gentle pat on the stallion's rump, he turned.

Ediva was staring out at the woods beyond the Colne. Up this far, the river wasn't much wider than the road to London and probably shallow. Adrien was sure he'd find himself swimming in it on some hot day this coming summer.

If William didn't call him to fight at Ely.

Regret burst within him, sharp and stinging, but he pushed it away. He wanted to get away from baronial life, if just for a day. He preferred the order within the ranks and spending his days in training or grooming his horse.

In front of him Ediva sighed. A tear had slipped free of her eye and now rolled down her cheek. Ignoring it, she only stared at the forest near the Colne, where some trees dipped close the river, as if their branches drank in the cool, meandering waters.

His heart tripped up. "Ediva?"

She looked up at him, a question on her face.

"You're crying."

Blinking, she lifted one small hand to her cheek and

looked down at the moisture wiped away. Her lips parted, and she hung her head.

His chest tight, he sat down beside her. He took her hand in his and held it quietly. "I have seen you on the parapet, Ediva. And looking out your window. Here, you look toward the forest with tears. You'd mentioned to me that you had thought of running away. Talk to me."

She studied her fingers. "As each day waned, I thought about escaping to the forest. I would wonder how long I could survive there. The winter would kill me if I had no shelter, but I dreamed I'd find some hermit's hut or abandoned sheep pen in some far-off field and live there without fear."

"Why didn't you escape?"

She looked at him, her eyes softened by tears. "What would have happened to the maids if I left? Ganute would have turned on them. And on other helpless servants, like Rypan. Or even Harry."

"Ganute is gone, Ediva. Gone and buried." It was then that he remembered a thought from more than a month ago. At Hastings he'd met several English barons head on in battle and ran them through. He could have killed Ganute.

The thought brought him no pleasure, though he hated the man. Death in battle was far too honorable for a man like Ganute. He should have been tried in court and held accountable for his crimes. Adrien squeezed Ediva's hand firmly. "He can't hurt you anymore."

"And you, Adrien? You're a soldier with violence in your blood. I saw how you grabbed your brother and how you let him tumble down and hit his face on the table. And you might have killed Olin had I not intervened. Indeed, you ordered a lashing where a simple fine would have hurt him more."

Adrien swallowed. 'Twas true. He was a soldier, used

to violence. In the past, he'd justified his nature and work well enough not to give it another thought.

Until now, sitting beside Ediva with her questioning eyes and her pain so deep he feared no one could heal her.

At a loss, all he could do was lift her hand to his lips and kiss it. She shut her eyes as if to savor the sensation and he continued the brush of his lips against her knuckles.

Finally, he lowered her hand and set it back on her lap. "I'm not perfect, Ediva. I want to keep my promises to you, but I fear now that doing so would cause you more grief."

"What do you mean?"

"If I leave, who will protect you? Aye, Geoffrey and your men can do much, but only a Norman lord of this keep can truly keep the likes of Olin away. And yet, as soon as King William calls me, I will leave."

She swallowed hard. She was far too lovely for his good. He looked out at the pastoral view they shared and focused on it instead of her face. "Years ago, my brothers and I—excepting Eudo, who was too young at the time—were called to escort William to his home in Falaise. We vowed to protect the Duke with our lives and kill any who would want him dead. I still stand by that vow, yet now I know some good Saxon people here might want him dead and I find myself unwilling to hurt these innocents. But William is my king and I have sworn fealty to him."

Surprising him, she lifted her hand to his face and stroked his growing beard. Aye, the king was his main concern, but what about these people? What about Ediva, with her warm, gentle touch? He could hardly breathe at the emotions coursing through him.

"You want to keep us safe here, but because of my pride and anger, I have not helped in that matter," she said softly. "My wrongs are my burdens, not yours. I shouldn't cause my fellow man to sin."

Adrien smiled at her reference to the previous week's sermon. She'd actually listened to the chaplain that morning. 'Twas a good start. She smiled back at him and he felt the breath flee his lungs. Then he did what he'd wanted to do since he returned from Colchester.

He lowered his head closer to hers.

Chapter Ten

Ediva held her breath and waited for the kiss. To her surprise, she wanted it to come.

Adrien's lips touched hers so very gently, 'twas as if the breeze drifting in had brushed her. She yielded to the limpness that wafted over her. Adrien removed the distance between them by wrapping his warm arms around her. She wanted nothing else but to have him hold her.

The sun broke free of the clouds and warmed her skin, just as Adrien warmed her soul. She wanted to sit there forever, feeling his strength taking over and his lips exploring hers.

How could a man coax such compliant feelings from her? 'Twas as if the grand world around her had stopped and held its breath to hope in Adrien's success.

'Twas not like anything she'd experienced before. There was no fear. All that coursed through her veins was a warmth that soothed her from her toes to the tip of her bare head.

His horse behind them whinnied and shifted, and that distant dog barked again. Soon, the sound of a mount approaching drifted into her mind.

Adrien lifted his head. "'Tis our noon meal. Whilst

the timing may not be perfect, at least we've worked up an appetite."

She flushed. Indeed, she was famished. She looked up to see young Harry grinning cheekily from atop an aging mare. Over both shoulders hung sacks. He also carried a large skin filled with something tangy and thirst quenching, she hoped.

She cringed. Harry had seen the kiss, no doubt. He'd soon return to tell all who'd listen, she wagered. Still, she found a smile creeping to her face, though her teeth nipped her bottom lip to suppress it.

Adrien stood and relieved the boy of his burden. Ediva took and opened one of the sacks. After finding and spreading out a crisp, white tablecloth, she busied herself with the task of setting out the food. From the corner of her eye, she spied Adrien's stallion move closer to the sway-backed mare, interested in her, but the old mare snorted her disdain. Adrien laughed. "Harry, take that old pony back before she hurts my stallion's feelings."

"Aye, my lord! And enjoy your meal, my lord and my lady!" Harry cried out jauntily as he turned the pony around.

Despite the emotions rolling over her, she laughed. *Shakily.* "That boy. I don't know why I keep him here."

"Because no one else will have him."

"He reminds me of your brother."

Adrien lost his smile. "Aye. Eudo was the spoiled baby but well-liked for his rascal ways."

The vanished smile gave her pause. As he sat down, she asked, "Adrien, why did you and your brother fight?"

"'Tis nothing, Ediva. Forgotten. We apologized whilst in Colchester. Let's forget him."

Again, curiosity sparked within her, but she said nothing more. Tearing her eyes from her husband, she focused on the task of unwrapping their meal. To her delight, she discovered sweet pastries, the likes she'd not seen since Ganute had ordered the feast the night before he left. The pastries shone with a golden, honeyed crust, thanks to Adrien's return with the sweet treat. Her mouth watered as she considered what may be inside. Her cook had a gift of making ordinary things taste delightful. She opened the next wrapping to discover fine cheese flavored with herbs. Inside a third wrap, she found small loaves of warm bread.

And she, still warm from Adrien's kiss, relaxed. "Our cook has outdone herself!"

"And some meats done in pastry, I see, stuffed with herbs and greens. More than I'd hoped."

"You brought good provisions back with you. Thank you."

"Aye, we're blessed. I'd planned to return with only ale and geese and cheese, but we spied a big doe and brought her down."

She leaned forward, her eyes widening. "Not on the king's land, I hope."

"Nay. She'd strayed onto the road just outside of Colchester. One of my guards is an excellent archer. It only took him one arrow. For a portion of her hind, I purchased the honey at an apiary along the way." He sat down across from her and his gaze lingered on her. "I knew you would be hard pressed to keep the soldiers fed, but you've kept them toned and fit thanks to the farm work."

"I had no idea that my plan was so transparent."

"Aye, but 'twas the effort both Eudo and I admired. And I knew 'twas good for our soldiers to learn the skill of planting and shepherding."

She nodded, lost for words as she recalled how she'd emptied her larder, killed more swine than she'd planned and used every last egg in the village. Soldiers had huge appetites.

Adrien sliced the meat and then broke a loaf apart. It steamed gently as he smoothed on some fresh butter. They ate in a comfortable silence, one broken only by the nature around them. The sun had shoved aside the clouds and the day lost its dreary pall.

They finished the meal in due time, but 'twas not a hurried affair. Ediva had knelt until her legs ached, and now she stretched them out. Her ankles showed, but she didn't care. In fact, after staring at her shoes, she bent forward and unlaced them, then kicked the leather free.

All the while feeling her husband's gaze lingering on her. 'Twould be nice to have this be the norm for them. To be comfortable in each other's silence. And to share long looks…

But Adrien had said that he was never meant for such a dreary life. Hadn't he dashed off to Colchester with his brother at the first opportunity? Only to return for—

For what reason, she wondered. He was hardly needed to escort a few tenants who were not required in Colchester.

"Adrien," she began, "what really brought you back this time? The truth, please."

He'd been watching her, but suddenly he slid his gaze over her shoulder to the forest. Distant geese called in flight, but she refused to listen. She wanted only to hear Adrien's voice. "Is this not my home? With the threat of more battles, I returned to be ready."

So he did live only for battle. Not for marriage to a Saxon who trusted no one save herself. Worse than that. Did she even trust herself with the way she was beginning to feel?

She shifted quickly and grabbed the cloths that had

wrapped up their food. The pastries were all gone, and though traces of honey still lingered on her tongue, the taste was now bitter.

"We should go. We've dawdled here for too long. That venison you brought will need to be prepared and I wish to compensate the tenants whose eggs I took. They will gladly take some meat." She chattered on, too quickly for even her ears to make sense of it, but she kept wrapping and working, fully focused on her task.

Beside her, Adrien sighed and began to help. Together, Ediva barefoot, they bundled up the remaining food. He slung the sacks over his horse's back and began to lead the stallion toward the keep, with the two of them walking on either side of the animal up the hillock. When the beast realized he was going home, he tried to increase his pace.

Adrien stopped the horse. "He's anxious to see that mare again. I'll leave the food with Harry and take him for a gallop to wear him out. Are you fine to walk?"

"Of course. I'll put my shoes on. I prefer the quiet anyway."

His mouth a thin line, Adrien mounted the horse before urging it to a trot. A few minutes later, she'd just reached the top of the hillock when she saw him race out of the bailey gate and down through the village. As suddenly as he left, she felt a pang of loss.

The worst had happened. She'd begun to care for the man bound to her in an unwanted marriage. The man who still saw Normandy as his home and who preferred life as a warrior.

Oh, how different they were. She'd not even seen Colchester and he was longing for more adventure than she could ever imagine. She'd heard of the sea beyond Colchester, with its stretches of beaches. A lady her mother knew who had visited once brought a selection of shells.

As a child, Ediva had admired them over and over, rubbing the smooth surface inside the shells with her forefingers until they cramped.

While Adrien, a man older than her, had seen battles and countries and crossed the channel she'd only heard about in a boat so large it could carry a hundred men. Adrien longed for adventure. How dreadful life here must be to him.

But she knew Adrien—and his honor. If he knew she cared for him, he'd be honor bound to stay and 'twould hardly be fair to him.

Suddenly, she decided as she watched him disappear into the forest, she didn't want to be unfair to him.

Nay, not one jot.

Adrien returned late, both he and his mount sweaty and tired. He'd pushed the stallion far too hard and though the beast didn't complain or slow, 'twas a difficult ride for both. Adrien ached, giving him a hint of what Ediva might have endured after her travel to London.

Dusk was near and without conscious thought, he looked up at the top floor of the keep, to Ediva's solar. The windows were already shuttered against the cool night. Should he seek her out? The kiss they'd shared still lingered on his lips.

But what good would it do? One kiss would not turn a sensible woman like Ediva into a woman willing to overlook her husband's flaws and love and trust him.

Although well-schooled, thanks to being born into an affluent family faithful to Duke William, he would easily drop anything and go to battle again. 'Twould be pointless to care for Ediva too much. She might begin to love him back, and then what? Men sometimes didn't return from war, or returned maimed. Was that what he wanted for his wife so shortly after they'd just begun to care for each other?

A strong distaste for war burst on his tongue. He dismounted and handed the reins to Rypan, who had raced out of the stables near the back of the bailey. Nay, he would not visit her. He would clean up and then send young Harry to check on the smithy's wife. And he'd see if Olin was healing. As soon as that man was fit to travel, he would be escorted off the Dunmow estates for good.

"Lord Adrien?"

Adrien turned, finding the chaplain hurrying toward him. The man's long robes swooshed in his haste to reach him.

"How is your guest?" he asked the stern man when he was close enough.

"As well as possible. Your lashes dug deep and were not necessary, but he will recover. I've given him a draught to ease his pain and help him sleep."

Adrien's jaw tightened. "As you say, he will recover."

"We have *frankpledges* here, milord. The men of Olin's *tythe* would have simply been fined—"

"I am well aware of *frankpledges,* sir," Adrien snapped. "But the ten men in his *tythe* are not here to pledge for his innocence or simply accept the fine on his behalf. I clearly saw him accosting the woman, and fining innocent men is foolish. Nay, without those men here, I assumed the role of constable." Indeed, his brother had already assumed that role in Colchester, with the support of the townsfolk there. "The few landowners left here sat as jurors and found Olin guilty. I meted out a fair punishment in accordance to Norman law."

"A fine would have sufficed, sir! The crime was not so great and not all of Olin's doing. Women should learn their place and not lure men to sin!"

Adrien dusted off his tunic, thankful to keep his hands busy while the chaplain spoke so ridiculously. "You say that Wynnth, with her babe in her arms and another in her hut was bent on luring a man of questionable honor?"

"Olin was Ganute's cousin! Not some reprobate of questionable honor!"

"The woman's ripped clothing would disagree. And Olin's kinship with Ganute is no recommendation to me."

The chaplain fumed. "Lord Ganute kept the estate well."

"He brutalized his wife regularly!"

The man stiffened. "He was well within his rights as master! She is willful, my lord. She needs a firm hand, as all women do!"

Adrien took a threatening step toward the chaplain. "Your Saxon laws balk at whipping a man, but a woman may be brutalized? You're addled, old man."

"And Norman law is better?"

Adrien pursed his lips. Nay, Norman law was harsher, and 'twas well known that Saxon laws protected women more. But Adrien would not be dragged into a useless debate. "I will expect you to keep your peace about *my* wife and treat her with respect."

The old monk leaned forward to force his point. "Your wife fights the order to attend services each morning. I ask you, how often has she been to chapel since you married her?"

Adrien stepped back, feeling the sting of the words. But he refused to let this man's rebuke weigh on him. He knew of gentle men of God, kind and loving like the man who taught him his numbers and letters. He also knew of harsh chaplains who kept their parishes tight with fear. Adrien had no cause to suspect that this man wasn't devout, but his way was harsh. 'Twas little wonder Ediva had turned from God.

"Lady Ediva should be setting a good example for the women here, but she does not. She didn't once come to chapel while you were gone, my lord. 'Twould be wise to reprimand her, as you have Olin. Otherwise, you will regret this marriage!"

The man spun and headed back into the chapel. Adrien crushed the urge to follow him and punish him for his harsh words.

But 'twas not his way to reprimand a man of the cloth. Adrien ground his heel into the dew-dampened earth as he turned to stalk into the keep. Having lost his desire for food, he ordered warm water for his ablutions. While waiting, he found himself staring out the narrow window at the hastening dark.

What the chaplain had said about Ediva not attending chapel services was most likely true. Whilst he was here she'd only come when he'd ordered it. But he could not order her to change her heart. Jesus stood at her door and knocked only. He did not burst in unwanted. His eyes shut, Adrien prayed.

What am I to do, Lord? Ganute hurt her, the chaplain threatens her and I keep talking of leaving. She deserves freedom from her pain, but I fear I know not what to do.

No answer came, and with a heavy heart, he opened the door to allow the two servants to carry in water. After he'd bathed, he sat at his table and pulled out his prayer book. With a wide iron hinge and yellowed pages bound to leather, it creaked open. How long had it been since he'd read this? So much had happened, and he hated that his life had taken him from his routines.

But he was learning much about Ediva. Surely that was good, aye? Nay. What he learned disturbed him.

* * *

Early the next morning, Ediva spied a young soldier gallop out of the bailey and into the forest, eastward toward the rising sun. Where was he going in such a hurry?

She watched from the grass outside the wall, where she supervised the spreading of linens and clothes to dry. The earlier they were set out, the better the chances they had to dry, and she was glad to be up early and kept busy. Running the keep was the task for which she'd been well-trained.

Helping the maids, she dug into the basket of wet linens for more. 'Twas a servant's job, but several had fallen ill last night, leaving Ediva to supervise necessary chores with a reduced staff. So she pulled free a large under tunic and fluttered it once.

"Milady!"

She looked over the cloth to her maid. "What's wrong?" she asked, fearing that the sickness had spread to her.

"You have tossed out some coins."

Ediva peered over the cloth to the grass, where her maid had spotted the coins, and quickly scooped them up. Ediva asked, "Whose tunic is this?"

"Geoffrey's, milady. I washed it this morning. They must have been in his pocket."

Ediva frowned. "Why were you washing his tunic? I thought his mother did that."

"Aye, but she's been busy with those who are sick, and she isn't young anymore. I offered to help."

Looking down at the coins, Ediva mused, "He must have forgotten he had them."

Though Geoffrey worked as steward, he also helped his mother, the midwife, keep fowl for their eggs in a coop behind her house. Ediva had begun to purchase the eggs to feed the soldiers, and as the midwife preferred payment in coin over meat, Ediva had sent the sum with Geoffrey to give her.

She nodded and slipped the coins into the drawstring pouch attached to her cyrtel. "I'll return them as soon as we're done here." With Geoffrey busy elsewhere, she'd walk into the village. 'Twould be a pleasant diversion from the chores.

By the time the sun had moved to shine upon the clothes they'd laid out, Ediva was crossing the path toward the village. She found the midwife busy in her garden.

The old woman smiled. "Good day, milady. What brings you here this fine morn?"

"My maid found some coins in Geoffrey's tunic." She stretched out her hand, noting the amount. "I believe they were payment for your eggs."

The woman frowned as she hastily pocketed the money. "Would you also be here for herbs for a nice tea? I have this new season's batch."

Ediva shook her head. The teas she'd drunk for the pain were no longer needed. "Nay, I have no need of them."

The woman's eyes narrowed. "I also have ones that can make you strong. Strong enough to give your lord good, healthy babes."

Ediva backed away. She had no desire to discuss with anyone Adrien's promise not to touch her, least of all the midwife.

Someone cleared his throat behind her and she spun. Geoffrey stood at the front gate. His mother smiled at him.

"Milady," he asked Ediva, "is there something wrong? Are you ill, too?"

She shook her head. "I came to return the coins that fell from your tunic when it was washed." She stiffened. 'Twas a menial task she'd done, and yet, as she spoke of it, she couldn't deny the edginess that had suddenly settled over the trio.

Her skin fairly crawled for some odd reason. Because she'd done something below her station? Looking at Geoffrey's pale face and stricken expression, she frowned. "Are *you* sick? You look ill."

His mother bustled past Ediva, her stout frame a far cry from her Danish roots. "Come inside, my son. I'll make you a draught."

Ediva bid her farewell, slipping past Geoffrey who bowed in respect. Behind her, she could hear the woman fussing over her son.

Some distance out, she turned and looked again at the midwife's small house. Something was amiss. She just wasn't sure what it was. She only hoped that the deadly fever that had killed her mother and mother-in-law wasn't returning.

Chapter Eleven

Thankfully, the illness that swept through the keep passed quickly with no one becoming too sick. Ediva wiped her moist brow during her walk back from the village the next week. She'd been to visit the young mothers, all the while wondering why neither she nor Adrien had caught the fever.

But did it truly matter? She was glad they hadn't—and that no one had died, as so oft was the case. As she entered the bailey gate, her gaze fell upon the exercise yard where the soldiers had gathered. 'Twas midway between noon and the late meal, and the bailey was bustling. With the crops planted and sheep out to pasture, the soldiers had less to occupy their time. So Adrien had ordered some drills.

In case they were called to Ely. Ediva's stomach clenched. Standing inside the gate, she watched her husband work with several archers, strengthening their muscles on an odd instrument full of wheels and cords. He'd shed his tunic and now stood with a short under tunic and lightweight braes that were popular in the warmer weather. A belt cinched at his trim waist. She could see his muscles straining under the effort of tightening the lines of gut.

He didn't see her, and standing still gave her the opportunity to study him. He worked well with the men, smiled often and enjoyed the exercises he shared with the archers. He was truly a wonder to look at. A far cry from Ganute, whose form had rounded and softened over the years. He'd cared not that he was growing fat as long as he was stronger than she was.

While Adrien worked hard to keep himself fit.

Then he turned. And spotted her.

Flustered, she hefted up the bundle of clothes that most of the babes in the village had outgrown. She'd ensure they were washed, mended if necessary and stored 'til the next babe's entrance. Yet, as she hurried about her work, she felt Adrien's stare upon her as brilliant as the sun that beat down this early May day.

The chaplain trotted into view. He had just exited the keep and was hurrying toward the chapel. He bowed and scowled out a greeting that was barely polite. She frowned at him as he hurried by. Mayhap he was sick, for as often as she'd known him, he was never surly with her. He'd long told her what he'd expected of her and faulted her for being barren, in a voice as cold as winter winds, but he'd never been openly sour and discourteous.

Aye, she often found excuses for not going to his services, but she was there whenever something important was scheduled. What more did he expect?

Pay him no heed, she told herself as she pressed on toward the keep. She had more important matters on her mind than his conduct. But at the entrance to the keep above her, she stopped. Some instinct caused her to turn.

Adrien had abandoned his training and was now striding with purpose into the chapel. Had the return of the old chaplain prompted Adrien to enter for prayers?

Oh, to have the faith he possessed! The strength within him came not from smooth and toned muscles, but from faith as strong as their keep. It gave him a peace when he went to war. But 'twas not a quiet strength. It troubled him to explain it.

She bit her lip. Adrien should not battle to explain his beliefs and she shouldn't expect him to minister to her. Mayhap he was going to pray about it.

She swallowed and entered the keep, the load of clothes heavier than before.

Adrien found the cleric in the front pew, praying. He would always assume the man faithful, but his attitude toward Ediva needed to change. Adrien approached the pew and waited for the man to sense him and end his prayer.

The chaplain lifted his head. In the dimness, Adrien could still not see his expression. "'Tis not time for services," the man said. "Or do you need me for something else, my lord?"

Adrien hesitated. A year ago he'd never have considered reprimanding *any* chaplain. He'd been a simple knight, knowing his place. But now he was Baron of Dunmow. And Lady Ediva was his wife, his Baroness. The man had no right to throw surly glares at her as he hurried by. 'Twas by her generosity this chaplain had stayed, and now by Adrien's own grace. Adrien hated the pride in those thoughts, but he hated the old chaplain's rudeness far more.

"I need to speak with you," he stated flatly as his eyes grew accustomed to the dark interior. "About your conduct."

The man looked genuinely perplexed as he rose. "My conduct?"

"I saw the look you cast upon my wife. She is the Lady of Dunmow. She deserves no such disdain."

The chaplain's expression hardened. "She has sinned."

Adrien's fingers dug into his palms. "We have all sinned."

"She resists her duty to come to services."

"And your attitude will remedy that? Did you also reprimand Lord Ganute?"

The chaplain fell silent.

"Answer me, Padre."

The man suddenly blurted out, "Nay, 'twas not my place! But Lady Ediva has stayed away from services and fights my preaching. Both she and that sinful midwife. They conspire together."

Adrien considered the old woman. Margaret had informed him that Ediva had returned some money that belonged to the woman. The old midwife was a secretive crone, sly and comfortable in her position of minor power in the village. Adrien had ignored her for the most part.

But was there another reason for Ediva to visit her? Did Ediva need more herbs for something nefarious? Did the chaplain suspect something?

Nay, the old chaplain was finding fault where none existed. He crossed his arms. "What did they conspire to do, Padre? Did you see your lady go to the midwife's house? Did you hear their words?"

The chaplain hesitated, not answering the question.

Adrien's stared hard at the priest. The man was unnecessarily hard on Ediva and ignoring the fact that he'd allowed Ganute far more sins. It had to end. "Answer me!"

With a shifting look, the chaplain answered, "Nay, I heard and saw nothing. 'Twas just what was said."

Adrien straightened, taking the time to pray quickly for the right words. He'd failed to say the right ones for Ediva, so mayhap God would guide him now. "Did Ganute always obey your counsel and come to regular services?"

The old chaplain colored. "'Twas not my place to order Lord Ganute!"

Adrien narrowed his eyes. "'Twas your place to scold the lady of the keep but not its lord? You are a hardly a shy man closeted away from the world. You knew Lord Ganute well for how many years? You can't tell me 'twas not your duty to counsel him."

"'Twere a few times…" the man began.

Adrien pulled back his shoulders. "And he would not listen, so you badgered Lady Ediva instead?" He pressed his hands to his hips. "Lady Ediva endured much in her marriage, and I don't care if you feel 'twas proper for her to be battered. Her lack of faith needs your prayers, not your reproof. More flies come to honey than vinegar."

He wanted to add that he had the power to send the man away, but the chaplain already knew how tenuous his position was. There was no need to say it. When the older man's gaze fell to the stone floor, Adrien left the dimness of the tiny chapel.

The sunshine outside prompted Adrien to pull in the warm air seeping through the open doorway. But his exhalation was shaky. He had no wish to reprove the chaplain—he only wanted to bring Ediva the respect she deserved. A respect so strong, his heart pounded in his chest at the very thought of his lovely wife.

But there lingered other questions he should have asked the priest. Who had told him that Ediva had visited the midwife? Her visit might have meant nothing but to check on the health of the other women. 'Twas almost as if the gossip was deliberately skewed to put Ediva in a suspicious light. Had it been Geoffrey?

Why did that irk him so? What was it about Geoffrey that had him so suspicious? Adrien's thoughts shifted to the record book, the entry reading naught and Geoffrey's claim that Eudo had taken it and he'd merely recorded the amount.

Adrien felt his jaw clench. 'Twas more than possible, but he didn't like being so unsure. Regardless, he'd soon find out. He'd already sent a missive to Colchester asking for clarification. Eudo would not lie to him. With the king's order to fulfill, he'd have no need.

"My Lord!"

Adrien spun back to face the chapel. The chaplain hurried over. He dipped his head in respect when the older man stopped. "If you please, Lord Adrien, forgive me. Your words are obviously something I need to pray about. But she *is* willful, especially about coming to services."

Adrien folded his arms. "And her first husband? What was he like?"

The old chaplain's lips pursed and tightened as he swallowed. "Lord Ganute was generous to the church."

"'Twas not what I asked."

The old man looked distant for a moment. Adrien reached out and placed a heavy hand on the man's shoulder. "'Tis all right. I have my answer. Though I don't care for it." Adrien felt a lump in his throat and swallowed it down. "We both know full well that Ganute abused his power over Lady Ediva and she's been hurt by it. Would you trust the men around you if you were her?"

The old priest stiffened. "I haven't given it such thought. But I have many prayers and I will use them." He reached up and gripped Adrien's arm with his hand. "Lady Ediva is bitter against men and will not forgive her husband. 'Tis what binds her to her sins."

Adrien nodded. He stared off beyond the chaplain's shoulder, unsure of how to ease his wife's burden. He looked back down to the old man. "We're not here to torment Lady Ediva further and drive her away."

He glanced around the bailey, his eyes lighting on the stables. Slowly, an idea formed. Adrien chuckled. "We've both learned something here, Padre. Let's use it wisely."

The old chaplain smiled. And for the first time since he'd come, Adrien felt the man showed genuine emotion. A small amount of satisfaction.

His heart lighter than it had been in ages, Adrien strode to the stables, allowing the idea forming in his head to blossom and grow.

After two days of rain, Ediva found herself sitting outside enjoying her task of brushing a servant's child's hair. The lovely little girl had long blond locks like hers. 'Twas a good day, though cooler than the early days of May.

She spied her husband closing the distance between them. Although they supped together, it had been so long since they had truly talked. Since that day in the meadow when he kissed her.

Her heart tripped up.

Adrien bowed when he reached her. "'Tis time you learned how to ride, milady."

Did she hear him correctly? "Ride? As in a horse?"

"Aye. I'm not suggesting oxen."

She swallowed as she continued the brushing. "I have done well all these years without learning."

"The mare King William gave us as a wedding gift is too fine to be standing about in a stable. I have taken her out for exercise because her muscles will weaken without it, but she needs a mistress."

Her eyes widened and she accidentally yanked on the little girl's locks. The child let out a yelp.

As she hugged the girl, she turned back to Adrien. "That mare is enormous! And willful. Harry told me that she kicked down several doors in the stables. I can hardly be her mistress."

"Harry told you tales. 'Twas only one door, and she'd not been out of her stable for days and was cranky."

"You're a good horseman. You take her. Or assign one of your men. That young sergeant is strong."

"She needs one owner with authority. I cannot always be around for it, and nor can my sergeant."

She sent away the little girl, her hair now gleaming. Once the child was out of earshot, Ediva stood. "What's brought this on? I am too busy. I have more important things to do than waste time riding horses."

"Such as play with little girls' hair?" He smiled. "You need to learn more skills than what were taught you as a maid. And you need to trust others. You can start by allowing me to teach you how to ride. 'Tis becoming a fashionable quality for a lady, I'm told by Eudo."

She rolled her eyes. "I'm not an addled woman who thinks only of fashion, and besides, how would your brother know of such things?"

"He has dealt with the queen and her ladies, I'm sure. And nay, you're sensible, and as a sensible woman, you know 'tis important to learn new skills. 'Twill do you good."

"Why do I need *this* new skill?"

"So your husband can take you riding, and 'twould please him if you trusted him to teach you." Adrien lifted his hand to stay any more protests. "Remember the pony Harry used to bring our noon meal to us in the meadow?"

With narrowed eyes and a suspicious sidelong look, she nodded.

"She's a good mount. Her mouth is leathered from too many tugs on her bit, and she's too old to bother to run. And she likes children."

She felt her eyebrows arch. "Oh, so you think I am a child!"

"Nay. I think, though, that she'll see you as one." He took her hand before she could snatch it away. "Time for your first riding lesson."

With his hand wrapped firmly around hers—lest she change her mind, she was sure—they walked to the stables. The air was still in this sheltered area and filled with the strong scents of horse and hay. There, Harry, grin firmly in place, held the nag's reins. A small stepping stool was set beside her. Her lips pursing, Ediva could see Adrien had arranged everything beforehand.

All only to teach her to trust him? The very fact they were standing here in front of the stable was proof that she did. But 'twas obvious that he didn't believe it. "And you think I will be able to sit on the saddle without tearing my cyrtel? When the king's men took me to London, I had to yank it up and expose my legs. Thankfully, those men were in fear of the king, for none gave me a second glance."

"Look around you, Ediva. Who do you see?"

She looked around. Their side of the bailey was completely deserted. "No one except you and Harry."

"He's a boy. He doesn't count. I have sent the men outside the bailey so you may maintain your dignity. Now, pull up your cyrtel and stand on the stool. I shall teach you how to mount a horse. Or in this case, a pony."

Ediva caught the humor and shot him a sharp look. "This nag may be short, but she's enormous compared to me."

"And once you're atop her, you'll be taller than her. You must show her that you are in charge. She will smell your fear."

"No doubt. I can smell it, too."

He held out his hand to help her, barely curtailing his smile. "Enough talk, woman. Get on the stool."

Pulling a face, she tried her best to climb up but ended up having the pony shift slightly away, despite Harry's efforts to keep her still. Finally and rather unceremoniously, Adrien helped her.

She squeezed her thighs together tightly to ensure she didn't fall off. And there, sitting rigidly up high, she dug her fingers into the wooden knob of the saddle.

"Give her the reins, Harry," Adrien said with a smile in his voice. "I fear she'll tear the pommel away with her bare hands."

She snatched the reins that were handed to her. "You should have been in a minstrel band with your humor, Adrien. I shall walk this mare around the yard here a bit, but 'tis all for today."

With Adrien's gentle direction, Ediva managed to walk the mare around. With no one about, she did manage to relax. After a short time, she even managed to return the pony to her start point and dismount without too much loss of dignity.

Adrien helped her from the stool and stood holding her hand. "A good start, Ediva. We will continue this on the morrow."

"In such a case, I expect I will need a special cyrtel for the training. One that splits like your mail armor does."

Adrien's smile widened. "'Tis a fine idea. You and your maid go design it, whilst I take this nag for a good grooming after her strenuous ride."

Sniffing at his final joke, Ediva walked around the motte to head into the bailey. Before Adrien's insistence she learn to ride, she had set aside today to inspect the tenants' children with the help of the midwife. In the hall, she spied the old woman with them, and one mother also there. 'Twas part of the mistress's responsibilities to ensure the children were cared for properly, a task she enjoyed very much.

One little girl, an older sister to the babe in the mother's arms, ran up to Ediva as she approached. "Milady, I don't want to be here! I want to be outside! 'Tis a lovely day. I wish summer would never go away! But M'maw says the summer will leave and I don't want it to. I want it to stay, forever and ever!"

Ediva laughed. The little girl had Harry's cheek and with her big brown eyes and sweet smile, she was sure summer would never disappoint her.

"Milady," the midwife called out. "Most of the children are in good health. Some have coughs and sores, but I fear that the sores remain because they pick them."

Together with the woman, Ediva administered salves for the sores and teas for the coughs. She listened to the midwife order the young mother to continue nursing the babe through his cough. And all the children needed to be bathed and have their hair combed briskly every morning. Ediva encouraged the mother there to do so. Then, succumbing to the urge, she took the babe from the mother's arms and cuddled him.

He opened his eyes. Ediva felt her breath draw in quickly. Such big, dark eyes, so dark that surely these wouldn't become the blue she often saw. With the dark, wavy mop the babe wore, he reminded her of her husband. This babe, born just after she'd married Adrien, babbled and smiled at her. Ediva's heart squeezed as she held tight to the child.

Would she ever have a babe like this one? If she didn't, her lands would fall to King William or some distant in-laws in Normandy.

"'Tis good to see a babe in your arm, milady," the midwife whispered in her ear.

She stroked the babe's head. "But what kind of life would my child have? The king now owns all. I have nothing to give a babe. Even its father would be off to war at the first opportunity."

Her words caught in her throat. Adrien had already asked her to return his body to Normandy. Should she be blessed with a child, she wouldn't even be able to give the babe its father.

"Give it love," the midwife said simply. "'Tis all a babe needs."

Love? Of course she'd love her babies. But it seemed wrong to bring a child into the world when she could not even give the child's father her heart. Nay, what would their child learn? Her tenants married and loved freely, and their children benefited from that love. 'Twould not be so for her child.

The midwife sighed. "I fear I will never see one with my son."

She lifted her gaze up in the old woman's bleary eyes. "Geoffrey's still young." She thought a moment. "Mayhap we could arrange for a maid to come from my sister's keep?"

The old woman's eyes sparkled. "Aye! I would be so grateful. Geoffrey needs a woman who can give him a family. But 'twould also be nice to see a babe from you."

Ediva looked away, unexpected tears surging into her eyes and closing her throat. The midwife's gnarled hand covered hers as she stroked the soft hair of the child Ediva held. "I don't see any signs of a babe growing within you."

Heat flushed her neck and cheeks. "Nay. There will be no babe from me this autumn." Longing to have her own child *did* fill Ediva. But she inwardly recoiled. Her husband was a soldier who loved fighting for his king more than anything else.

At the thought of him, she glanced furtively around, and her breath caught again in her throat. Adrien had entered the keep and now stood in the doorway.

His muscles showed his training well. They strained against his light tunic enough to have her wonder if she should make him a few more clothes. He'd put so much into his training that he was fairly bursting at the seams.

She'd studied his form often enough. His body language was masterful, a man who knew his control and was ready to enforce it.

The midwife followed Ediva's line of vision. "I know not what goes on in milady's marriage, but some say that—"

Blushing furiously, she tossed the old woman a harsh look. "Stop spreading rumors, woman."

"I'm just warning you 'bout what's being said, 'tis all."

"Of course," she answered derisively. Passing the babe to his mother, Ediva stood and called to her maid for some sweet pastries to reward the children for their good behavior. The cheeky little girl who'd spoken of summer laughed and danced in anticipation. Ediva would have smiled, but beyond the girl stood Adrien, still deep in his thoughts as he watched her. She could no longer summon a smile. Her heart pounded so much it nearly hurt her chest.

What would it be like to have him truly love her, to have a marriage that was as happy as some she'd seen? It didn't hurt the wives to love their husbands. In fact, they delighted in the love they shared.

Did love really give such pleasure?

Only after the maid slipped past him did Adrien move from the door. Blinking rapidly, Ediva returned to her other duties and spent the rest of the day ordering a stream of cleaning and sewing a new cyrtel. That evening, after a quiet meal with Adrien in the hall, she retired early but soon found herself walking the parapet. She then remembered her promise to the midwife to find a wife for Geoffrey. She returned to her solar and set out a parchment. It had been used before, a letter from Olin to Ganute, and she needed to remove the old text before she could begin. But first, Ediva turned it toward the waning sun to read it.

'Twas about the new court of King Harold, late last summer. Olin warned that Ganute would be called to fight in York that fall. Ediva frowned. Olin's missives that she had seen were usually less interesting. This one must have reached Ganute directly rather than being read first by her.

She read on, straining in the dying light to see the scrawl of Olin's poor script. He confided that he would not fight, for he believed Harold's hold on the throne was weak. To that end, Olin wrote, he would hide in the tower.

Here in the keep? Ediva lifted her head, trying to remember if her cowardly cousin-in-law had visited then. Nay, he had not. He must have found elsewhere to hide, for he certainly had not fought. He was so ill-trained, he would have been quickly killed, and had he tried to desert or avoid fighting, he would have hanged as a traitor.

Shaking her head, Ediva took her powdered pumice and some milk ordered from the kitchen to scrub away the writing. Once it was dry, she worked quickly before the sun set completely. She offered her sister greetings and asked about her family. Both her sisters had found happiness and already each had children. Ediva said little of her own situation before she began the real reason for the missive. She asked if her sister had a suitable wife, perhaps the daughter of a steward, for Geoffrey. Mayhap the girl could come and they could see what might happen.

She blotted it and set the letter by the window to dry.

Should something not stir between the girl and Geoffrey, Ediva wouldn't force them into marriage, as she and Adrien had been.

'Twas not fair that Adrien suffer for her stubbornness, tied to a wife that was his in name only—one who barely shared his life and did not share his faith. The thought of such soured in her stomach and she rose to pace away the feeling.

When the sun washed her solar with red, she made her decision. Tomorrow was the Sabbath. She'd go to the services. Neither may want this marriage, but she'd at least make it as palatable as possible, and that would start with Sunday services.

Chapter Twelve

A smile jumped unbidden to Adrien's lips when he spied Ediva step onto the main floor that Sabbath morning. He'd just come from his chamber beside the hall and had locked the door firmly. Having secured the record book into the strongbox and taken Geoffrey's key until the riddle of the missing money was solved, he'd decided to lock up everything, including his chamber.

Smile widening, he held out his hand to Ediva as she approached.

"I'm on my way to services. Can I assume you are also headed there?" she asked with remarkable calm.

He bowed. "Aye, and I'm pleased you have chosen to attend them with me."

She nodded, taking his arm to allow him to lead her out to the warm, sunny bailey. There, he glanced down at her hand. Her knuckles were cracked. She worked hard, right along with her servants, to ensure the keep ran smoothly.

As they strolled toward the chapel, she said, "Very early this morning, I sent one of your soldiers to my sister's home with a letter."

He stopped. "My sergeant? Aye, I haven't seen him yet today."

"Kenneth is his name."

"Ediva, he is my responsibility. I should have been told."

Her eyes flashed for a minute before she lowered them. "My apologies. 'Twas wrong not to ask you first, but you weren't available and I wanted him to be on his way immediately."

Impressed with the apology, Adrien lifted his eyebrows in surprise. After services, he'd ask her what had been so important that she needed to send a missive immediately, but for now he was grateful for the small mercy that was her contrition.

Though slipping into the pew beside her, he kept his distance. The memory of their kiss by the river would steal his focus far too easily and he didn't want his mind to be wandering about in a daze of adoration during the time intended to be worshipping the Lord.

The scent of candles wound around him as he struggled to keep his mind on the service. But with Ediva beside him in a cyrtel of pale green and a veil and diadem as delicate as her features, she proved to be a difficult distraction. Even the tiny space between them fairly hummed with life, as the air did after a thunderstorm. Alive, tense, brushing his skin and the tiny hairs on his arms.

Finally, the service ended, but Ediva still sat quietly. Adrien held out his hand to her, but she shook her head. "Nay, my lord. I will sit here for a bit. I won't be long, I promise."

Adrien slowly dropped his hand and left her alone. Her back was sword straight and her shoulders were equally rigid. He could see in her profile how her jaw was firm and unmoving. 'Twas not the stance of a woman bowed in reverence.

But he would not rebuke her. She'd come to services and wished to tarry in the chapel. 'Twas all that mattered.

* * *

Not wanting Adrien to urge her to leave, Ediva bowed her head. She'd come today to the services because of the need to strengthen the rapport between them. But now a desire to sit seeped into her soul. She didn't want Adrien to hate their marriage so much that he would seek any pretext to rush away. Sitting and waiting for some answer seemed a viable option—if God would send one, that is.

Perhaps one small prayer…

Her eyes strayed toward the pulpit. The old chaplain had left his Bible there, neatly closed and guarding its secrets.

The candles glowed, although now stubs. The flames would soon sputter and die and plunge her into darkness. Careful not to make noise and encourage someone to peer back into the chapel, she slid silently to the end of the pew. With a fast glance toward the slightly open door, she confirmed no one lingered there. Only sunshine peeked in at her.

She stood and reached for the Bible. It was heavy for its size and the leather binding groaned as she opened it. She glanced up again at the door, but she remained alone.

Scripted in Latin, the words forced her to adjust to the lesser practiced language. Aye, she understood it, but in her daily life she spoke English to her staff and French to Adrien, though he was quickly learning her mother tongue. Latin needed to be drawn from her memory.

She turned a page. The drawings there were exquisite. Ediva allowed her fingers to trace the elaborate pictures that showed love and forgiveness. The words she read were even more confusing. 'Twas not the God who'd put her in Dunmow Keep. The God who lived in this book loved freely.

Her lips pursed tightly, she flipped back to search where Jesus taught how to pray. Finally, the familiar words leapt from the page to her. The congregation often recited that prayer from memory. But now, the verses reached into her.

"...*as we forgive those who trespass against us.*"

She slammed the Bible shut. The draft she caused extinguished the candle nearest her.

At that very moment, a shadow appeared at the door, and she snapped her head up. The small silhouette tipped its fluffy head, allowing the sunshine to radiate from the curly locks. Ediva jumped, unsure of what she was seeing.

Then the creature spoke. "The candle blew out, milady."

Ediva sagged. 'Twas just the little girl who'd wanted summer to last forever. She stepped away from the pulpit. "I see that. Go home, my dear, or your mother will worry about you."

The girl disappeared, but a cloud chose that moment to plunge the chapel into a dimness that even the remaining candle could not fill. Ediva quickly extinguished it before hurrying out.

She found Adrien waiting for her in the hall. It was busy, noisier than it had ever been in the months since Ganute died.

Ediva liked the quiet. But with the scents of delicacies floating about her, the sounds of happy people, the warmth and light from the torches burning merrily, Ediva's emotions surged upward, surprisingly.

Dunmow a happy keep?

At the table set up on a dais, Adrien rose. Beside him, the chaplain also rose, as did the rest of the people in the hall, but Ediva found herself staring only at Adrien. When she reached him, he offered her a seat beside him.

Such protocol. After Ganute died, she'd let it slip away, caring little for it. But to have Adrien treat her so well...

The mood *was* lifted. And as the hall brimmed with people and food, her spirit lifted also.

Flushing, she waited until grace was said before sitting. The meal was served, each course tastier than the last. Geoffrey directed the servers well. Adrien kept the conversation innocuous and she appreciated that. Not once did he ask her why she'd chosen to remain in the chapel or even why she'd come to services. He offered her the meat served to them and she found it spicier than her usual preference. Indeed, 'twas almost as if the food reflected the mood. Warm, spicy, interesting.

But Adrien ate little, and she noticed the chaplain's appetite was also minimal. They talked on about the keep, and Adrien offered teasing tales of Ediva's minimal success in turning his brother's soldiers into farmers.

She smiled between bites of food and the sips of the juice she needed to keep the spices in check. Adrien was showing a lighter, more humorous side of himself she hadn't seen before. Soon, all were laughing at how one young soldier spent an entire morning trying to catch a nasty rooster that had escaped his coop. Finally, at the end of the morning, impish Harry told the young man the rooster would simply walk into his coop at sunset.

And all the time Ediva watched her husband's handsome profile. His straight nose and strong chin, the dark eyes that could hold her captive with a single, warming look.

A haze usually accumulated from the torches above, but today was fine enough for the windows high above them to be opened fully. A strong breeze carried away the smoke and left a freshness Ediva appreciated. Yet was it getting warm in here?

They sat about lazily until the sun had shifted far to the west and the wind had cooled. Around them, the servers gathered up the platters and what was left of the trenchers. Geoffrey began to clear away hers and Adrien's place.

"Another sweet?" Adrien offered her the last on the platter before Geoffrey could remove it.

She looked down at the trencher they'd shared. Crumbs filled it as she realized she'd eaten the majority of pastries. "But you had hardly any!"

"I couldn't get them quickly enough. I fear I need to increase my training if my wife can best me at the sweet-meat tray." His eyes twinkled.

"'Twas not that bad, sir." She flushed. "But I do fear that my appetite is as large as young Harry's over there."

Adrien glanced over to see Harry sitting between a pair of young soldiers, studying them whilst still shoveling food into his mouth with great force.

"He's certainly enjoying himself. However, I do not share his delight in eating today. The meat was strongly spiced and I prefer a blander roast."

"Aye, and I think I drank the most juice as a result."

Beyond, one of the maids sneezed several times in succession, slopping the pitcher she carried. Ediva frowned. "She may be getting sick. Several of the children have coughs."

"Hot water and onion was always my mother's cure for everything." He smiled. "My brothers and I dared not to sneeze or cough within her hearing."

"I would think the spices used would do much the same. They are certainly clearing *my* nose." Her stomach clenched and she touched it. "I fear that mayhap I have indulged too much."

Adrien stood. "'Tis the day of rest. And it looks as though you could use it." He pulled back her chair and she stood. Beside Adrien, the chaplain excused himself, leaving them alone at that end of the hall.

"I *am* tired," she admitted.

"Sometimes you need to stop, Ediva. Did you stop at all whilst I was in Colchester?"

"Of course I did." She sighed. "Though I shouldn't have made the promise of keeping your soldiers strong. I didn't look in the larder first. 'Twas far less foodstuffs than I realized."

Aye. 'Twas far less supplies than she'd expected. She thought hard, remembering several hinds of ham and barrels of ale down in the cellar after her wedding that were not there when she inventoried her larder a month ago. They had not used them all up, surely.

But Adrien was smiling, his expression warm as he leaned close, and her concerns scattered. "'Twas why I returned with foodstuffs. Eudo also knew you couldn't keep your promise but was impressed by your boldness. Norman women are more subdued, less easily provoked."

"Really? Do you have any sisters?"

He pulled a face. "Too many. And come to think of it, they are *often* provoked. Mostly by Eudo, not me. But I bore the brunt of it because he was the babe of the family."

They walked leisurely up to her solar. There, she stopped and leaned her back against the heavy jamb. "Adrien, your brother knows how to provoke you. Is that what he did before you grabbed him?"

Adrien swallowed. With little light from several small slit windows, Ediva found it hard to read his expression. "Aye. He sought to anger me by telling me that he was offered your hand before I was given it."

She gasped. "Was that true? Or did he say it only to annoy you?"

"Both, I expect. Eudo suggested that he might ask the king to annul our marriage, thinking he could build a castle in Colchester and have you as his wife at the same time. The castle was important and 'twas why he wasn't given you."

"Could that happen?" A myriad of thoughts raced through her. She had no desire to change husbands, even if it were possible.

"I do not know."

"Nay! Having met Eudo, I would say he was merely provoking you."

"Nevertheless, he won't do it again."

As she searched her husband's expression, her breath seemed to lodge in her lungs, and her face felt heat rise from deep within. But Adrien remained impassive. Oh, what she would give to know his thoughts.

Still, shock lingered. An annulment? Eudo instead of Adrien? 'Twas not a marriage she could fathom. Nor could she fathom giving up the husband she now had.

She touched his arm. "Adrien, I…I cannot think of having any husband…save you."

The dark corridor refused to reveal her husband's expression, but she heard his indrawn breath. She could sense his strong frame tense. Finally, he stepped back and said, "Enjoy your rest, milady."

Chapter Thirteen

After bidding good day to Adrien, Ediva entered her solar and sagged against the door. She was coming to care for her husband far more than she had ever intended. She swallowed to relieve her dry throat. But with the heat and the tightness within her belly, she strode to her pitcher set and poured some weak juice Margaret had left for her.

She drank deeply. Still, it did not soothe her throat.

In fact, heat and dizziness surged into her head and she fought to keep the room from spinning around her. Staggering to the bed, she gasped. Pain shot through her belly and she curled like a newborn atop the furs.

Then, with telltale tingling at the back of her mouth, she realized the worst. She rolled over quickly and pulled out the pot from under her bed before retching into it.

When she could, she rolled over and shut her eyes. Oh, she hadn't felt this sick for a long time. The day before her first set of nuptials she'd retched with anxiety, but 'twas different now.

After lying on her bed for a while, she tried to sit up. That being successful, she stood tenderly and took a mouthful of the juice again. This time, it stayed. Uneasily.

She pulled off her outer tunic and fell upon the bed

again. The room took up its spinning again. But as she closed her eyes to the terrible sensation, her thoughts turned to Adrien. Then darkness floated over her and stole the spinning room from her vision.

"She's waking, Lord Adrien."

Movement around her. Ediva forced open her eyes and found her solar dim and quiet. Her hair fell across her face, and a rough hand swept it back, causing a streak of pain to slash through her. She tried to speak, but her mouth felt glued shut with dryness.

Her attention shifted. Her maid took a cool cloth to her face, gently dabbing her chapped lips.

"Thirsty," she whispered.

Her maid hurried to the ewer and poured a small amount into a cup. Ediva grabbed it and drank deeply, but the relief was short-lived. "More."

"Nay," a male voice beside her said. She turned, finding herself in Adrien's thick arms. He shook his head. "Too much will only make you sick again."

"I was only sick once. I feel better now."

Her maid gasped. Adrien tossed a sharp look of reprimand at her. "Nay," he answered softly. "You have been sick many times these past few days."

"Days?" She blinked. The sun had set, though the windows were unshuttered. "How many?"

"Five. We weren't sure you'd even awaken, but Margaret was able to get some herb broth from the midwife into your belly."

She tried to sit up but was punished with more pain. "My head."

Adrien helped her. "A headache. 'Tis not good to go so long without drinking."

Her maid fluffed the pillows behind her back and

Adrien eased her against them. She touched the pillow with her hand, finding that her fleece pillow had been replaced with several feather ones. "Not mine," She croaked.

"They're mine," Adrien explained. "I'm afraid you messed yours."

"Sorry." Margaret gave her a dram of water and Ediva sipped it, though she ached to quaff the entire contents of the jug just beyond her reach. Adrien ordered her maid to the kitchen for herb broth and some bread.

"I'm grateful for your help, my lord," Ediva whispered.

"You're my wife, Ediva. I wouldn't be anywhere but here."

The words sounded sweet to her ears, but she remembered the truth he had told her so many times. He was and would always be a soldier. Her keep was not somewhere he wished to stay. And yet he was too honorable to leave her when she was ill.

She forced the painful thoughts away. "Was it a fever I had? Were many others sick?"

"Some. I didn't feel well, but it passed quickly. Harry was sick but not like you. Mayhap one of the children you examined with the midwife had a fever."

She opened her eyes. "Was the midwife sick?"

"Nay. But she has her herbs to keep her healthy."

Ediva found that hard to believe. The midwife had given many herbs to her mother and mother-in-law, but they'd died anyway. But 'twas good that the old woman hadn't fallen ill. She was needed in the village. "So I was the sickest?"

"Aye. We prayed for you thrice daily."

Ediva looked away as she rubbed her forehead. Oh, how it ached! "God spared me? Why? To prune me more?"

Adrien took her hands in his and held them snugly. "I'm sorry I told you that story of the vine. 'Twas not the right passage. You're hurting and you're still angry at Ganute. When I discovered what he'd done to you, I was angry, as well. But we should pay kindness for evil."

"When I buried him, I paid him more kindness than I should have. Many were left on the battlefield."

"Look at me, Ediva." Adrien sat close, and she could smell the scent of cedar on him. "Ganute will continue to hurt you as long as you allow it. But freedom from hurt starts with a small prayer, even a single word. You will find peace, and that peace will grow with you." He paused and tightened his grip on her hands. "But if you stay bitter and angry, you'll be no better than Ganute."

Ediva wanted to pull back her hands but Adrien held them fast. Her head still ached, but the water had helped. A cool breeze chose that moment to sail in and soothe her hot face.

Finally, she whispered, "Nay, I do not want to be like Ganute."

"Ask God for help if it's hard."

The door opened and her maid entered with another tray from the kitchen. They set steaming broth and warm bread on Ediva's table, along with herbs and hot water and cloths. Adrien rose and lit the lamp.

He brought her a small cup of broth and a tiny portion of bread. She ate hungrily, but then he took it from her as she was reaching for the last piece. "Nay, let that digest first. I'll leave so Margaret can help you retire."

"Will you come back?"

"On the morrow. If you feel better, we'll go to chapel and give our thanks."

She smiled at him as he left. 'Twas not so bad to go to chapel with Adrien. He would guide her prayers.

Her next thought surprised her. She looked forward to praying.

* * *

Ediva stepped out of the chapel to welcome the sunshine of the day. The service saw more people than she expected, all praising God for her restored health.

She felt a blush rise in her. Adrien took her arm. "Are you unwell again?"

"Nay, my lord. 'Tis seeing everyone thankful that I've healed makes me feel…" She paused. "Unworthy."

Adrien smiled at her. "'Tis a good sign."

What did he mean? She'd merely sat in the service, feeling regretful for all the angry words she'd tossed at Adrien. But whenever she tried to concentrate, she found her thoughts wandering about.

Though she could not form a prayer, she listened to the chaplain.

And slowly, like the dawn on a cloudy day, she considered the old man's position here. Dunmow was more comfortable than the abbey from where he'd come years ago, and the man was no longer young. Dunmow was his home now—just as it was hers. Aye, they saw things differently and mayhap they always would, but could he have been well-intentioned, though misguided? He had seen to her tenants with care for many years. When she thought of him, she thought only of their conflicts, but there was much good he had done, too.

Now, in the morning sunshine and oblivious to her thoughts, Adrien spoke. "Let us take some food in the hall. You shouldn't stay hungry for long. Did last night's herbs help?"

"Aye. I must thank the midwife for them."

A shadow settled on Adrien's expression as they walked, and she stopped him. "What's wrong?"

"'Tis nothing." He took her elbow. "Let's break our fast."

* * *

After a pause, Ediva nodded. But Adrien knew she'd guessed his thoughts. She had used herbs to ease the pain. Even the thought of such being necessary ate like vinegar in his stomach.

'Twas not the fact she needed them for pain or to sleep, but that the midwife also had herbs that could kill.

And Ediva had been very ill.

His attention snapped back to his wife. Ediva found it hard even to manage the few steps up to the keep. She smiled shakily at him, pulling him from his other concerns. "My legs are as weak as a newborn foal's," she puffed out.

Adrien slipped his arms around her back and legs and swept her up. She grabbed his tunic tightly, but he smiled. "Never fear. I won't drop you."

He carried her into the hall. There, they ate a simple meal of broth, bread and cheese. Nothing spicy, just as he'd ordered. After the meal, he ordered her to do no work and employ her staff for everything.

With a nod, she said she would sort through the baby clothes she'd brought from the village, and he left her with her maid as they began the task.

That evening, Adrien returned early to carry her up to her room. He ordered her maid to help prepare her mistress for bed. "'Twill take several days to regain your strength, Ediva. We'll talk in the morning."

She sat askew on her bed, her big blue eyes full of shock at the gentle handling. She was so beautiful. Her expression still of vulnerable uncertainty, she parted her lips and blinked. He gave into the urge coursing through him. He bent to kiss her.

Their lips had barely touched when Adrien was swept away in a torrent of emotion. He gripped her. He wanted to be her husband, fully, as God intended, but until she released her anger, she'd never be able to accept any love.

He must be patient. He forcedly lifted his head from his short but firm kiss. They looked at each other for a lingering moment. Did he see a tiny spark of trust in her? Or was it something his hopeful heart conjured up?

He stood, refusing to speculate. He needed more soothing thoughts to occupy his frayed mind. Quickly, he took his leave, forcing his mind onto more unsettling concerns.

He needed to get to Colchester. He needed to talk to Eudo face to face. If Eudo had taken the money, Adrien would see it in his eyes.

But to leave Ediva now? Nay, when she was stronger.

He began to walk away only to hear the solar door open.

Turning, he found Ediva's maid gently closing the door and hurrying up to him.

"Milord? May I speak with you? Away from the keep's ears?"

He hadn't heard the expression before, but he understood it. Keeps had enough people and everyone heard the other's business. "The parapet, then?"

The young girl nodded and led the way to the top. Adrien dismissed the guard he'd set there as sentry should the rebellious forces from the north descend.

The maid began again. "'Tis about Lady Ediva."

He stiffened. "What of her?"

"Milady wasn't sick from the fever."

"How do you know?"

"I helped Milady care for her mother and her mother-in-law. Their fevers were much different."

"How so?"

The young woman struggled to find the right words, and worry creased her face. "They did not vomit. Their fevers were higher and their lips went blue. They coughed a lot, too. Lady Ediva was sick with something far different. When I went to the midwife, she gave me herbs that were not the ones she gave Milady's mother and mother-in-law. If we didn't give her the herbs, she'd die, the midwife said. I can't help but wonder if she knew Milady had something different. But she is very good with herbs, so mayhap not."

Adrien furrowed his brow. Margaret's expression was etched with concern as she grabbed his arm. She rarely spoke to him and 'twas always with reserve and had never touched him, but at this moment, her actions burst with urgency.

"Milord, you must take care of Lady Ediva! I have served her for years and seen all she's dealt with. She stayed with Lord Ganute to stop him from turning on me or the other maids. She sacrificed herself for us."

His blood ran cold. He knew in his head the reasons she'd stayed with the man, but to have it spoken from her maid's lips was like dunking his heart into a pond crusted with ice.

"She doesn't deserve to die a frightful death, and such would have happened if we hadn't caught that illness in time. Please let her not come to harm!"

"I cannot stop a fever."

"Nay, none of us can." She shot a swift look around her, as if fearing the keep itself could hear her. Then she pinned him with a look so sharp he nearly felt its prick. "But we can stop *other things* from hurting her."

He squeezed her hand, understanding the words she didn't dare speak, though all the while it seemed his heart would pound right through his chest. "I promise," he whispered. "Return to her, lest she get suspicious, whilst *I do* the protecting."

She nodded and released his arm. As she bustled away,

he clenched his jaw. He'd been part of several royal house-holds. Too many kings and dukes and even babes who would one day reign had succumbed to such illness as the one Margaret had just mentioned.

Ediva had been poisoned.

Adrien strode outside, determined to ask Geoffrey if his mother kept a record of the herbs she administered. Or mayhap, because Geoffrey visited his mother each evening, she'd commented that her more dangerous herbs had gone missing. She was, after all, the only one in the village growing plants that could easily kill. The rest used every scrap of viable land to grow vegetables for personal use, as was their need.

But reaching the center of the bailey, where many soldiers were enjoying the early evening, Adrien could hear the thundering of hooves down the road that led to the west. He folded his arms to await the visitor.

His sergeant was returning from delivering the message to Ediva's sister, requesting a suitable wife for Geoffrey. The sergeant, Kenneth, dismounted. After handing over the reins to Rypan, he reported to Adrien. "Milord," he began. "I have a letter for Lady Ediva from her sister."

He held out his hand and the man set the folded parchment in his palm. "Your journey was good? Any news from the west?"

"Our Duchess Matilda arrived from Normandy and was made queen on Whitsunday. The people of the north are gathering, daring the king to come. King William left for Nottingham and plans to move toward York. Much of the English nobility has fled to Scotland. There is talk of plunder by the king's army, also."

Adrien grimaced. Plunder wasn't honorable. He would prefer to disarm the enemies—not lay waste to the land and hurt the innocent. But if the king willed it, there was little he could do. And what else would the king will? Would he rally his carefully placed soldiers for another battle?

If the king was planning to march north, he'd need soldiers and knights, like he and Eudo. Eudo may be a steward, but he also was capable in battle.

All the more imperative that he speak with his brother soon. The sooner this issue of money was settled, the better. The keep also needed its men back and plans for more battles would delay the building of Colchester's castle, anyway.

And with his suspicions of Ediva being poisoned, mayhap the return of the men would placate whoever had tried the foul deed.

"You've done well, Sergeant. I may leave you here in charge of the soldiers whilst I go to Colchester to consult with my brother." He dismissed the soldier and returned to the keep.

'Twas the next day before he was able to give Ediva the letter from her sister. She read it and nodded. "My sister knows of a suitable woman for Geoffrey. But 'tis hardly the time to send for her. Mayhap, by summer's end we'll suggest it, after the harvest and the work has slowed."

Adrien stood by the open window. "A good idea."

"My sister warns of more skirmishes and battles. She's heard that one of King Harold's sons has returned from Ireland to claim the crown." She looked up from the table where she was sitting. "The forces in the north will fight hard for freedom, too. William may not win."

"He will." Adrien turned to study his wife, his expression sober. She sat now at the table, still in the veil she'd chosen for the day. Her blond braids fell to her waist like cords of gold. She looked nearly restored to full health. Last night's sleep had been beneficial.

His heart swelled and he thanked God that she was better. He hadn't realized the strength of his devotion to her until Margaret had warned him of the poison.

"I must go see my brother," he blurted out.

Her mouth fell open. "Why?"

"I need to consult with him on various matters. First, we need to know the amount of money he took. We're allowed to keep a portion to feed the men staying here."

"I would think you would go to recoup the losses, not ask him."

Adrien's mouth tightened. "I'll get the truth, Ediva, but I won't demand anything from my brother without asking for his story first."

"And if he admits to taking the money with only mischief in mind?

"I will take it back."

"Do you promise to take some back if the king ordered it?"

Adrien didn't answer right away. He wanted to obey the king's decrees, but the people would starve this winter without help, for with the men gone, half the harvest would rot in the fields. Ediva had not only wormed her way under his skin, but so had her people, the children especially, who were to work the lands with their mothers, but chose to play instead, to his secret delight. The women, like the quiet Wynnth, and the servants, who he hoped had seen the fairness in him, had begun to mean something to him.

"I'll do what's right," he finally said.

"And the other reasons you must leave?"

"We need the tenants back. With talk of more battles, the castle won't be built this year. I see no reason for Eudo to keep our men."

Ediva stiffened. He knew he'd sparked an urge to emphasize her point. But to his shock, she merely said, "Be careful. I've lost one husband. I have no desire to bury another one."

"You will *not* bury me," he ground out before sighing. "I will leave on the morrow. My sergeant will take care of the men in my absence. And I *will* return."

Ediva bit her lip. Across the room, he stood stock-still, keeping his arms folded and his knees locked to stop him from closing the distance and hauling her into his arms. She'd lost weight while he'd been gone before and this illness had caused shadows under her eyes, adding to her vulnerability. If someone had really poisoned her, she needed protecting now more than ever.

To prevent that, he'd already ordered the kitchen to give her only the blandest of food, without herbs, under Margaret and the cook's careful supervision. Only plain bread with butter. Eggs would be hardboiled and still in their shells, and there would be no herb tea unless Margaret prepared it herself. He doubted it would cause any suspicion. 'Twas a believable story that her stomach wouldn't be able to take spicy food.

As their gazes locked, all ferocity drained from him. "I'll return as fast as I can, Ediva."

She walked over to the window and looked up at him. "Promise?"

He could smell the faint scent she wore, she was that close. "Aye. Promise me that you'll follow the orders I've left with the kitchen. And not work."

"Of course. I doubt my legs will allow me to work hard. And I fear my stomach will refuse fine foods. Besides I have no desire to have special food prepared for me alone whilst the servants get pottage every day. They rely on me."

"But they must learn to trust me. And you can set the

example." He tightened his jaw. "Ediva, you can take care of your people well whilst still trusting me. You know that by now, surely?"

She studied his expression with great intent. And slowly, she wet her lips. Her eyes filled with tears. "Aye. I know that."

Their gazes lingered on each other and Adrien found himself holding his breath. A small frown furrowed her brow as she leaned closer to him. "Is there more you need to tell me?"

His arms tightened in their fold. "Nay." 'Twould not be wise to suggest that someone had poisoned her. 'Twould break her heart to suspect her staff, but who else could it be? He'd have torn apart the kitchens if he thougth it would reveal the poisoner, but he knew that it was best he stay silent and not make the cur suspicious.

Again, he didn't want to leave. A part of him screamed not to, but he kept it in check. 'Twas necessary to speak with Eudo and he'd only be gone a few days, returning before the next Sabbath.

And to make sure his body knew that, he leaned forward and pulled her close. Their lips met in a sound kiss that sealed his promise to return.

Chapter Fourteen

Adrien left early the next morn. After exiting the bailey, he stopped and turned his mount. He had to look upward. As his courser stomped restlessly, he found what his eyes sought.

On the parapet, Ediva lifted her hand to him. His heart leapt as he saluted her back. Then, tapping his mount, he urged the horse to a gallop.

The ride to Colchester, thankfully, was quiet and uneventful. He stopped only to water and rest the horse and eat the small meal Ediva had ordered for him, then set off again. He reached Colchester by late afternoon.

Adrien entered the town by the main gate, a young soldier snapping to attention as he trotted in. The town's wall was formidable, with more masonry work added recently than in the centuries since the Romans left.

He followed the main street that rode atop a slight ridge. Halfway along, he spied his brother standing near a large Saxon church. Beside him lay a pile of rubble.

"Hello, Prado," his brother called when Adrien rode into earshot. Adrien shook his head. Mayhap Eudo had been provoking him by taking the money. Was he still not doing so with that awful baby name? Once the pleasantries were complete, Adrien dismounted and looked around. "I don't see my men."

"They're up the street at the castle site. I came here to Runwald's Chapel to assess this rubble's worth. Do you know there is simply no natural stone here?"

"'Tis a flat area near the sea. Did you expect any? And you're still planning to build the castle?"

"The foundation's there and 'tis the king's will. Why not?"

Adrien looked around. "Because of the threat from the north. Have you not heard?"

"Aye, but William hasn't summoned me or my men yet."

"*My* men, Eudo. And I'm here to retrieve them. The harvest will be upon us soon and your soldiers would rather lop off human heads than grain heads."

Eudo pulled a face but then slapped his brother's back. "Come, we'll eat and have your horse groomed. I am living near the castle foundation. You can stay with me there."

Over a late meal, Adrien told his brother all the news from Dunmow. He did not delve into his personal relationship with Ediva. There was little to tell, and 'twas no business of Eudo's anyway. "I have another matter to mention," he added.

Eudo picked up his mug. "The missive you sent about the taxes?"

"Aye." He set down his knife. "I didn't receive an answer."

Eudo frowned sharply. "I sent the courier off the day after he arrived with a long note to you."

"He didn't return."

With a concerned expression, Eudo called for one of the guards. He ordered a count of the men and ordered the sergeant in charge of the rider to report to him.

When the sergeant arrived, he stated that he'd watched the messenger leave, but no one had seen him since. Because it had only been a few days, the sergeant hadn't yet reported the man missing. 'Twas not uncommon for a trip to take longer.

Eudo turned to Adrien, his mouth tight and thin. "I'll send some men to search for him. I fear the worst. The roads can be dangerous for a Norman traveling alone."

"I had no trouble. There are few settlements along the way."

"But that rider is less experienced and you and your horse are much bigger. There are many English who would defy William's curfew laws and love to place themselves as heroes. I have heard of several Normans disappearing, only to find their bodies later."

Adrien remained passive. Eudo's words were quite true. He looked at his brother. "What was the answer that you sent with him?"

"I didn't take all the tax money. William instructed me to take only what I needed to start the castle, from Dunmow and several other estates." Eudo's expression showed deep concern. "Adrien, I knew Ediva had no proper means to feed my men, despite her boast. Of course, I'd leave some money to feed them. They're my men, after all."

"Geoffrey, the steward, said you took it all and thus recorded it as such."

"Nay! I ordered my sergeant to leave a quarter of it. Geoffrey counted out the money, for my sergeant's counting skills are not as good. I watched them until Ediva walked in." He lifted his brows at Adrien. "I'm guessing she also distracted you."

Adrien grimaced. "Aye. We should have been watching the money."

Eudo shrugged. "You can't blame either of us. She's a comely woman." Immediately, he held up his hand. "'Tis all I'll say on the matter. My body still aches from your previous admonishment."

"As it should. She's *my* wife."

Eudo's smile returned. "Is she well?"

"Now she is."

Eudo lost his smile. "Now?"

Adrien told his brother of her illness and the maid's suggestion that she'd been poisoned.

"There's no reason to kill Ediva. 'Twould be wiser to poison you, Prado."

"True. But we shared a trencher and a cup. Anyone who'd want me dead, but not her, would not use our food as a weapon. So either way, it could not be a Saxon wanting me dead or a Norman wanting her dead. Besides, others were sick also. Mayhap 'twas just a fever and her maid was mistaken."

Eudo studied his brother. "Whatever it was, be wary, brother. 'Tis a dangerous country in which we now live."

Ediva's strength returned as the day advanced. After she'd seen Adrien leave, she had returned to her solar, but there was too much to do to lie about. So she spent the day ensuring that the rushes on the main floor were changed and all floors swept. She also saw to the collection and drying of the small fruit now reaching their peak. The currants would be needed for both food and teas this coming winter. Such minor work, part and parcel of her duties, was the only way she could keep her mind focused. She would not allow it to so foolishly wander back to when she'd kissed Adrien with far more passion than she believed she possessed.

Aye, she'd never felt such thrill. For the span of the kiss, the keep, nay, the whole of England, faded away. There was nothing save her and Adrien.

He'd promised he'd stay safe and she'd promised she'd eat only as he prescribed. Feeling hungry and unable to find Margaret, she headed for the kitchen for a small morsel to ease the pangs. The noon meal for her had been light and her stomach now complained.

She found Geoffrey in the larder, recording the provisions with the cook.

"Milady!"

She held up her hand. "I'm only here for a bite of bread."

"I will see to it immediately. I'm finished here, anyway. Will you take it in the hall?"

"Nay. My solar."

"As you wish, milady. 'Twould be a good time to rest, too. Lord Adrien wants you to eat and work lightly and has ordered me to ensure it."

She smiled. As if Geoffrey could ensure that. But the thought that Adrien had informed the staff brought a smile to her face. "True. I'll rest awhile after I eat."

Later, when she sank onto her bed, and into Adrien's pillow, she inhaled deeply, filling her head with his scent of orris root and cedar. She'd love to simply lie there, but too soon she must oversee the evening meal.

And it must be a hearty one. If Adrien didn't return with her tenants, she would be forced to send the soldiers to the fields with sickles. The early grains were ready and she needed to confirm that the best seeds would be saved for planting next year. The harvest could start tomorrow if the weather held, though it was cloudy out. She may as well get up.

The corridor beyond her solar was dark, the torch head barely a glow of embers still stuck to the shaft and any light from the small slit window was dull and gray. She stepped onto the stairs and found it darker still. She felt the rounded wall for the torch and found its hilt. A tender, dabbing touch told her that the wick was still warm.

The torches were to remain lit. Her chandler would

hear of this and so would Geoffrey. With careful steps, she made her way down the flight, keeping her hands on the walls and feeling the next stair with the toe of her shoe.

Before she stepped onto the landing that would take her to the main floor, a growl sounded. She froze.

A dog? There were several about the keep, and she always ordered the servants to shoo them out. This one must have slipped in.

"Go! Out!" she told it sharply, but the animal did not move. In the dim light reaching her from the distant hall, she could see shiny white teeth as the animal curled its lip at her. 'Twas odd. She recognized this mongrel—but it was usually shy, even timid around the feral cats. She rarely offered it food but allowed the children to do so occasionally. It had never shown such ill temper.

She glanced beyond, hoping to catch a servant wandering past, but the keep was unusually quiet. Deep in the kitchen, she could hear the sounds of the evening meal being prepared, and down the corridor that led to the main door, she caught noises of men talking excitedly. Someone or something had diverted their attention. A distant tinkling of percussion instruments suggested a traveling minstrel troupe had arrived.

Then the lilting music of flutes drifted in. Indeed, a minstrel troupe *had* arrived. She looked back at the dog. His ruff was up and his hackles looked like a hedgehog's back. She didn't want to call out for help and look foolish. She'd simply brush past…

But someone grabbed her first.

Adrien spent the evening meeting with his tenants and learning how highly the townspeople thought of Eudo. He was a fair leader, Adrien was told, even taking on the role of mediator in several small quarrels. The Norman presence didn't seem to bother the townspeople, who, because of their proximity to the North Sea, had seen many foreigners. Dutch and Danes and even Jews communed in relative peace, with only minor complaints against each other, mediated equitably by Eudo.

He'd taken to the role of constable like a duck to water. Adrien felt his pride swell at his younger brother, even though the man was oft a nuisance. More important, the townsfolk no longer saw him as an enemy. Adrien only wished others were as accepting, like those who hid in the forest and may have ambushed the missing messenger.

Satisfied that the tenants had been treated well, Adrien returned to the house that Eudo rented. 'Twas large and clean, with a good pallet for him to sleep on, complete with fine wool blankets and a down pillow. After the day in the saddle and walking all over the walled town, he longed to retire.

But his mind returned to Ediva. What was she doing? Had she already retired? He knew that once he was out of sight, she'd set about her work as though her illness had never happened, but Adrien knew fatigue would catch up with her.

Was she well?

He lay down, but his eyes refused to close. His lovely wife's pale, golden hair, her beautiful smile and gentle grace lingered in front of his mind's eye.

He'd told her that the memory of her was good enough to take into battle. But oddly, battle was losing its appeal. Nay, that couldn't be so. He would fight for his king and be the first in line to volunteer—

Why would the mind's eye recall Ediva instead of some patriotic action? Shouldn't it recall the stirring of a coming battle, like that at Senlac in Hastings?

He shifted restlessly on his pallet. Leagues away, Ediva

lay in her bed, and the idea that someone had wanted to hurt her ate at him. He should never have come here. But the matter of the missing money and the need for the men to return had to be dealt with.

Still, Ediva was in danger as long as the person who poisoned her remained at large.

As he punched his pillow, he said a prayer for her safety and a vow that he would return to her as soon as possible.

Ediva fought off her attacker, but her cyrtel twisted fiercely, trapping her legs. She reached back to grab the man's hair but found nothing but a wrap of cloth about the head.

He held her fast, his arm nearly choking her. She tried to scream, but he pulled tighter still. When she was spent, he began to drag her up the stair. Her heels pounded on the stone treads until pain forced her to stumble with him.

At the corridor to her solar, he stopped, jerked her close and hissed into her ear. His breath was sour, his voice oddly pitched. "Listen, *milady*. Listen well to what I say to you."

She stilled.

"I know you and Lord Adrien are not lovers, so 'twill not be hard for you to do as I say. If you don't, I will ruin all you hold dear." His voice broke like a boy coming into manhood.

"What is it that you want me to do?" she gasped out.

"You will kill your husband."

Chapter Fifteen

Ediva gasped. "Nay! I'm no murderer!"

He wrenched her closer. "If you don't, I'll kill one tenant at a time until none are left in Little Dunmow."

"'Tis a sin to murder!"

A laugh of mockery followed. "And you are so very pious? I know your Godless heart. You've murdered Ganute many times in your dreams. 'Tis the same."

Tears stung her eyes. She'd wanted Ganute dead so many times. 'Twas the same and she hated the truth. He squeezed his arm. She stiffened as the chokehold tightened.

"Listen!" Spittle sprayed across her cheek. His accent was Saxon but the voice sounded cracked and rough. And that smell about him… "Kill the Norman you married. I don't care how. You have enough herbs in your larder to use against him. Should you choose not to, I'll kill your tenants. And should you tell anyone, I'll kill *more* of your tenants."

"Nay, you cannot kill your own countrymen!"

"We must all sacrifice to purge our lands of these Normans."

She clawed at his arms and pulled in vain. "Do it yourself, you filthy cur."

"I cannot, for Adrien only lets you close to him." He pressed his face to hers. "So 'tis your decision, my lady. Choose Adrien or your tenants. You should be thankful I am not killing *you* for your betrayal."

"What betrayal?" she rasped out as he shifted position slightly.

"You married a Norman. You threw yourself at William's feet to keep your land. You are the most despicable of the lot."

She gritted her teeth. Most of her tenants wouldn't know she'd had no voice in the decision of marriage. They didn't realize that King William would have razed the land here and killed all in Dunmow had she refused to wed. Did they really hate her for her perceived cowardice?

"I'll have you hung on a tree for this!" As she spit out the words, her assailant shoved her to the cold steps. She coughed. It hurt to move, but she strained to turn around. All she saw for her painful efforts was a shadow fleeing down the remaining stairs.

She sagged onto the wooden planks of the upper floor, panting to catch her breath. Beyond, the revelry continued, the sounds of music rising from the traveling minstrels.

She'd been attacked in her own keep! Told to kill Adrien or others would die!

Ediva struggled to stand, then staggered back into her solar. Thankfully it was empty. Should her maid have heard the ruckus and come to her rescue, Ediva feared the woman would have had her neck snapped. The vile cur that had attacked her was that strong—and that ruthless. No doubt he would follow through on his threats.

She sank onto her chair by her table. Shaking, she lifted up her polished silver glass and peered in it. With her other hand, she undid her tunic's high top and gasped. Welts and bruises were beginning to form.

Memories of Ganute's brutality washed over her. He'd been dead nearly a year and the image of him leering as he leaned over her still swamped her mind.

Nay, the man was dead. She had been attacked and threatened by another equally strong.

She smacked down her looking glass. She would not bow to this threat as she had to Ganute's for so long. She'd vowed to protect her people, and 'twas not Adrien's fault he was given this keep. Nay, both meant too much to her to bend to this cur.

Astride his stallion, Adrien trotted into the bailey three days after he left. He'd planned to stay in Colchester for the week but ached to see Ediva too much.

Most of the children were gathered around a brightly garbed man and it took Adrien a moment to realize the fellow was a traveling minstrel. How long had this troupe been here? They showed no signs of packing and leaving.

Adrien searched the bailey for Ediva in vain. Calling to Harry, who was absorbed in the revelry, he dismounted. The squire, his attention still on the minstrel, hurried over.

"Pay heed to your duties, boy," Adrien snapped at him. "You'll make a poor knight if you're so easily distracted."

"Nay," he answered brightly in the French Adrien was still teaching him. "I want to be a minstrel. That man can play the lute and pipes *and* do magic!"

"Fool boy, you can't even carry a tune! And the magic is merely sleight of hand. Beware of that, if you value your soul."

Harry took the reins, his grin still wide. "Aye, sir. But with you to keep me well-behaved, I'm going to heaven when my duty as a knight is done."

"'Tis not good behavior that gets you there, boy. God sees the heart, so keep yours pure." Adrien shook his head.

He should send the boy to Colchester for Eudo to deal with him. They were apples from the same tree. "Where's your mistress?"

"I haven't seen Milady today. But her maid's in the kitchen."

Expecting to find Margaret preparing the simple meal for Ediva as he'd ordered, he was surprised to find her helping with all the meal preparations. The smells of roast goose and onion pies made with rich butters wrapped themselves around his senses. He was hungry, but his hunger to see Ediva loomed far greater than his need for food.

The maid spied him and quickly wiped her hands before hurrying over to him.

"Where is your mistress?"

"She's abed, my lord. She sent me down here to help with the main meal."

"Is she ill again?"

She glanced away. "She didn't seem so, though her voice was hoarse."

Adrien strode out of the kitchen. He spied Geoffrey busy with several servants as they arranged the tables for the troupe. He looked surprised. "My lord! Welcome home! Some minstrels arrived and Lady Ediva asked them to stay, but I fear she won't enjoy them. Milady said she was tired."

Berating himself for assuming she'd mend as quickly as he might, Adrien strode past the hall and bolted up the stairs. Fresh torches lit the way as he hurried along the corridor to the solar.

Ediva lay on her bed, her back to him. He skidded to a stop. Mayhap he should not have stormed in, but concern wracked him so. He drew back the half-open curtain, expecting her to be asleep.

She turned and looked at him, and his heart went cold, she looked so pale. "You're still sick!"

"Good day to you, too, sir!" She smiled her welcome weakly. "I'm surprised to see you so soon. I'm not sick, just tired."

Despite the warmth in the room, she'd wound her hair around her neck as if she felt a chill. The furs were also pulled up.

"I'll order some warm broth."

"Nay!" Her hand shot out as he turned. When she relaxed her grip, she smiled ever so slightly. "Stay with me, Adrien." She hesitated before continuing. "I've missed you."

He smiled. "I've only been gone three days."

"'Tis good to see you home safe. The roads are dangerous."

Adrien thought back to the young soldier who'd been dispatched with the answer he'd sought. That soldier was still missing and others had been sent to find him.

"How was your visit?" Ediva whispered. "Will the men be returning soon?"

Was that the only reason why she missed him? Disappointment sank into his heart. "Aye, they will. And I learned Eudo's explanation on the money." He paused. "But first, Ediva, you need to be cared for."

The door behind them opened and Ediva's maid and with one of the scullery girls padded in. Having anticipated their patrons' needs, two bowls of steaming broth sat on a tray, trailing their savory scent behind them. Despite his concern for Ediva, Adrien inhaled deeply. He'd not eaten all day.

Never mind, he told himself sharply. He had more pressing matters than to fill his belly. He looked back at Ediva. She'd sat up, keeping her throat well wrapped in that glorious hair of hers. But she was still not looking him in the eye. Behind him, the women worked in silence. Ediva needed to convalesce and she'd object to any fussing he'd do. So, with his heart heavy, he stood and bowed to her. "I'll take my leave, then. We'll talk when you have healed."

Ediva sighed a mix of disappointment and gratitude as she unwound her hot hair. She hadn't wanted Adrien to leave, and she needed to know what Eudo had said. Yet, she couldn't have sat in bed with the furs and her thick hair hiding the bruises from her husband's eyes much longer.

Margaret shooed away the other girl and served the broth. "I have a salve for those welts." She shook her head. "Milady, I beg of you to tell Lord Adrien what has happened! You won't confide in me, but consider your husband."

"Nay!" What had that man said? More people would die should she mention his threat? Who would he choose first? Margaret who fussed over her? As much as Margaret could annoy Ediva with her hovering, there was a mutual caring. All through the brutality she'd endured with Ganute, the woman had done her duty faithfully, helping Ediva as best she could.

No, Ediva couldn't bear it if Margaret was killed. She was terrified that the man would take those closest to her to sink the dagger of his threat more deeply. Who was this evil cur?

Thankfully, the next day, the welts had faded somewhat and her throat soothed enough for her to speak without hoarseness. She needed to see Adrien, to assure herself that all was well with Eudo. And that Adrien had not been chosen, should her attacker decide to kill her husband himself. 'Twas a foolish fear, because her attacker had said that he could not get close enough to Adrien to do him harm—yet her heart would not rest easy until she saw her husband again.

She found Adrien in his room, one of the keep's maps spread across his table. He looked up when she entered, and he slowly straightened.

Relief sluiced through her. *He was safe.* And she found she no longer cared about the missing money.

Today, Adrien's tunic was a light brown, trimmed with a thin line of embroidery. Her breath caught in her throat. Was this not the one he'd worn when they'd first met, which turned out to be his wedding tunic? She looked down at her own cyrtel. And smiled. 'Twas the one she'd worn that fateful day. How had such a coincidence come about?

He walked around the table and took her hands. "I'm glad to see you up and well."

"Aye. The herbs and broth did wonders for me."

"And my wife has come to see me for what reason?" His smile widened, and his eyes shone. "Or was it just to say hello?"

She squeezed his hands back. "You came to see me yesterday. It touched me." She looked at the table. "Why do you have a map?"

"I need to see what roads there are between us and Colchester. A soldier who should have delivered a letter has disappeared."

A letter that explained Eudo's version of the missing money? She didn't want to know about that right now, for the news of a man missing was more serious.

She released his hands and walked to the table. "This map shows the county's new roads, made by King Harold when he was still Earl of Wessex."

Adrien stood close to follow her finger as she traced lines on the heavy parchment. He smelled good, like the forest after a rain. She inhaled deeply.

"How well do you know these roads?"

"Only from what I studied when Ganute left to fight." She shrugged and pointed to one broken line that stopped in the middle of the forest on its way to Colchester. "I know that this one goes into the king's forest. 'Tis said it hides thieves and wolves. A dangerous place, even for rebels."

"I doubt that the soldier Eudo sent would have strayed off the main road," Adrien said. "Mayhap a band of thieves or a wild animal attacked him."

Ediva touched his arm. "I'm sorry."

"I'll send out some more men to search for him." He rolled up the map and secured it with a leather thong. Then he walked to the door and called out for Geoffrey and his sergeant. As Adrien handed over the map, he ordered a search for the man. Then to Geoffrey, he wanted refreshments for them.

She thought again of her attacker. He'd demanded that she kill Adrien or others would die. But so far, he hadn't done anything.

An idle threat? Nay. With Adrien's sergeant and several men out searching, would this be the time to carry it out?

A day later, the men returned. Ediva hurried into the hall, anxious for news. Looking up from a map, Adrien shook his head. Fighting her sinking heart, Ediva sank onto one of the benches.

Adrien smacked his palms onto the map. "I fear 'twas not a wild beast that killed the soldier but a man."

She glanced up at him. "Why do you say that?"

"If a wolf attacked him, the horse would have fought back then returned to either Colchester or here. These horses are fighters themselves. But if several men went against him, there would have been little hope for the man, and the horse would have been kept." Adrien walked over to her and held out his hand. "Come, pray with me for the man's safety."

She hesitated. He tilted his head. "'Tis the right thing to do. God loves all men, Saxons and Normans."

Those dark, delicious eyes melted her resolve. But she couldn't… "Nay, Adrien, 'tis not that. 'Tis…"

"'Tis what?"

She bit her lip. "Why should God listen to me? I had thought too many times of Ganute's death, and…" She stopped, remembering her attacker's words and hating how they convicted her.

"Go on," he encouraged softly, his hand still stretched out.

She blinked. "I didn't have the courage to make a true plan or put it into action. The consequences would have been too high should I have failed." She studied her feet and found her vision swimming in unshed tears.

Reaching down, Adrien lifted her chin with his finger. "Ediva, look at me." When she obeyed, she could see only kindness in his dark eyes. "'Twas not cowardice that stopped you. 'Twas the desire to do right."

If only she was so valiant as to care for what was right, but she didn't dare mention the attack two days ago. And what if that soldier had been the first to die because she refused to kill Adrien? How could she call herself brave then?

"Ediva, we've all sinned. But Christ loves us all. He died for us. And as your husband, I'm to love you the same way."

She let out a small gasp. "I don't want to be a widow again!"

"I would die to protect you, Ediva."

She swallowed to ease her suddenly dry throat. Was he saying that he loved her? Or was he just being obedient to his faith? She didn't know and found herself too scared to ask.

Abruptly, he hauled her up and held her. Nay, his statement of laying down his life for her was surely just obedience to his faith. 'Twould be too dangerous to give her heart only for obedience and not for love.

A voice within whispered, *Haven't you already given your heart to him?*

Nay! 'Twas just the romance and her silly female heart taking over her good, practical sense. She would not love a man who was so willing to dash off to war and to his king.

He broke the embrace and led her to the chapel. But there, her thoughts scattered, with prayers as loose-limbed as a newborn foal.

Lord, help me sort this out. 'Twas all she could manage. But she felt better for it.

The next day, early, Adrien sought her out to pray again and oddly, she looked forward to the quiet moment with him.

But afterward, when he escorted her to her solar, Ediva knew she was headed for another riding lesson. Her maid held out her split cyrtel.

Adrien had given her simple lessons so far, and she'd almost hoped he'd forgotten this desire for her to learn to ride in light of all that had happened. But 'twas not so.

"If you did not enjoy chapel so much," she said with a mock frown a short time later in the bailey, "I'd think you planned services in order to lure me out and give me another riding lesson."

He grinned lazily. "Never. We're going on the road to Colchester today. Your lessons are going well enough for us to try you outside the bailey."

She spied Harry leading the gift mare out. "With her? Are you addled?"

He laughed. "Nay, not her. She still needs more training with younger riders. I often put Harry on her to get her used to a smaller lead, which is what he's doing today, though he'll go out to the fields. Today, you'll take another mare." He looked down at the cyrtel she wore. "I'm glad you put on your new riding outfit."

Although still nervous, Ediva mounted an old roan mare and followed Adrien out of the bailey. As they left the gate, she threw one longing look back. Holding the gift mare's reins, Harry stood beside Geoffrey and waved. But being too nervous to release her reins, Ediva offered a hasty nod.

She called to Adrien. "Is this safe? We have already lost one soldier and you may as well be traveling alone for all the help I'll be."

"He traveled at night, alone, and was young and unseasoned at defending himself. We are only riding as far as the new road. I want to see it for myself." His expression was serious. "I *will* protect you."

Indeed, Ediva thought, eyeing his long sword. He could unsheathe it in a heartbeat and by its length, it was a formidable weapon. Aye, she felt safe, but still did not trust her equestrian skills.

They plodded along, disgusting Adrien's stallion, who obviously longed to run. But Adrien kept the beast under tight control.

Summer heat dissolved in the shady forest and Ediva was glad for it. Ahead, she heard Adrien sigh before he turned.

"'Tis a good day for a ride and the forest is cool."

"What are summers like in Normandy?"

"Much like this, but less green. Our winters are harsher."

She swatted an insect quickly, lest she lose her grip on

the reins. "Wait until autumn. There are no insects, yet the weather is still pleasant."

"I look forward to it. I hope to be here for the harvest. I want to help. As a soldier, I've never done that."

She refused to think that Adrien would be any place but here. "We have a festival for it."

But 'twas difficult to think of festivals when they were out on the road alone, and her attacker from the other night was possibly lurking nearby. Someone wanted Adrien dead. Her heart hitched. If she warned him, Adrien would order her to her solar, and search out this attacker. He'd stop at nothing.

But as trained as he was, he was still just a man. He could die from a knife in the back as quickly as the next one.

Nay, she could not bear that.

Adrien pulled to a stop at the new road. 'Twas mucky from some recent rains. Long branches shadowed its narrow length, which bent out of sight a short way up.

A chill rippled through her.

Adrien urged his horse forward.

"Nay, Adrien. Don't go!"

He stopped and turned his horse around. "I'll only go up to the first bend. There are big hoof prints here. Apart from me, only Eudo uses coursers that size."

"The road is too sloppy."

Adrien's stallion disagreed, whinnying loudly and stepping sideways impatiently.

He drew his horse around to distract it, then pulled up aside Ediva. He scanned the woodland, studying each rustling leaf. "I'll only be a moment."

He trotted the horse up the trail and she watched him, offering a small prayer that he wouldn't disappear around the bend. He stopped there and tipped his head as if listening for something.

Then he returned to her side. "The road dwindles away, just as the map shows. The hoof prints go into the woods and disappear. There's no one around."

"How far is Colchester?" she asked.

"Several leagues. More than thrice the distance we have already traveled."

"'Tis unlikely the soldier would take that road when he'd come so far."

Adrien looked along the road he'd just inspected. "Why is this road here?"

She shrugged. "I don't know. We can ask Geoffrey."

He grimaced, deep in thought. "So we're back to the beginning in our search."

"Let's return, Adrien. I fear my riding skills are dwindling and 'tis as if this road is watching us."

They began the ride back. Ediva kept glancing over her shoulder at the quiet forest, but thankfully, no one followed them.

Inside the bailey, Harry and Rypan ran up. Ediva waited until Adrien dismounted so he could help her off. Her legs gave way and she slumped toward him, but he held her fast. "I think I'll take a cool drink of juice in the hall before the noon meal," she said, leaving Adrien to see to the horses.

Inside the cool hall, she took the mug of black currant juice Geoffrey brought. As she drank, he stood there frowning at her.

"What is it, Geoffrey?"

He hesitated. "There's talk about a battle brewing in Ely, milady. The soldiers want to fight, and I could see them leave without a tear shed for them, but the villagers fear they'll be forced to fight for the new king. 'Tis wrong, and they'll blame Lord Adrien."

She wet her lips. Aye, some *would* blame him, for Adrien *would* do as ordered if he was commanded to muster the men.

Geoffrey wrung his hands. "And some will take matters into their own hands."

She stilled. "Do you mean they'd start their own rebellion?"

Geoffrey looked stiff as he cleared his throat. "Milady, no good has come having a Norman as lord of this keep. 'Twill cause nothing but trouble should the north meet our new king at Ely."

Adrien had done so much good here, ensuring the bailey was organized and the villagers given a venue to voice their converns. But the county was rife with revolutionary talk and discontent. "Go on," she whispered.

"Those who oppose the king would also want Lord Adrien dead before he could fight. He has a reputation as a powerful soldier. Should he battle at Ely, the English rebels would suffer greatly."

Worry rippled over her, forcing her body to go from hot to cold in a single breath. Would they have Adrien dead before he was called to Ely? Was that why her attacker had tried to force her to kill Adrien now?

After glancing around at the empty hall, she leaned forward. "Who has started this talk?"

"People defending their land, milady!"

She knew she wouldn't change the steward's opinion, so she lifted her brows and announced, "*I* vowed to protect these people, not some band of curs who know nothing of *real* care. Do you know who has started this?"

He didn't answer immediately. "Nay, milady."

"Then you have work to do. Report to me when you have discovered who's behind this dissention. There aren't enough men to make an uprising possible and so aren't enough men to hide this cur." She spun away from the table and plowed out of the keep.

'Twas time she warned Adrien. And tell the real reason she'd spent yesterday in bed with her neck covered.

She'd tell him everything.

Chapter Sixteen

Adrien needed to run his stallion. And he knew exactly where to go. After he left Ediva to head into the keep, he took a skin of fresh, tangy cider. Carrying that, he set off to meet the new road.

One question had lingered in his mind from the time he'd spied the new road on the map. Why create a trail that led nowhere? He'd returned home only to take Ediva back, telling her there was nothing so as not to alarm her. But now he meant to find the truth.

Reaching the road, he slowed his horse, forcing his mount to walk only for fear he'd wrench an ankle in the muck.

As the horse stepped forward, Adrien pulled out his sword and held it upright. His courser heard the familiar noise and immediately tensed.

At the bend in the road, his battle-hewn senses came alive. Someone cunning enough to stay hidden was watching him. He and his mount were sure of it.

The tracks his horse had made earlier were still visible, as were the tracks of another horse, one that ran. Like he'd told Ediva, it was a big one, and he knew it had to belong to Eudo, having loaned it to the courier. The prints continued around the bend, and so did Adrien, his sword at the ready. Had the young messenger taken this route, or been attacked, leaving the horse to gallop up here?

Adrien stopped at the bend and studied the soft muck. Several footprints crossed over the other horse's hoof-prints. All led into the woods.

Sensing its master's excitement, his courser nickered softly. The stallion had battled with him at Hastings. Bred for their aggressiveness, coursers loved to fight. The horse sniffed the air. Aye, he smelled someone. And together, they'd find the cur.

As they had this morning, the branches drooped heavily, and the air lay humid on his skin.

Adrien listened, slowing the horse until it picked its way along the road. Nay, not a road anymore. 'Twas barely a path now.

And it was closing in around him.

He turned his horse around, slowly, all the while studying the woods. The feeling of being watched lingered like a bad smell. He wanted to dismount and investigate, but he'd lose the advantage if he did.

His horse nickered again, softer, turning to Adrien's right. In response he turned the horse to face that way.

And tensed.

Ediva grimaced as she walked away from the stable. Adrien had been gone for far too long.

"Which way did Lord Adrien go?" she asked Harry.

"I saw him take the road into the forest like this morning, milady."

Concern deepened. Had he seen something up that new road? She'd seen it on the map, drawn in by Geoffrey as was his duty, but had thought nothing of it. The road led nowhere, Adrien had said. So why return?

She pulled in her own nervous breath, remembering her attacker's words. Her gaze strayed toward the chapel and an unfamiliar ache swelled within her. She swallowed. The chaplain had a small garden at the edge of the village and this time of day, he'd be busy there. The chapel would be empty.

Before she could talk herself out of it, Ediva slipped inside. The thick, stone walls kept the chapel cool and she welcomed the relief. Rather than the family pew, she chose one of the simple benches at the back. There, she shut her eyes and did nothing, thought nothing.

Before too long, a horse whinnied outside and she hurried to the door but found a mare was responsible. She sagged and returned to her seat.

Tears sprang to her eyes. *Lord, please keep Adrien safe. I know I have done nothing to warrant Your ear, but please, he loves You. Protect him.*

But there was no answer, no wash of comfort. Just worry. She gripped the bench until her hands hurt. *Lord, haven't You made me suffer enough? What do You want?*

Forgiveness. The word spread over her like warm honey. Forgive who?

She knew exactly who. But could she? What would be the point, since his body lay in the grave outside the bailey?

Would it really ease her pain?

The silence irked her, and she stood. No answer today.

A man leapt from the woods, his sword held high.

Adrien's mount reared in surprise. Automatically, Adrien leaned forward. He took a heavy swipe at his attacker. Their blades clashed, and Adrien saw immediately that his attacker's weapon was a shorter Saxon sword with curved guards and shorter grip. But equally deadly.

The man's face was wrapped in plain, well-secured

cloth, and Adrien growled at being unable to recognize him. His attacker lunged, sword swinging again, but Adrien shoved him with his foot. With leg pressure only, Adrien turned his horse. The stallion knew exactly how to battle, with or without the hindering armor it would normally wear.

It pivoted and kicked the man, sending him flailing backward, but not before catching Adrien's thigh with his sword. With more leg pressure, Adrien ordered the animal around again. When their assailant staggered upright, Adrien swiped hard with his weapon, catching the man at the shoulder. The man let out a painful cry before falling into the dense woods.

Adrien held back his horse as it danced with the desire to chase. The thick overgrowth would not stop his battle-trained and aggressive stallion, but the animal had no barding to protect its length, and Adrien refused to risk injuring it.

He allowed his mount to trot around the end of the trail, all the while searching the woods. The only sounds over their breathing were of the man scurrying through the underbrush.

He turned his horse once more and felt a sharp pain in his thigh. Looking down, he discovered he'd been sliced open and the sudden shift of his leg exposed the wound further. His hose cut through, he could see blood streaming out. His mount sniffed the air. Smelling blood, the courser danced edgily.

"Easy, boy." Adrien examined his stinging leg. He, too, would like nothing better than to press into the wood and finish off his attacker, but at least the man would not be doing anything tonight except tending his wounds. It was likely that his horse's hooves had cracked some ribs

and, if not treated, they could become a death sentence
for the man.

Nay, enough for now. *Though odd,* Adrien thought. The
taste of battle was no longer the sweetness it had been. He
urged the horse back along the main road again toward
Little Dunmow, giving it the lead and allowing it to gallop to burn off some pent-up energy.

As he broke free of the forest, he saw a young boy, a
tenant's son, playing at the edge of the village and called
to him to fetch his sergeant and Harry. Harry would see
to the horse, though the beast may give the boy some trouble. The sergeant would take some soldiers and find his
attacker, be the man dead or alive.

Then Adrien would see to his wound.

With the child bounding toward the bailey, Adrien
walked the horse toward the midwife's hut. She'd have
poultices and bandages suitable for his wound, and once
bound and stitched if necessary, 'twould be hidden from
Ediva. If he could get by without too much limping and
manage to change his hose before she noticed it, 'twould
be all the easier.

He didn't want her worried. The battle they would
surely face at Ely was worry enough. Unbidden, a smile
grew on his face. She'd worry, and the idea that she cared
warmed him.

The midwife's house was deserted. He called out to
her but received no reply. Not willing to wait, he eased
from the saddle with a grimace of pain. After tying the
reins to the fence post, he knocked on the midwife's short
plank door.

No one answered. Behind him, he heard pounding feet
as Harry raced around the hut to skid to a stop. The horse
took exception to the sudden movement and reared, snapping the wood that held his reins. Harry tried to catch the

dangling leather but looked more like he believed the beast would trample him.

Adrien limped over, grabbed the reins and held them tight, soothing the horse with calm words. But 'twould not last. His mount smelled blood and wanted battle.

"Take him away, and keep a good grip on him, boy. I don't want him bolting out."

"What happened, my lord?"

"Never mind. Be gone." His leg stinging, he thrust the reins at Harry and sent the boy on his way. To his credit, and having spent all summer with the big mount, Harry was able to lead the anxious beast away.

His sergeant appeared then, letting out a gasp as he stared down at Adrien's leg. "My lord! Let's get you inside." He pounded on the midwife's door, but as with Adrien, received no answer.

Not giving up, the young sergeant charged inside, calling for the woman to come immediately. When she didn't, he held the door open for Adrien, who eased in and onto a chair at a nearby table.

"Get me a cloth to sop up the blood," he told the sergeant. The man found one hanging by the fire pit and Adrien pressed it against his leg. It stung like vinegar in a cut.

Where was that woman? He stood and limped to the tiny room beyond. The midwife was one of the fortunate few to have a hut with a bedchamber behind the hearth, likely because of her son's position.

Adrien drew back the hide curtain to peer in.

The old woman lay on her pallet, her mouth open and her wide eyes directed heavenward.

She was quite dead.

Ediva nearly collided with Adrien as he limped into the bailey. He'd refused to allow the sergeant to bring down a cart for him, not wanting word to reach his wife. Clearly the effort had been wasted. Harry's wagging tongue was starting to grate on him.

"I just heard! What happened?"

"'Tis only a cut, Ediva. There is no need for a fuss."

She led him into the keep and into his private chamber, but hovered at the door. "You should come up to my solar. 'Tis far more comfortable."

"Not unless you're willing to carry me there," he grunted as he collapsed onto his pallet. He didn't want her to fuss over him, but frankly, his leg throbbed. The cut was deep and whatever had been on that rag still stung.

Ediva called out into the corridor and ordered boiled water, clean cloths and honey to seal the wound, along with herbs for the pain. Then, instead of waiting with wringing hands, she carefully removed the torn hose and covered him with a warm fur to ward off the chill that may follow.

"Water is no good to clean wounds, Ediva," Adrien gritted out.

"Not usually, but this water is. It's from the spring that feeds the river past the rock where we kis—we ate. The cook said 'twould be good for fevers like I had and has ordered it be brought up daily and boiled. Once sealed in a keg, it never goes stale."

He leaned back against the wall at the head of his bed and shut his eyes. Bad water had caused many a soldier's wounds to fester. The choice for cleaning them was often wine or spirits. But at least he didn't have to deal with their sting.

Peeking at the wound, she paled. "We need the midwife. She's healed many wounds."

Adrien caught her arm. "Nay."

She frowned. "Why not?"

"Because the midwife is dead."

She gasped. "Dead? When?"

"'Twould seem sometime last night. We found her lying on her bed."

"We?"

"I went straight there upon returning, so she could tend my wound. My sergeant found me there."

Ediva paled further. "After returning from the new road? Adrien, this wound looks like a sword cut—'tis so clean. Who attacked you?"

"Whoever was watching me."

"So you confronted him? Look what he did to you!"

Adrien leaned back and smiled grimly. "Aye, but you should see how injured he is." He winced. "My courser is a good fighter. He kicked him and sent him flying into the woods. The man has broken ribs."

She shook her head. "Broken ribs make it hard to breathe. He'll die."

"I've been in battle, woman. I know the usual outcome."

The supplies arrived, with the sergeant carrying many of them. The cook helped prepare the honey poultice and the herb tea, saying she'd picked the willow bark herself a fortnight ago. 'Twould do well to ease the pain.

"Sergeant," Adrien ordered, the strength in his voice softened by the pain. "Send some men into the wood, up the new road to the bend. Search the wood until you find the man who attacked me. I want him here."

"Aye, my lord." The man disappeared, but not before ordering most of the staff who'd bustled in to leave the chamber.

Adrien watched his wife wet the cloths. He hadn't wanted her to know about the midwife so soon. "I'm sorry about the midwife, Ediva. I know 'tis hard for you to lose one of your tenants."

She didn't look at him. "Aye, 'tis a shock. How do you think she died?"

"We found her on her pallet, still in her night shift." Seeing her pained expression, he caught her arm and squeezed it. The veil she'd donned after the ride smelled of lavender and sunshine, and he inhaled it deeply. "She died quietly. A good way to go for an old woman."

Ediva gave the barest shake of her head. She'd bit her lip, then swallowed before saying, "Mayhap she had the fever also."

"She looked neither flushed nor fevered."

Still, Ediva didn't look at him. "Something terrible is happening, Adrien. You were attacked, she was—"

"She was old, Ediva." His voice was firmer than he expected. "I'd heard it said that she'd seen King Edmund rule and how long ago was that? She died of old age."

Ediva bit her lip and blinked. Did she think differently? But thankfully, she said nothing else. The sergeant returned as she began to cleanse the wound.

"It needs to be sewn up, milady," the sergeant said quietly. "I can do it. I've done it many times after battle."

She shot the man a worried expression. Her hand was shaking. "Will it be dangerous?"

"Nay. 'Tis a simple wound, really."

She stole a quick glance at Adrien. He tightened his jaw and nodded, knowing what was needed. She swallowed again, and Adrien watched her go pale.

The room spun as she watched the gruesome task. Bile rose in her and she felt as light as air. Adrien tightened up, his grip so hard on his pallet that she was thankful he wasn't holding her hand. She'd have broken fingers for sure.

She stole another glance at him and found his pained expression drilling into her. "I'm sorry," she whispered.

"Nay, I'm sorry, Ediva," he gritted out.

"You? Why?"

"For making you look like you're ready to faint."

She laughed, but it sounded wobbly to her ears. "I don't understand this. I've seen babes born, cuts and broken bones, but this…"

"'Tis done, milady," the sergeant said quietly. "The honey poultice will keep the wound sealed. We'll give him some more of the draught the cook prepared."

Ediva helped Adrien take the drink. Soon, it became obvious that the draught was helping with the pain. Adrien also accepted a small dose of spirits the sergeant urged him to take.

Satisfied that there was nothing more they could do, the sergeant ordered the cook out, but he stayed at the door. Ediva pulled the chair close and sat, thankful she hadn't retched. With eyes closed, Adrien spoke. "You're upset with me, aren't you?"

"You went to the midwife because you didn't want me to see the wound," Ediva said quietly.

He opened his eyes briefly. "Aye," he slurred.

She glanced over her shoulder to sergeant, then turned back to her husband. "Adrien, I need to tell you something. I know 'tis a bad time, but you should know this."

He didn't answer. The draught and the spirits were taking their toll. All she could do was watch him fall asleep.

With a concerned look to the sergeant, Ediva asked, "'Twas just a sleeping draught?"

The man looked grim but satisfied. "Aye. He needs to rest to heal well."

"How do you think he got this wound?"

"This one was caused by a sword. I've seen enough of these."

She shuddered. "The forests are deadly."

"Aye, milady. There are many Saxons who now live in the forests in defiance of the curfew laws. They prey on Normans."

She sat back and watched her husband, chilled as she realized how close he'd come to dying. "So you were with him when he went searching for the midwife?"

"Nay. I found him at the midwife's hut. When she didn't answer her door, we went inside. She was on her pallet, dead."

Ediva swallowed, her attacker's threats returning to her. "Did she really die in her sleep?"

The sergeant hesitated.

She frowned, waiting. In the quiet of the room, she could hear her own heart pounding. "Sergeant?"

"Nay," the man finally said quietly. "She did not die in her sleep."

"Then how?"

"She was smothered, milady."

Her heart stalled. "Smothered?"

He leaned forward, his dark eyes serious. "Whilst I was in Normandy, I was sent to escort some guests of Duke William's from their chambers back to their estate. They'd fallen from the royal court's favor. But the man and his wife had died in their bed. They looked like that midwife."

"How do you know they were smothered?"

"The physician who attended the death pointed out the blue lips and noses and marks about the throats and cheeks. He said 'twas death by smothering and warned me to say nothing for my own safety. The midwife had the same bruising around her face and neck."

Ediva's hand found her own throat. "That means..."

"I detected no odor about her that suggested a poison. Losing one's breath to an herb can happen, but 'twas not the case here. Her lips were blue and her throat was marked. What else could it be?"

Ediva shuddered. "Tell Lord Adrien none of this, Sergeant. We need to allow him to heal without worry."

"Aye, milady."

Ediva spent the next day tending Adrien. She tried to keep him sleeping all of the first day, but when he declined the draught she'd prepared for his afternoon rest, she soon realized that trying to keep him abed was fruitless.

She *was* successful in keeping him in his chamber by bringing him in food and berry juices. The cook said those fruits would help him heal faster. She'd picked the berries herself, then crushed and juiced them, adding only boiled water to help him swallow the tangy drink—the tangier, the better it was for healing. But by the late afternoon, whilst sitting with him, Ediva knew his time lying there was short.

It added to her worry. Death lingered on her threefold, a fulfillment of a warning whispered in her ear should she refuse to kill her husband. Someone had smothered the midwife.

Second, the death echoed eerily in her recent illness. She'd been poisoned. 'Twas obvious that Adrien suspected the same, for why else had he ordered for her only bland food with no seasonings, prepared only by trustworthy servants?

She rose from her place by Adrien's side and paced the small chamber. This third attack hit her the hardest. It pointed to the danger against Adrien whether or not she acted. He had fought against the assailant but not without injury. Would he be so fortunate next time?

"Ediva?"

She hurried to his side. "Are you in pain?"

"Nay. Ediva, I fear you have filled me so full of willow bark tea, I shall not feel pain for a year."

"I didn't want you to suffer."

"I'm a soldier. I can take a bloody nose."

She stiffened. "'Twas not a bloody nose you suffered, sir!"

He threw off the fur she'd covered over him and sat up. His attention immediately went to his wound. Ediva had carefully reapplied the honey salve enough to know that it was healing nicely.

"Will you remove my stitches when it is time?" he asked.

She swallowed. "I shall try."

"Until you faint?"

"I didn't faint before," she sniffed. "I was shocked by your wound, 'tis all."

With a soft chuckle, he swung the leg over, sat on the edge of his pallet and looked down. During his time unconscious, she'd ordered a bed spring made and his men had lifted the pallet onto it. "I see I have a new bed."

"Aye. The bending down was torture on my back." She reached for him suddenly. "Nay, don't stand!"

"I've been abed long enough. I'll be fine. See, the wound is still sealed and I have weight on that leg."

She tugged on his tunic to cover his bare legs. Shaking her head, she added, "Very well. But we need to keep the wound tightly wrapped if you are going to march around the bailey like nothing's wrong with you."

"Nothing is wrong with me, and I need to show the men here that a small cut can't best me."

She crossed her arms, disliking the way her heart thumped hard in her chest at the thought of her husband's valor. "Since I can't change your mind, I should leave you alone to get dressed and be about the bailey."

Adrien, fully clothed and outside a short time later, turned to find Ediva at his side. He'd sent her to her solar, but he'd no sooner spoken to a few soldiers, than she reappeared.

"I can't rest," she explained when he looked pointedly at her. "I have rested too well these past few days."

"Liar," he admonished softly. "Very well. Where's Geoffrey? We should offer our condolences."

"He's in his mother's hut. I've given him leave, and he agreed to postpone her funeral until you were up." She paused and seemed about to speak again but stopped.

"Is there something more?" he asked, trying out the sloping land beyond the bailey gate. He'd already managed the motte steps well enough.

"What I have to say can wait, but, Adrien, we will need to talk as soon as possible."

Probably about the attack in the forest, he thought. All that was needed now, though, was to bury the midwife and send a message to his brother that he needed the men back for the harvest.

They reached the midwife's house shortly, and Adrien hesitated at the garden gate. Herbs grew wildly about, so many varieties in strange pots or tucked under trees. One even grew in a shallow pan of water.

"Such a shame," Ediva whispered. "The garden was perfect for her. She knew exactly what each herb needed to grow strong."

A shame, indeed. The midwife had been murdered. He'd noticed that at the same time his sergeant had, although the man had said nothing. Her neck had been marked with bruises. They weren't harsh enough to stand out, but her eyes had popped open and her lips had been blue. 'Twas not a natural death. He needed to see his sergeant and order him not to mention it to Ediva. She may connect the midwife's murder with her illness.

Had someone stolen some foul herbs and given them to Ediva, then murdered the midwife when she discovered her loss? Had she confronted whoever it was who'd been in her garden? Anyone could have slipped in and taken anything, for the garden was not fenced in.

Adrien took Ediva's arm and knocked on the jamb of the open door. They found Geoffrey gathering things in the kitchen, between the cold hearth and the small casket.

Ediva was the first to offer condolences. He nodded. Then Adrien did the same, but Geoffrey gave him only the barest nod. "I will bring the herbs she'd already dried to the larder," he said. "The cook will be able to dispense most of them. Several of the tenants have offered to help me bury her."

"Take whoever you think is best," Ediva said softly. "Mayhap the soldiers can help."

"Nay, milady. We Saxons bury our own, and her neighbor has been very helpful."

Adrien nodded. The man next door was one of the few landowners in the village and had sat in the hasty jury Adrien had assembled for Olin's case. Older, with a constant sour expression but a steadfast reliability, the man would be valuable to Geoffrey.

"Excuse me, please." The steward bowed to Ediva and Adrien and left them alone in the hut for a moment.

"We have no midwife," Ediva noted. "And we'd been spoiled too long with such a good one. She trained no one to take her place. I hope she kept a journal of her dispensing, but I doubt it. Her skills were more to herbs, not reading and writing."

Adrien grimaced. "I'll ask Eudo if there is anyone in Colchester willing to come to the keep for this work." His grimace deepened. He'd have to spare several good men for such a missive—he would not risk sending one man alone. Fast horses also, to blaze through the woodlands too quickly for any Saxon churl who may want to ambush them.

They returned to the keep and Adrien agreed that a rest would be in order. Alone in his chamber, he wrote out a missive to his brother and ordered the sergeant to find the fastest men and good steeds to carry it there.

Normally, he'd wait a while for a replacement to come from the village itself or allow the villagers to find one on their own. 'Twas a small village and none were sick. But with Ediva already ill once, he would take no chances on being without a healer.

No chances.

Chapter Seventeen

Ediva listened to her maid quietly sob throughout the funeral the next day. The chaplain offered brief prayers, but Ediva wondered if mayhap the old man was thankful the woman was gone. The chaplain had had several altercations over the years with the midwife. Her crafty ways and secrecy often made the chaplain suspicious.

Immediately, she reprimanded herself. 'Twas unfair to judge people, especially when she had been so cruel in her own thoughts.

She stole a glance at Adrien. What kind of advice would he offer?

As if hearing her private question, he took her hand in his. Her heart swelled at his strength, his stamina, the rough feel of calluses scraping her knuckles. He was healing faster each day. Today there was no limping and she'd loosened the bandage more this morning, allowing the air to reach the cut. In a few more days, the stitches could come out.

But until this moment, he'd kept his distance from her. He'd seemed on edge, too much for her to wish to trouble him with the story of her attacker. There was no time for such things, or even for the mild flirtations they'd formerly exchanged. Oddly, she missed the light banter.

Before long, the funeral was over and the villagers and tenants gathered in the keep for refreshments. Adrien stayed only a brief time before announcing he needed some air.

She found him on the parapet, staring out at the woods, deep in thought.

Ediva noted the frown that creased Adrien's brow when he scanned the edge of the forest. Was he looking for a sign of the messengers he'd sent to his brother?

She slipped up beside him. A light wind buffeted his long tunic. "You're concerned for your men?"

"Aye." He nodded. "The forest is filled with churls who defy William's curfew. And we have not found the first courier who went missing."

"We will see the men soon enough, perhaps they will be more successful than the other men sent out." When he didn't answer, she wondered when the best time to approach him about her experience was. Together they could discover if the attack on him was connected to the attack on her. Was it all related to the fact she hadn't bowed to her attacker's demands?

Until this moment, she'd had the luxury of time, doting on her husband to the exclusion of all other thought. She hadn't left his side, except to gather herbs or berries and, even then, she'd posted a guard on his chamber. She'd allowed him only the privacy he needed to attend to his routine.

Now, she had no other tasks. If the midwife had died as part of the threat against her, she needed to speak up. What would Adrien do? He'd be furious, and mayhap see her secrecy as traitorous.

The thought gripped her stomach and she regretted

holding her tongue. She would not kill her husband. But if she didn't, she'd become a traitor to her own people. It had been one thing when the threat was merely words spoken. But now the midwife was dead. Had her attacker shown himself willing to follow through on his threats? Perhaps he had offered clues in his words as to who he might attack next. Fear had clamped not only her throat that day, but also her memory. She struggled to remember that man's awful words.

But all she could recall was that he'd said something about her being the only one to get close to Adrien.

She thought of her illness, most likely a poisoning. That day, she'd eaten nearly all of Adrien's meal and hers. Mayhap her attacker had tried to kill Adrien but failed.

She felt her insides go icy cold.

"You looked furious, then fearful, Ediva. What are you thinking?"

She glanced up, surprised. Aye, she told herself sharply, she'd been reluctant to speak and still was.

Lord God, give me strength.

Adrien took her hand and kissed it. "I should like to hear your thoughts."

She couldn't bring herself to tell him. He'd turn Dunmow Keep into a fortress. Then her assailant would surely attack again, knowing she'd told Adrien what he'd done to her. Who would he choose?

She shook her head, ignoring her sweaty palms and pounding heart. "'Tis nothing. In fact, it's left my head, already."

They stood in silence as the sun dipped lazily below the horizon. All the while Adrien watched the road to Colchester. "You need to rest," she finally said. "You have been standing on that leg all day."

With an indrawn breath that seemed to savor the cooling air, he nodded. "Walk with me to my room."

There had been no banter to make her smile, and longing for it rolled over her.

Nay! Don't think of your own foolish heart, woman. There is too much danger about. With an unsure smile, she took his arm and with gentleness and a hint of gallantry, he folded her hand into the crook of his elbow. They made their way carefully down to his room.

Only when he'd said good-night, and she'd pretended to walk away, did he finally close his door. Upon hearing it shut, she spun. She sought out the sergeant and ordered him to put a guard on his lord's door.

The sergeant nodded, and she started up the stairs but turned. "Sergeant," she began after a thought. "Have you seen the small, wiry dog anywhere?"

"There are several around, milady. Has one bothered you?"

She nodded. "I know 'tis hard to remove them all, but should they become nasty, we need to be rid of them."

"Aye, milady. The only good they do is bark out warnings."

She bit her lip. Warnings? That dog usually ignored her, but had it seen her assailant behind her and tried to warn her?

She bid the man good-night, feeling even more unsettled. Taking a deep breath, she climbed the stairs, happy that the torches had been replaced. Both the chandler and her steward had been warned, but she was grateful that her maid waited for her in her solar.

Whilst a not-as-pale Ediva examined his wound the next day, Adrien gritted his teeth and sent up a prayer for faster healing. The pain was no longer sharp, but the muscle had been cut and he hated to keep still whilst it healed. 'Twould take longer to build it up again.

But a small commotion outside curtailed the examination. They hurried out to see who it was. The men he'd sent to Eudo had returned with a letter. The leader of the messengers handed over his missive in the Great Hall. "My lord, I bring you Baron Eudo's greetings."

Adrien unfolded the letter.

My brother, I greet you in the name of our Lord. I am saddened to hear of your injury. We're still searching for the missing soldier, but I fear the worst. Saxons who oppose the king will do anything to drive us from this land. Beware, Adrien. If a Saxon wants you dead, he may not care who he kills first. Lady Ediva could easily die, too, being seen as a traitor. And keeping your tenants here adds to their hatred, I fear. The rebels may see them as slaves, not hired men. So I'll keep the men only as long as necessary. The work of moving rock is nearly complete.

I'll also see to a replacement for your midwife. A good apothecary will help, but I can't guarantee that one would come. The guilds in this town are tightly knit. They asked for me to allow them control over their own people and I granted it, so they may not wish to send anyone.

Keep on guard. Your brother in Christ and in blood, Eudo.

Adrien crushed the letter into a ball and shoved it deep into his tunic's pocket. Thankfully, the words were written in French and only Ediva would be able to read it.

"What's wrong?" she asked.

He led her inside. "Nothing. Eudo says that he'll return the tenants soon."

"That's good news. So why are you frowning?"

"He says he'll ask the guilds for someone to send here as midwife but fears no one will want to come. Eudo granted the guilds a measure of autonomy over themselves."

"No doubt your brother will use his charm."

Adrien sighed. At least Ediva believed his distress was due to the fact that they may not acquire a midwife. She must not know the truth. She already knew that the woods were dangerous but not to the extent that her life was at risk.

He needed his wits about him. He needed to be vigilant for Ediva's sake. Should something happen to her, he would surely die also.

To that end, Adrien's decided as he watched Ediva wrap a fresh bandage about his leg that he needed to stop wooing his wife and focus on her safety. He dared not be distracted. Yet, hadn't he already realized that since he had been hurt?

Still, she was softening toward him and a powerful moment of temptation rolled over him. He wondered how much more would it take for her to fully accept him.

Nay, 'twould not be wise. He would be gone soon enough to battle at Ely. He dared not risk turning the sensible wife he had into a love-softened woman who'd too easily let down her guard. She needed to remain alert. His sisters had been besotted with their husbands and he'd see how carelessly they wandered about in those romantic early months of marriage.

The moment the bandage was tied, he stood. "'Tis healing well. It feels as if I was never cut."

She scoffed lightly. "I doubt that, but I think I can remove your stitches without feeling ill."

"In a day or two, perhaps. Now, I must attend to my duties—and you must see to yours."

Her brows lifted, she said, "The wound's still mending and you keep moving the muscle. Let me stay and tend to you."

"My prayers and your ministrations have worked well. Now, your duties are sorely in need of you." He had no desire to be brusque. Indeed, the memories of the kisses they'd shared squeezed his heart, but neither of them could afford such indulgences.

Ediva stepped away, and with a look more hurt than agreeable, she left to supervise the noon meal.

She didn't stop at the kitchen. Instead, Ediva fled through to the garden. She dropped onto the stone bench where the cook often sat to peel the vegetables. Since Adrien had ordered all waste, peelings included, to be thrown in the heap at the other side of the keep, the small garden had taken on a fresh air. A maid had been assigned to weed it, and the scents of summer greens and blooming violets soothed Ediva's battered nerves.

She sat back, her head pressed against the stone wall. Though the sun warmed and soothed her weary body, but her heart remained troubled. Why was Adrien so gruff?

Because he was anxious to get her tenants back so that he may march to Ely to fight alongside the king?

The only good the war did was make her a widow. And she did not wish for Adrien to die.

Her throat tightened. Her eyes watered and loosened their hold on her tears.

A shout cut through the quiet garden, followed by a dog barking and the thundering of hooves. Ediva jerked forward. Could it be the tenants returning? She hurried around the keep and onto the small patch of green motte that allowed her a clear view of the bailey below.

Norman soldiers were galloping into the keep, barely

missing Rypan, who'd opened the gate. The standard they flew was the king's, but she'd already met the king, and knew these men were merely on Eudo's business.

She trotted down the slope to stand in the center of the bailey near where the messenger stood as he prepared to return to Colchester. The only good news these riders could bring her was news of the return of her men.

With knuckles pressed against her hips and feet planted firmly, she waited for the men to stop before her.

The first rider did but looked over her shoulder. "My lord."

Lord? Ediva spun and found Adrien standing there, magnificent in his light tunic, his belt slung about his slim waist and his beard trimmed. He'd taken on the Saxon style of a beard but kept his hair short, though not as short as a Norman's usual cut. He also stood akimbo, but with his height and breadth, he was far more intimidating.

He glanced down at Ediva, then stepped in front of her. Piqued, she stepped to his left to stand there beside him.

He glared down at her. "Woman, times are dangerous. Stay behind me or I will have you carried into the solar and kept under lock and key."

His voice was so fraught with warning, Ediva relented and stepped back. The mounted soldier's horse skittered about, forcing Adrien to grab its bridle as the man spoke. "My lord, we have been searching the king's woods for several days and bring disturbing news."

"What has happened?"

Several other riders trotted into the bailey, two men on one mount leading another. Ediva peeked out from behind Adrien and gasped.

The last horse carried the bloodied and beaten body of a soldier.

Chapter Eighteen

The missing courier, Adrien thought. He shot Ediva a glare to warn her to stay before striding up to the horse that bore the body.

Indeed, it was the soldier, and the marks of violence on him were enough to shock even Adrien.

"We found him closer to Little Dunmow than Colchester, my lord," the first rider announced as he dismounted.

Disgusted, Adrien turned to find Ediva's face as pale as she'd been when she first saw his leg injury.

He turned back. "Take the body into the chapel and set a guard on it. Ask my sergeant if he can tell how he died. He has experience with that. Though 'twould seem his injuries alone could kill a man."

Nodding, the man ordered his troop into action. Adrien returned to Ediva. "Go inside. 'Tis not a sight for a lady to see."

"I saw Ganute's body. Though I must say, it didn't shock and sadden me as this poor fellow's death. He looks so young."

"He was. Ediva, your countrymen did this."

She shot him an eye full of daggers. "My countrymen are defending their land. Would you not do the same?"

Adrien glared back. "William was promised the throne!"

They stared at each other for a long moment. No one moved. Then, from somewhere behind him, a dog barked excitedly.

Ediva jumped. Her gaze lit on his sergeant. "I told you to chase that dog away! And if you find its owner, bring him to me!"

She steeled her spine and pulled up on the hem of her cyrtel. "Adrien, regardless of our opposing views, this man has died, and he deserves our final respects. I will prepare for his funeral. Since it isn't safe to send him to Normandy, we'll bury him in Ganute's family cemetery."

"'Tis a Saxon graveyard, Ediva."

She rolled her eyes. "'Tis true. In fact, I plan to bury him right beside Ganute." Then, her voice dripping with sarcasm, she added, "They can sort out their differences on the judgment day."

Adrien watched her stride away. What was Ediva thinking? Ganute's cemetery was full of Saxon nobles, and to bury a lowly Norman foot soldier there was unthinkable.

Unless Ediva was punishing Ganute and his family with it.

His heart fell. She needed to let go of her anger toward that man.

Lord, show her how to do that. Heal her heart.

The dog returned to its yipping, pulling his attention away. And since when did Ediva hate dogs so? There were plenty of mongrels about, some small enough to capture rats, whilst others were trained to herd sheep. They were hardly a threat.

But suddenly, Ediva thought differently. Why?

Ediva ordered the men who'd carried the young soldier into the chapel to clean his body and dress him in some decent clothes she found in her keep. Hardly the boy's style, she knew, but 'twere better than the ripped and blood-soaked tatters he wore.

Then she sent a servant to find the man who'd made the casket for the midwife. She entered the chapel later that day to ensure her orders had been carried out, only to find Adrien standing over the remains. She stopped and held her breath, afraid she'd disturb him from his prayers.

But he looked up at her, his expression grim. "I'm only here to offer my respects. This man belonged to Eudo, so 'twould seem appropriate that I stand in my brother's stead."

She walked to the front. The rough-hewn wooden casket had already been delivered. 'Twas a simple one, not the fancy one Ganute had had hewn from limestone many years ago.

"'Tis kind of you to buy him a coffin, Ediva. I know that many Saxons use only a strong cloth."

She nodded, not wanting to test her voice for fear it would shake. She couldn't allow this boy to go to his grave a pauper. She pulled from her right pocket a small scroll and set it on the coffin.

"What's that?" Adrien asked.

"'Tis just a Saxon prayer. When my father died, my sister said it at his funeral. I had memorized it." They stood in silent reflection for a moment and before she did or said something foolish, she turned and walked out.

For the rest of the day, Ediva kept busy. Her servants stayed quiet, but she knew 'twas not in reverence as it had been for Ganute's funeral. None wanted a Norman soldier buried with their lord, but the more Ediva thought of it, the more adamant she became. And the more her servants sensed her stubbornness the more they kept out of her way.

'Twas odd, of course. Had this death occurred earlier

in the spring, she'd have been the first to send the remains back to Colchester, but an ache deep within her grew and formed the desire, nay, the need, to bury the man here.

Still, one important question remained. She sought out Adrien and found him outside strengthening his upper arms.

"Is it wise to exercise?"

"The wound is healing well and I'm not using my legs. Besides, I must do something useful until we bury the soldier."

His muscles were fairly bursting from his tunic, leading Ediva's mind to wander. Why was he spending so much time training? To stay busy, as he had said? There was enough to keep all, servants and master, occupied. Nay, he was training himself—preparing for battle. Her heart turned to stone and sat heavy in her chest. "Adrien, the man who was killed was coming here to deliver a missive. Was the letter found?"

Adrien set down the weights he was heaving about and grabbed a cloth from Harry to wipe his face and hands. He led her to a stone bench set against the bailey wall near the steps that led up to its battlement.

"Nay, but Eudo told me what he'd written."

"Which was?"

"He said he left a quarter of the money behind. He guessed you were speaking hastily when you promised you'd make the soldiers stronger and fitter. So he left you some money to do so."

"But Geoffrey recorded only what was in the strongbox after that, which was nothing. Eudo must have taken it all."

"I see no reason why my brother would lie to me."

She couldn't explain it, either. But there were others in the room at the time, and she knew her arrival had distracted them. "Mayhap the guards took the rest?" she asked quietly. "'Twould only take a sleight of hand to snatch up the few coins left."

Adrien thought a moment. "My soldiers are trustworthy."

"Are they? I know you have forbidden plunder for your men, but King William allows it."

"Taking from a defeated man all he has is wrong. 'Tis fine to take enough to prevent the man from raising arms again, but I see no reason for greed."

"Mayhap your soldiers disagree." She eyed the men as they continued their training. "They will return to the garrison in London with nothing but their meager wages, whilst others have fine clothes and jewelry or money from the sale of such items."

His mouth tight, Adrien stood. "My soldiers respect my orders. Talk no more of this, woman."

Frustrated, Ediva flew to her feet. "Someone stole from us, Adrien, and you can't see it was your men or your brother. Nay, all you want is to serve the king as his slave! You're only here at his bidding until you can fight again. Go, then, fight for William at Ely! I'm sure we'll soon hear of the orders to move north!"

Adrien's face grew dark. "I am no man's slave!"

"You are, and you are proud of it! You think that your faith can hide that fact? Go, die at Ely for your king! You torment me by staying here with your silver-tongued promises. But soon, I'll be left alone!"

She stormed away, hating that she'd allowed herself to care for Adrien, so much that 'twould cause her to lose control, only to have him turn cold.

In her solar, she dismissed her maid. Tears had already filled Ediva's eyes and she swiped them furiously away. The door opened and closed again, and she spun to throw her maid out again.

Adrien stood there, hands on hips, determination reigning over his face. "I will not have you argue with me. Nor will I have you storm away like a spoiled child."

She drew back her shoulders. "I'm mistress of this keep, and I'll do as I please. Having Normans treat their women harshly doesn't allow you to treat *me* that way."

"When have I treated you harshly?"

Nay, he hadn't, except with her heart and his desire to go to battle. "You say you can stand a bloody nose, my lord, so you should be able to stand a woman's scorn."

His lips tightened. "If I have earned the scorn, I'll accept it, but I see no reason for your foul mood." He pulled in a breath and let it out with great control. She blinked as he grimaced. "Ediva, 'tis not the way I want us to be, but I can't change who I am. I'm a soldier."

"You are also Baron of Dunmow! You promised to keep these people safe, and yet you plan to go to battle again! How can that give me—us—security?"

"Fighting will secure the land." He shook his head. "But we've had this argument too much. I know something else lies beneath it. What's wrong?"

She couldn't say it. The coarse voice of the man who'd nearly strangled her lingered in her memory. She was to kill Adrien or villagers would die. Such was the determination of the Saxon men who hid in the forest and fought to rid their land of a foreign king.

She had to protect her people. But she didn't want Adrien to die. The very thought clutched her heart with cold fingers. Yet the midwife had already died. Smothered to prove the threat against Ediva was real.

Finally, she spoke. "The midwife was murdered, wasn't she?"

Adrien waited a moment before answering. "Aye. How did you know?"

"Your sergeant told me whilst you slept. We have a killer here."

"I'll protect you."

"I'm not concerned for me. I have soldiers about me for guards, but the women in the village have nothing! They don't even have their husbands and sons."

"They'll return very soon."

"And you'll leave for Ely. While the man who has killed will still be here." Her voice sounded flat to her ears, and she turned away.

But she heard Adrien approach, felt his warm hands upon her shoulders as he turned her and hoped that her eyes didn't shine too brightly with unshed tears.

"I won't allow you to carry the burden of this keep alone. Nor will I die at Ely. I promise."

She shook her head. "You can hardly promise that!"

"God will protect me."

She rolled her eyes. "And I have been so good a servant of His that He would allow you to stay safe for me?"

Adrien reached to cup her face with big, warm hands. Despite the lingering summer heat, she felt cold and found herself grateful for Adrien's strong frame.

"God doesn't hate you, Ediva. But I hate that you have been hurt by people who should have protected you. From your parents who sanctioned your bitter marriage, to the chaplain who feels 'twas fine for Ganute to be cruel. But you must find peace and love and learn to forgive them all for what they did to you. Starting with Ganute."

She tried to pull away, but he held her fast. He lowered his hands to her upper arms and kept her close. "Aye, forgive Ganute or you're as trapped as he is in his own sin."

"You don't know what he did to me!"

"I have seen plenty in my time, Ediva. And I saw the scrap of clothing he tore from your body. I know what he did, and it turns my stomach to think on it, but unless you allow God to heal you, the hatred will eat you alive. I find it difficult to forgive him, but with our Lord's help, I am slowly doing so." He wrapped his arms around her and pulled her close. She could smell the late summer sun on him. She could feel the beating of his heart against her cheek. She slid her arms around his torso and held him as tightly as he held her. Her veil fell from her head.

"Ediva, you can't love as God wants you to love until you set aside this hatred," he whispered into her hair.

"How does God want me to love? To have compassion? I have had that with the young soldier. To protect my people? I do that also."

He set her away from him slightly and then lifted her chin so she could see his eyes. "This love, too."

He dipped his head and met her parted lips. She could taste tart cider on him and felt the brush of his beard on her cheeks. But the surge of emotion was far more compelling. Should she feel this desire? It was a longing she couldn't explain, a want for something that she'd never felt before.

She wanted to love him. She could sense the deep satisfaction that a divinely sanctioned love could offer.

She kissed him back, snaking her hands over his shoulders to catch the nape of his neck. She wanted so badly to love him fully, heart and soul. But what was the point? He'd soon be off to Ely, giving in to his king and his love of battle.

'Twas what had angered her so. But no anger could tear her away from his kiss. He pressed further into her, tightened his grip and demanded an answer that matched all he was giving her.

She held him fast. All she wanted that moment was to stay in his arms. For as long as they were this close, he couldn't leave her. Nor die in battle.

Weakened from the kiss, they broke apart. He blinked, wet his lips and drew in a breath that was as ragged as her own.

"We should go and offer prayers in the chapel before the funeral," he finally said. "Change and meet me in the hall. 'Twould be wise to be seen together, to be seen as a united keep."

He lifted his hand to her face, brushed her cheek with his knuckles and studied her well-kissed lips before backing away and leaving her alone.

She reached for her chair and sank into it, trying all the while to steady her breath. She was a fool to fall for Adrien. But her heart cared little for good sense. Her head ached with confusion and she turned to her ewer and bowl to splash water on her face. It soothed her but she still found her hands shook as she donned a more appropriate cyrtel for a funeral. With a fresh veil and modest diadem, she was ready.

With her insides still feeling tight and her heart still pounding blood up to her face, she opened her solar door and stepped into the corridor. When she reached the stairwell, she saw a leather-clad hand close over the nearest torch and extinguish it.

Chapter Nineteen

The darkness of the stairwell swamped her and Ediva grappled to find the cold wall as she eased herself back up the stairs.

She stumbled and fell, her hip cracking on the stone tread. Feeling the closeness of evil, she stilled her frame.

Whoever was there leaned into her. She could see nothing but felt him pressing on her. His foul breath plowed through her skewed veil, making her gag.

"I warned you," was his hoarse whisper.

She fought to free her feet from her tangled cyrtel, but the more she fought, the more trapped she became. She tried to scream but a hand clamped over her mouth and pressed her against the steps.

"If you scream, I'll strangle you. And after you are dead, I'll kill your husband *and* your tenants."

She strived to listen to the voice. 'Twas Saxon for sure, but it sounded strange. An accent? She jerked her head from the sour smell of filthy wool and squeezed her hands up between her and this evil creature to shove hard. But he barely moved. And under the stench lingered something she couldn't identify. Something sharp and foul on his breath.

Ediva turned her head. "If you want Lord Adrien dead, try it yourself. But he'll kill you before you lift your blade."

"He cannot kill someone he doesn't see coming."

She listened, realizing that her assailant had chosen this timing well. Everyone was outside, on edge from the death of the young soldier and either preparing for the funeral or avoiding the keep altogether.

"If you tell him, I'll kill another villager."

"They're innocent!"

"They'll die for freedom, my lady. A noble cause for any Saxon. 'Tis why you'll murder Lord Adrien before any more deaths happen."

"I won't murder anyone!"

"You will, milady." The voice sounded different, cracked as before, yet different. "You are the only one he lets close."

"'Tis not true! He's a fine lord who—"

The man smacked his hand on the stonework, making her jump. "Do not insult me! Did he not come up here just now? I can smell his stench on you. You betray your own people!"

She felt the heat rise into her face and shimmied up another tread. Her hip ached. As if he could see in the blackness, her assailant followed her up.

"You *will* kill him. Before those at Ely do."

"Why do you force this on me?"

"Because you are the only one who can do it. Do not worry, milady, for the village will say nothing when his brother comes looking for him."

She shoved hard against the man and managed to shift him off her. He laughed, the cackle cutting through her, hoarse and broken. "Your midwife is dead, thanks to you. Who will be next? The young wife, Wynnth?"

She gasped. Did he really kill the midwife? Would he… nay, not Wynnth! She had two small babes!

A short whimper escaped her and she knew she had to stop this evil. She lunged at him with a screech, but, too late, she learned that he'd stepped to one side.

She found herself toppling headfirst down the stairs.

Adrien released a sigh of thankfulness as Ediva's eyes fluttered open. He'd feared she'd never awaken. A servant had found her at the bottom of the stairs and called to him immediately. His heart had nearly stopped at the sight of her crumpled body.

He gently carried her no farther than his own chamber. After he ordered extra furs for the pallet, he lay her bruised form down as tenderly as possible.

She'd moaned and shifted her legs. Although he cringed, he'd sent up a prayer of thanks. Her movement meant she wasn't paralyzed. He'd heard of men injured on the battlefield, struck on the head or spine and unable to walk. They'd died slow, agonizing deaths.

He also ordered her pillow be brought down. And when it arrived, he adjusted it to support her shoulders, all the while setting her braids neatly down her prone form.

"Ediva?" he asked gently. "Can you hear me?"

She blinked, as if bringing him into focus. One look at him and she burst into tears. He tried to pull her close, but she cried out. "Nay, I ache all over!"

"Of course," he said, berating his foolishness. "You fell down the stairs."

"'Twas dark. The torch…"

"The torch is lit again. It went out."

She looked around the room with confusion. "How did I get here?"

"I brought you in. I didn't want to risk more injuries by carrying to your solar."

"How long have I been here?"

"Only as long as it took your maid to fetch your bedding. I've sent them off again for cold water and cloths."

She gasped. "How long was I at the bottom of the stair?"

"It couldn't have been more than a few moments. I was there not long before."

She grabbed his arm. "He might still be here! You must find him!"

"Find who?" He sat back in shock. "Did someone push you?"

"Aye! A man." She shook her head. "You must—"

He flew out of his chamber. The first person he spied was young Harry, who'd sat himself down along the wall, his face pinched with worry. The boy scrambled to his feet when the door opened.

"Get me the sergeant! And seal the gate! No one leaves nor enters this keep!"

Harry bolted away. Adrien ordered a young soldier who'd come at the sound of shouting to guard the door. Then he stalked straight to the armory to find a more suitable blade. His own 'twas best when mounted. A shorter Saxon blade was better when on foot.

The sword firmly in hand, he charged back to the chamber. His sergeant was already waiting at the door to his chamber.

"Lady Ediva has been attacked. I want the keep emptied top to bottom, except for your most trustworthy man to guard this door. Line everyone else up outside. Now!"

Behind him, the door opened. Ediva stepped out. "Adrien! You must listen to me—"

Shocked yet relieved she could stand, he barked at her, "Stay inside! You're safe there, Ediva."

"But how safe are you?"

Disgusted, he scooped her up and set her back on the bed. "I'll be fine. I'll return shortly." He stalked out, shutting the door firmly behind him.

Ediva jumped as the door slammed. She dare not chase him, for she'd discovered that her body ached with even the slightest movement and moving to the door had been pure agony.

And her stomach churned like a waterwheel in spring. She swallowed the taste of rising bile as she pressed her head against her pillow. Adrien was gone to find her attacker, an unknown man. How would he even recognize him?

What would happen if that man felt threatened? Would he run Adrien through should he turn his back? Geoffrey's warning returned to her. Saxons wanted him dead.

A sob rose in her. She shut her eyes tight against the tears and pressed her hand to her mouth to keep from crying out loud.

Her heart twisted for peace. Her attacker could easily kill again.

Kill who? A tenant who'd trusted her with his or her very life? She'd fought so hard to protect her people, to help them and care for them. Was it possible that one of them truly hated her that much, simply for marrying a Norman? Slowly, she realized something. Her attacker could never forgive her for *betraying* her people with her marriage. As she could never forgive Ganute.

Lord Jesus, what should I do? Help me forgive.

She stared up at the ceiling, the walls catching what little light angled in through the slit windows, all the while recalling to her mind the chapel's mural with its compassionate faces and open arms. The subtle offer of help.

She'd been burdened by hatred and unforgiveness for far too long. She could now see what the hatred did.

To her, and to her attacker, too. Many of the villagers thought she'd married Adrien willingly, and some of them must hate her for what appeared to be a betrayal.

So how could she expect forgiveness from them, while not forgiving Ganute?

Adrien had offered her a solution. *Adrien!* She sat up. The keep was quiet. She stood, grimacing at her aches.

Lord Jesus, protect him.

A small measure of peace settled on her. 'Twasn't any great strike, just a seed within her. And it comforted her.

She stepped tenderly toward the door and opened it a crack. The corridor was dim and quiet, the guard staring down it to the keep's open door and the men formed up outside.

Adrien stood in front, with his sergeant and Geoffrey accounting for each man. She breathed a sigh of relief. Beyond him, several guards stood by the closed bailey gate.

A commotion started. Someone was being dragged out by one of the soldiers. 'Twas Rypan. He tripped and fell before being hauled up by the shoulders to stand in the ranks of servants. He stood, hunched with fear.

Ediva gripped the door as she carefully scanned the backs of those she could see. Her attacker had worn rough, damp wool, easy to discard. All who stood there wore light under tunics and braes. But she couldn't see all of them, and Adrien would never allow her to inspect them.

After quietly closing the door, she settled back on the bed. What would happen to the man should her husband find him? Adrien had flogged Olin for his vile act, and he barely knew Wynnth.

A shudder rippled through her at the thought of what

he might do to the man who had harmed her—and at the revenge the man might later take in return.

'Twas dim when she awoke again. She could feel a gentle warmth emanating from a small brazier that had been brought in. On the hook above it, a lamp glowed a low, smoky flame.

She looked around. Her stomach growled, and thirst parched her mouth as she realized how late it was. A body shifted on a low pallet beside her and, still aching, she peeked over the edge of the bed.

Adrien. She recognized his strong, slim form. Her heart lurched with gladness at the sight of him dozing below her. *Thank You, Lord, for protecting him.*

Again, she felt that seed of peace within her as she sank back onto the bed. *I trust You, Lord. Please help me learn to forgive.*

"Ediva?"

She peeked over the edge again. Adrien rose and adjusted the small metal lamp's air tube to allow it to burn brighter.

The light landed on him, warming his tanned skin to a burnished glow. He'd shed his outer tunic and stood beside his table with hands on hips and feet planted firmly on the stone floor. His dark hair caught the yellowy light, a wonderful gleam like of polished wood.

He was so handsome, Ediva wondered if she wasn't dreaming this moment. She allowed herself the pleasure of taking in every inch of him. His strong arms, his wide chest, his legs...that bore no bandages.

She blinked. "Your leg isn't bandaged. Did you have your stitches removed?"

"Aye. They'd begun to itch. The wound is well-sealed now."

They sank into an uneasy silence until she could stand it now more. "Adrien, did you find him?"

"Nay. All the men were working in groups. There were a few in the fields with the animals, but they were too far away to have reached there so soon."

She fell back onto the pillow.

"You didn't see him?" he asked.

"Nay. The torch had gone out. I smelled something strange, besides the smell of the wet wool he was wearing."

"Wool?" With dropped arms, he took a step closer. "Was it wet with sweat?"

She wrinkled her nose and shook her head. "There was a familiar smell, but I couldn't say where I'd smelled it before."

He eased back as if her words disappointed him. "On the morrow we shall walk about to see if you can smell it again. Was it food?"

"I hope not. 'Twas more sharp and foul." She bit her lip. "Is it late?"

"Aye. I ordered all tenants to their huts and a rotating guard around the keep. The men are not to leave the hall after dark. The women are in servants' quarters behind the kitchen."

Throwing off the furs, she swung her legs over the side of the bed. She felt far better than she did earlier, despite the aches and hunger. Adrien had turned the keep into a fortress, but she wouldn't complain. He did what he felt was proper.

As she should. She should tell the truth. "Adrien, I fear I haven't been fully honest with you."

He sat down beside her. "How so?"

She cleared her throat. "I was attacked before."

He jerked forward. "Before! When?"

"Do you remember the day when you found me with a

sore throat? 'Twas because that man nearly throttled me, not because of a fever as I had led you to believe. He caught me in the stairwell."

He gaped at her, but his expression grew from shock to fury. She could see his fingers curl into fists.

"What happened?" he bit out.

"I was coming down the stairs, and a dog stopped me. It was quite angry and wouldn't let me pass the last few steps. But I think it was growling at the man behind me.

"Then the man grabbed my throat and I nearly passed out from lack of breath. He said I must kill you. And if I don't, he'll kill the tenants one at a time."

"He has attacked you twice!"

She bit her lip. "I'm not sure. It almost felt as though there were two of them. But it couldn't have been. He knew what he'd done before." She rubbed her head.

Adrien dragged his hand down his face. "Why didn't you tell me this before?"

"I was going to. But then you told me that the midwife was dead, and your sergeant confirmed that she'd been killed. I thought it was the attacker, punishing me for not harming you. I was so scared!" She gripped the edge of the bed. "He threatened to kill more if I mentioned anything. These are my people, Adrien. When Ganute died, they worried they'd be killed by Normans or plundered as we were hearing other villages were. I promised them that I'd protect them."

"And I promised you *I* would."

"You weren't here when I promised this." She pulled in a deep breath. "There is more."

"More?" he fumed.

"Geoffrey told me about some men starting to rise up against you, led by one man. They say that they'll fight against you, especially when you leave for Ely."

"I can protect myself."

"It's not that at all, Adrien. We don't know who is behind this, and there are only so many strong Saxon men here. Geoffrey promised he'd find out, but even he believes these men have the right to defend their lands."

"Those who think that are fools. William won't tolerate them. But I can protect this keep and village, even from the king. Do you not trust me on that?"

"Can you truly protect us from the king?"

"Aye. I'm not just a simple knight, Ediva. My brothers and I escorted William to safety years ago. William remembers that. He trusts me."

"But—"

"But what, woman? Have I given you my word so you could treat it as if 'twere that of a child's?"

"You swear allegiance to a Norman king who has stolen my land! You allowed your brother to take away my tenants, save a few men and women. 'Tis hard to trust you! And if *I* find it hard, consider those who don't know you. That man said if I told anyone, even you, he'd kill the villagers. I couldn't allow that. They have no one."

"They have me." He paused, and then his voice dropped so low she could barely hear it. "And I thought *you* also had me."

Adrien had tightened his jaw. But his eyes softened and showed not anger, only hurt. It cut her to the quick.

She should apologize for her doubts. And tell him of her new faith. *Her new faith!* Did she really have new faith in God? Even that simple prayer in her head seemed to grow the seed of love within her. Adrien deserved to know this. And yet, his scowling hurt told her he wouldn't listen right now.

She deserved this pain. She'd hurt him.

Snatching up her pillow, she fussed about the bed. "I

should return to my solar. 'Tis not right to have the lord of the keep sleep on the floor."

He didn't answer immediately. In the dimly lit room, his expression was unreadable, but she felt him tense.

Finally, he held out his hand and helped her up. In his other hand he bore a short blade, one Ediva recognized from Ganute's armory. The hilt was decorated with the family crest. "Aye, you should return to your solar."

Shivering despite the warmth in the room, she put her hand in his, marveling again at how gentle he could be. Instead of pulling her close as she'd hoped he would, he opened the door to find Harry asleep in front of it.

"I'd ordered him into the hall," Adrien growled, stepping forward.

She touched his arm. "Let him sleep."

"He was worried for you." With his foot, Adrien nudged the boy, who jumped up, startled. "Bring your lady's maid to her solar. She needs her tonight."

Harry scampered away, and Adrien led Ediva to the stair. She hesitated. "Are the torches all lit?"

"Aye. I ordered them to stay lit all night."

She stopped at the first tread. Beyond, in the hall beside Adrien's private chamber, several men snored loudly. Other than that, all remained eerily quiet.

She stared deep into the spiral that had only a flickering glow to welcome them. 'Twas hardly a welcome, considering how the torch had gone out before.

Lord, be with us.

"Let me go first." Adrien set her behind him and began the climb. With tender footsteps, she followed him up.

"Adrien!"

He turned.

"Do you smell that?"

He sniffed the air. "I smell the torches. Tallow stinks when it burns."

"Can't you smell something sharp and tangy over the tallow? It's so strong here."

She scanned the stairs and gasped. Between two torches, at the edge of one pool of light, something lay in a heap. Adrien lifted the torch nearest him from its mount. "What's wrong?"

"What's that thing?"

He handed her the torch and lifted up a long, dark cloth. "'Tis a wrap." He leaned forward and sniffed it. "Ahh, I smell it now. 'Tis sharp like spirits. You have a good nose."

"Aye," she whispered hoarsely. "My assailant smelled of this."

"He may have, but he also smelled like he didn't know how to bathe. This wrap has never been washed, I'd wager."

"'Tis more than that, Adrien. I have smelled that smell before! But I can't remember where. Do you recognize it?"

He shook his head. "Not a smell I know." He held the cloth up.

She shrank away. "He wore that about his face."

"'Tis unfortunate that we hadn't found this yesterday. I suspect that our cur was thirsty from the heat after covering his face. Had I known, I'd have watched the well or the pantry. Or I could have sniffed the line of men to locate him."

"Take it out of my sight, Adrien, please. 'Tis an awful thing to look at."

The sound of people approaching caused Adrien to drop the cloth and push past Ediva. He raised his sword slightly, but when Ediva's maid hurried into the circle of torchlight, he lowered it.

Margaret jumped and stepped back onto young Harry, who let out a small yelp.

Adrien lowered his weapon, and ever cautious of it, Margaret stepped around it to take the torch.

"Nay!" Adrien stepped forward. "Follow me."

The three followed him along the upper corridor. "Wait here," he ordered them.

Adrien threw open her solar door, and after a few minutes of searching, stood back and gestured the obedient group to come closer.

Much relieved, Ediva stepped through, while Adrien ordered Harry to remain outside the closed door.

"My lady, I'll see you on the morrow."

She thrust out her hand but stilled it. She wanted so badly to tell Adrien of her prayers, but 'twas not the time.

He noticed her movement, but said nothing as he closed the door.

Chapter Twenty

For a long time, Adrien stared up at the ceiling of his chamber, thinking only of how Ediva had kept the truth from him. *She didn't trust him.*

Of course, even if he had been aware of the threat, he wouldn't have felt himself to be in any true danger. He wasn't intimidated by some Saxon cur. Hadn't he driven off the man in the wood? 'Twas easy with his mount, aye, but he could have easily sent the man to his Maker without his horse.

Adrien sat up on one elbow. Was the man who'd attacked Ediva the same as the one in the wood? Had he not been as injured as Adrien suspected? How could a stranger simply wander into the keep and—

A stranger couldn't. But someone from here, or Little Dunmow, could easily wander about freely. The bailey gate was open and many had business here, people like the midwife who'd often deliver herbs. Or her neighbor, who was called to sit as juror against Olin. That man had not liked the task one bit.

The herbs the midwife delivered. He was sure Ediva had been poisoned and had wondered why.

Because she was a traitor in their eyes. As soon as the

righteous indignation rose in him, shame also swept over him. Hadn't he also thought her a traitor to him?

With head dropped to his hands, he could do only one thing.

Father in heaven, I have sinned against You and against Ediva. Forgive me and guide me with wisdom here.

Yet, despite the prayer, the hurt still weighed heavily on him. Ediva still didn't trust him because all he'd said to her was about his return to battle.

How could he expect her to believe he'd protect her people if he was off fighting their countrymen? He looked up. Through the slit window above dawn was lightening the sky. He should rise and begin his investigation. Today, he'd find who'd attacked his wife.

By chapel time, Adrien had studied and counted all the men. The village men who Eudo had dismissed early were at their homes. They'd been in the fields and far away from the village when Ediva had been attacked. Adrien doubted these men would have entered the keep and threatened their mistress. Those few men had been injured in Colchester and could barely work the fields, let alone attack anyone.

He returned to prepare for services. The sky was light when Adrien reached the chapel. The chaplain opened the door. When the man's widened eyes strayed to the keep, Adrien turned.

With Margaret and Harry following, Ediva was descending the keep's steps, her lightweight blue cyrtel matching her sheer, silvery veil. His breath stalled, a single, savage catch in his throat at his wife's fair beauty. Blue made her skin glow, her eyes brighten. It was an expensive color but it became her.

He bowed as she approached, saying nothing as they entered the chapel. What could he say? He dared not even breathe for fear this was a foolish dream. Ediva walking, albeit carefully, toward him, sitting with him, showing reverence and awe and interest.

Adrien shifted edgily beside her. Something had changed. He'd seen her sit stiffly and pay attention. She'd done all that was proper. But something was different today. He stole a glance at her.

Her expression. She looked at the chaplain with softened eyes. Yet, her lips lay straight in a contrite line and her chin wrinkled slightly as it would before she cried.

When the service was over, she stayed seated a moment and bowed her head. Then, standing, she blinked several times.

"Ediva?"

"I'm fine."

She waited for him to leave the pew and allow her to exit also. The men and women behind them also waited.

He did not move.

"No one can leave until you have exited, my lord," Ediva quietly reminded him.

"Then let them wait," he answered softly. He continued to study her.

"Why are you staring? Have I grown an extra nose overnight?"

"You're different."

"Dismiss the people. Then we can talk." She lifted her chin and blinked as he motioned for the people to leave. When they were gone, she continued. "I'm still the woman who has hurt you. I'm still the woman whose husband looks forward to a battle at Ely, rather than protecting his own people, something he'd vowed to do."

Ire rose in him. "I can do both." Then, remembering his contrition from last night, he crushed his anger. "I'm also the man who realized last night that I was angry at a man who considers my wife a traitor, when I also considered her one. I was hypocritical." He shook his head and lowered his voice. "And wrong. You were doing only as you'd promised."

Her stiffness watered and she took up his hand. She seemed to begin to speak, but instead turned him and gently shoved him into the aisle. She nodded to the chaplain as she took Adrien's hand and led him from the chapel. He allowed her to guide him out the gate, but instead of taking the well-worn path to the villagers' huts, she led him to the right, and soon they were alone, walking along the sheep trail that led to the stone bench that overlooked the River Colne.

She didn't speak until she reached the stone and sat down. "I should have told you immediately what had happened. But I was afraid for you. I didn't know what to do. I didn't want anyone else to die."

"What have you decided then?" Had she brought him here to attempt to take his life? At half his size, she was no match. Besides, he knew she would never hurt him.

"I prayed for help." She looked up at him. "You were right about me needing to forgive Ganute. I need to forgive if I expect God to forgive me. And I most definitely need God to forgive me. Before Ganute died, I had wanted his death many times. When my attacker pointed that out to me, I knew I was a sinner."

He sat down beside Ediva, hardly believing her words. "Go on."

"I knew I could get help only from God. And peace from Him."

He smiled, took her hands in his and kissed them warmly. He held his breath for a moment. "I'm thrilled beyond measure, but there's still something that's bothering you. What is it?"

"I have peace, but just not as much as I thought. I am still afraid you and others will die. I don't have much faith, I fear."

"We all die, Ediva. Faith will help you learn not to fear it. Remember it takes time for a seed to grow. Within the Scriptures, there is a man called Paul—"

"I know the Scripture stories, Adrien. At one time, I enjoyed chapel services. But my life became bitter when I married."

He looked across the river, where an apple tree stood, its fruit now taking on the first blush of ripeness. "Just as it takes a summer to grow good fruit, we need to allow ourselves time to change."

"I know this. I just…" She looked at him. "You have so much patience. I admire that."

With a smile, he shook his head. "No, I don't. Eudo still calls me Prado, that horrible childhood nickname. I have *little* patience with him. But he is slowing understanding how I feel. Last time we met, he called me Adrien. It's a good start for both of us."

She smiled back. They sat on the rock for some time. He took her hand in his and held it between them, and they watched the river roll lazily past on its way to the town of Colchester and finally out to the North Sea.

He thought of why she had not trusted him. He couldn't blame her for it.

But he also couldn't change what was. He was loyal to the king, born to be a soldier. 'Twas all he'd ever wanted to do. Ediva needed a husband who could be there for her and he could never guarantee that.

Slowly, he peeled free his hands. "We should return to the keep."

"And what should we do about the attacker?"

He didn't want to tell her the conclusion he'd come to

early this morning. He still believed the cur lived within
the keep or in Little Dunmow, so very close to them.

"I plan to keep the men separate and always accounted
for. I'll order the soldiers to patrol more often. We'll find
your attacker, Ediva. I know you don't think much of my
promises, but I promise you I won't let another person be
killed in Dunmow Keep."

She set off ahead of him, her frown deepening as she
hiked up her cyrtel to move more easily through the long
grass. "I don't doubt your sincerity, Adrien. I only pray
you *can* do it all."

They returned to the keep and found it quietly busy.
Adrien looked up at the wide wall and found the soldiers
patrolling as ordered. A wave of uneasiness rippled over
him as everyone began to gather for the noon meal. The
soldier's funeral had been completed without Ediva, and
it now left a pall on everyone.

After the chaplain said the blessing for the meal, Ediva
reached to choose the meat for them, but Adrien stopped her.

"I'll taste it first." He tossed a hard look at the young
server who stood with the platter extended and eyes as big
as the brooches on Ediva's cloak. Beside him the steward
stiffened. As he should because 'twas his responsibility
to ensure the safety of the food. Even the chaplain beside
him tensed.

Adrien cut off a small portion of the choice meat and
sampled it. The only thing he tasted was a light salting.
And it sat well in his stomach.

He tasted the drink and found it simple and bland, with
no spices to hide a poison. Satisfied, he served Ediva the
small piece of meat and some boiled vegetables.

Adrien was testing her food? Ediva found herself holding her breath as he sipped from their cup. *Please, Lord,
make this meal safe.*

Smiling uneasily at him when he set down the cup, Ediva felt a little more of that elusive peace drift in, and she welcomed it.

"Milady?"

Ediva looked up, startled. Geoffrey stood in front of the table, his expression emotionless, holding out the savory pastries.

She shook her head. Geoffrey moved to serve the chaplain. Her gaze followed the man around the room as he completed his task with calm efficiency. Then her attention returned to the chaplain, who, oddly, had also refused the pastries.

"Eat while the food is still warm," Adrien suggested, knocking her out of her study.

She picked at her meal. She'd ordered Geoffrey to find who hated the Normans so much that they planned to attack the keep.

Was it someone she trusted? Was it her attacker? The thoughts churned within her.

The meal's conversation remained innocuous, with everyone lingering far too long for her liking. Finally, it was over and many returned to their chores. But Adrien remained at her side all afternoon.

When the night had deepened and fatigue seeped into her, Ediva excused herself to retire. She found Margaret in her solar, and after Adrien left them alone, she ordered her maid to her side.

"Bring Geoffrey here."

Geoffrey arrived with Margaret shortly after Ediva had settled in her chair. With her maid remaining for propriety, Ediva turned to him, her words blunt. "You were to find out who wants Lord Adrien dead."

Margaret gasped, but Ediva shot the young woman a

silencing glare. The woman hastily returned to the embroidery she'd started days ago.

"Milady, I've found out only a few things. The man
who has started this plan to attack now bides his time."

"I can see that. But I want to meet whoever spoke to
you. On the morrow."

"I—I fear I cannot arrange that."

Ediva pulled back her shoulders. She didn't believe that.
"You're a resourceful man. We both know the man who
spoke to you is probably the one who wants Lord Adrien
dead and not just speaking for someone else."

His face remained impassive. "What should I say?"

"That he should expect to be offered coins if he comes
to me. I wager that money—not loyalty to England—mo-
tivates him for Dunmow has not seen any brutality since
Ganute died."

The steward lowered his eyes. Geoffrey knew they had
no coins to offer him, but thankfully he said nothing. "Aye,
milady."

She dismissed the man. No sooner had the door clicked
shut did Margaret rush up to her. "Is it true, milady? Someone wants Lord Adrien dead? I knew you'd been poisoned,
I just knew it! I even told Lord Adrien of it!"

Ediva snapped up her head. "You did what?"

The girl stepped back. "He needed to know. You were
so sick, and I had helped you nurse your poor mother and
Lord Ganute's mother, remember? 'Twas not a fever that
struck *you*." Her hand reached for her throat, her expression full of worry. "I was terrified. You don't deserve to
die!"

"I'm a sinner like you." She turned away from her maid.

But Margaret was not done. She scurried around to face
her mistress. "Not in my eyes, milady. How could anyone

want you dead?" She moaned aloud. "Who attacked you? Why didn't you tell me? I would have surely died for you!"

Ediva smiled grimly at her. "That's exactly why I said nothing." Standing, she laid a heavy hand on her maid's shoulder. "I couldn't let you get hurt."

The woman's eyes misted over as she nodded. "You can't shoulder this all yourself. Nor can you meet with this brute alone. Let me go with you, please, Milady. I'll take a sword from the armory—"

Ediva laughed. "Neither of us can *lift* a sword from the armory, and certainly going down there to ask for one would only alert the guards. They'd tell Lord Adrien in a blink of an eye."

Margaret gasped. "So you don't plan to tell him?"

"Nay." Her eyes narrowed. "And nor will you."

Her maid lowered her gaze.

"If he were to learn where I plan to go, he'd go instead and that cur would wait in ambush for him."

"Lord Adrien has outwitted one man who ambushed him." The girl wrung her hands and moaned again. "When Lord Adrien first arrived, I feared his hand would be as heavy as Lord Ganute's, and I hoped that the many Saxons hiding in the woods would rid our keep of all Normans." She shook her head. "But Lord Adrien is kind and good and keeps his men well-disciplined. Nay, if one of them even looks sideways at us maids, he reprimands them."

"Then you don't want him dead?"

"Nay, I want none of them dead! I want an English king on the throne, but right now, this Norman duke keeps the Danes away. M'maw says that the Danes were far more brutal. Oh, milady! If 'tis God's will for us to have a Norman king, then we must trust in Him."

"Aye. So not a word to Lord Adrien."

"But he can help!"

"And he can also get hurt or even killed." She felt her mouth turn into a thin line before she continued to speak. "I require your silence not only for Lord Adrien's protection but also for ours. He has the king's ear. I can't allow him to die and risk far worse for us here."

Margaret studied her, her silence pensive.

Ediva frowned at her maid. "You want to say more, don't you? Say it then."

Her maid blushed. "'Tis not fear of the king you have, milady. Methinks you're falling for your husband."

Ediva felt the rush of heat and turned away. 'Twas hardly the time for romantic notions. "I'm merely saying that I'll confront the man who tries to ruin our safety."

The maid waved her hand. "How, without Lord Adrien?"

"I'll buy him off. Even addled men see the value in quality goods. I have jewelry and finery he can sell as he sees fit. We'll gather it together on the morrow. Now, 'tis late. We need our sleep."

After the lamp was extinguished, Ediva lay on her bed, still as stone. All that had happened, all that *would* happen, churned within her, until she felt the gentle, coaxing love of God come to her, reminding her to take her rest in Him.

So she began to pray quietly to herself, until she fell asleep.

By the noon meal, Ediva had gathered together her finest linens, some embroidered with gold, along with her best diadem and jewelry. She ordered her maid to hide it all in a rough sack and store it in her bed.

From below the window, shouts rose, and Ediva hurried up onto the parapet.

"What's going on?" she asked the guard there.

"Your tenants are home, milady!"

Smiling, Ediva leaned between the merlons and peered down. They were back!

By the time she reached the bailey, the gate had been opened and not only the returning men, but their families had poured in. The chaplain held up his hand and offered a prayer of thanksgiving. When it was finished, she lifted her eyes to meet with Adrien's own smiling gaze.

One of Eudo's guards sent to escort the men home rode up to Adrien and handed him a folded missive. Across the bailey, she could see Adrien's expression darken as he read it, and her heart hitched in her chest.

She hurried over, her progress delayed by several villagers who hugged her in gratitude. The air about was fast becoming festive, with songs and joy and laughter bouncing off the stone walls. When she reached Adrien, his scowl had truly deepened.

"What is it?" she asked.

He refolded the note and tucked it in his tunic. "The uprisings have strengthened in the north. William has spent the summer in Normandy but is returning soon. Eudo fears that some Normans to the west have treated the English nobility poorly. Word of such has reached an exiled Saxon lord by the name of Hereward the Wake. He plans to return to England."

"I heard once that a Hereward was exiled for poor behavior. He made Ganute look like a gentle maid." She shook her head. "Will Eudo send the soldiers here to Ely?"

"He awaits the king's orders, but likely he will. He says I'll accompany them."

Geoffrey's warning rolled over her. Her attacker wanted Adrien dead to ensure he never fights at Ely.

"And you'll go?"

"Of course."

She bit her lip and spun, heading toward the chapel. If

Adrien called out to her, she did not answer. The chaplain met her at the chapel door, a question on his face.

A dog ran about the bailey, barking madly. It raced past her and she shied away from it.

"Milady?" the chaplain asked. "Is there something wrong?"

She shook her head as she hurried inside. "Nay. I want to offer my thanks for the men's safe return."

'Twas obvious to her that the old man didn't believe her. But his opinion mattered little. 'Twas God who she wanted to hear her prayers. Only God could give her peace in her mind and heart at the thought of her husband returning to war.

Ediva didn't want him to go to Ely, Adrien thought grimly. But what choice did he have? If he was ordered to fight, he would.

Still, those words sat like bad food inside of him. He no longer wanted to fight.

How was that possible? He'd spent a lifetime honing his skills and training his horse. Fighting was in his blood.

Over the din of festivities in the bailey, a dog's snippy barking broke his thoughts. He watched Ediva speak briefly with the chaplain before slipping into the chapel. He should be happy she was going to pray, but the consternation on the chaplain's face unnerved him.

Ediva was worried.

The revelry around him stole his concentration. A young girl grabbed his tunic and offered him some flowers she'd picked. He accepted them with a smile and allowed himself to be led into the impromptu festivities.

In the midst of the revelry, he waited for Ediva to exit the chapel, and when she didn't, he ordered the cook to start a feast worthy of this homecoming. He wanted to bring Ediva out to enjoy the festivities, but before he could, he found himself distracted by yet another small child.

Ediva heard the chapel door open and close. She turned around, but with only one lamp lit, all she could tell was that a man, not as tall as Adrien, had entered.

She held her breath, hoping it would still her pounding heart. She had the benefit of being used to the dimness, as opposed to the man who'd just entered. Staying deadly still, she watched him scan the interior and prayed he would not see her.

"Milady?"

She sighed. 'Twas Geoffrey. "Aye?" she called out to her steward.

He came hesitantly forward, his hands reaching out to the back of the front pews for the security that the dimness refused to offer. "I have news, milady. The man agrees to meet."

Her heart hammering, she stood. "Where?"

"On the road that leads to the tithe barn is an abandoned watch tower."

"I remember the place. It sits at a fork in the road. I passed it when I first came here."

"Aye. It's been abandoned for years and is open and gutted. The man who plans a rebellion will wait there for you, tonight."

She blew out a sigh and nodded. "Good. Thank you, Geoffrey."

He hesitated. "'Twill not be safe for you to go alone."

"True. That's why I'm taking you with me."

That startled him. "Will you try to kill him?"

She nearly laughed aloud. As if she could. "Nay. I'll go to pay him off. With the price I'll offer him, he can leave Essex and start anew elsewhere or buy arms and fight in some other place. I don't care what he does as long as he leaves this county and does not return."

"But, milady, if you plan for us to leave at night, how will we find our way?"

"We'll leave at dusk. The night should be clear and the moon is full."

"He'll want you dead, milady!"

"I'm of no value to him dead. He knows that or else he'd have killed me already. Aye, I know he is the one who attacked me." She stepped out of the pew and touched her steward's shoulder. "Say nothing of this, Geoffrey. We have God to protect us."

She saw his features harden but brushed past him. Geoffrey didn't believe her, and why should he? He'd seen her skirt her religious duties for years. Never mind. She had no time to convince him of her newfound faith.

She found the addled boy, Rypan, in the stable, feeding the horses, completely unmoved by the celebration in the main bailey. His father had died at Hastings, and his mother shortly after. His aunt, the cook, had asked Ediva if she'd keep him on. So Rypan remained doing whatever was needed. He'd never been quite right, but he was a good boy, willing to work. He was fast approaching manhood, but Ediva hoped he'd stay the sweet, shy boy he'd always been, despite now being slightly taller than her.

Ediva hesitated at the entrance. The old nag Adrien had given her to train on was still in her stall at the back. She looked up at Ediva, expecting another lesson with the nervous rider who tugged too hard at her bit. Immediately, she snorted her disapproval.

The boy noticed her. "Rypan," Ediva said gently, "I need that old nag and another pony. Geoffrey and I will ride out at dusk. Have them ready, but take them behind the midwife's house."

Rypan was thin and wiry, older than Harry by several years but younger in spirit and mind. Ediva knew he could saddle the ponies, just not Adrien's courser or the gift mare. Rypan nodded mutely for he spoke little, as his voice often cracked. Immediately, he set about the task of finding the tack needed.

She returned to the keep to find Adrien had ordered a feast that would combine the noon meal with a supper one. The cook looked up from her work of dressing a bird. "Do you need a bit to hold you over, milady?"

She was about to decline because since Adrien had arrived, she had returned to the protocol of sending her requests to the cook through Geoffrey. But she stopped. "A large, sweet pastry, please. Send it to my solar." She planned to enjoy the banquet, then slip away, saying she was tired. With the whole of the keep and village celebrating the men's return, she'd be able to reach the watch tower, buy off the man and return before anyone missed her. 'Twas not so far that she couldn't accomplish such a task within the span of an early evening.

Now, for the other matter she needed to accomplish before leaving... Though she was taking Geoffrey, he would not be the only one armed. But acquiring a blade from the armory would raise suspicions. She glanced around the kitchen and spied a fine filet knife. The cook was preparing game and birds, so there was no need for a fish blade. Carefully, she slipped it and its sheath to her side as the cook busied herself, and she trod quietly out.

Chapter Twenty-One

After leading two ponies from behind the midwife's empty hut later that evening, Rypan handed Ediva their reins. With a shy smile, he accepted her thank you gift of the large pastry filled with sweetmeats that she'd ordered sent to her solar earlier.

With Geoffrey, Ediva had been able to slip out of the bailey. Her steward's comings and goings had long been ignored by the Norman guards. So the steward and his slight companion dressed in old braes and tunic would hardly warrant a second glance. Many would think she was Rypan.

Ediva allowed the boy to help her mount, and once she was seated, Geoffrey handed her the plain sack that held her treasures. Swallowing her apprehension, she nodded to him.

The scents of roasting meats drifted over from the keep now mixed with an unpleasant smell. She sniffed the air, but when she couldn't immediately identify it, she curtailed the thought. She had no time to waste with trivialities.

Looking down at Rypan, she said, "Stay until we return."

He nodded, and she spurred her pony into an ungainly trot northward.

The sun had set, but 'twas not yet night. They trotted along, Ediva aware that the last time she was on this road was for her first nuptials, five years ago. She hoped that her memory of the distance was still intact.

Ahead trees closed in on them, blocking the rising moon from lighting the path. She thought of Adrien, her last words to him wishing him a good night.

Lord, be with me.

The nag beneath her sensed her apprehension and slowed. "Nay, old girl," she said softly, patting the dun-colored neck. "Just a bit longer. I need to do this for Adrien's sake."

"Milady?" Geoffrey trotted up to her side.

"Just talking to my pony. How much further is it, do you think?"

"At the end of these trees, I believe."

Ediva urged her mount on. *For your master's sake, old girl,* she thought instead of talking to the mount. *We both need to protect him. I fear Margaret is correct when she says I'm falling for him.*

The pony returned to a trot and they soon cleared the wooded area. Moonlight bathed the open field, and Ediva dared a glance over her shoulder. The forest behind them lay like a thick, dark blanket. She could no longer see the keep, and Geoffrey had become like a dark, bobbing mound.

Inhaling deeply to steady her nerves, she tried to soothe herself with the clean smell of summer. She needed her wits about her. Ahead, catching the moonlight on its battered front flank, the old watch tower very nearly glowed.

Ediva slowed the nag and pulled alongside a low wall east of the tower. Thankfully, the old boy's clothes aided her dismount. She set the reins onto the top of the wall and secured them with a rock before freeing her sack from the saddle. Adjusting her belt, she pulled gently on the hilt of the knife secured there to ensure it could be freely released from its scabbard.

Lord, protect me.

By now, Geoffrey had dismounted. He said nothing, but Ediva could feel the tension in him.

She found the broken doorway in the back, well-shadowed by the position of the moon. Pausing, she strained to hear something, anything, but only silence answered. Had something happened to keep the man away? Or did he lay in wait for her? She turned to Geoffrey. "Stay here."

"Allow me to go first, milady!" he whispered back.

"Nay, 'tis my duty."

She stepped inside the door as soundlessly as she could. Chips of broken wall crunched under her foot, causing her to stall her footsteps and hold her breath.

Nothing happened. No movement, no scurrying of vermin to warn her assailant.

She slipped further inside. The bottom floor was overgrown with decades of debris. Moonlight filtered down, hitting a sapling that had taken root in the center of the main floor. To her right stood a flight of narrow stairs.

Climbing softly, she shifted her sack to her left hand and eased the knife out of its sheath with her right. She passed a slit window. Moonlight glinted onto the blade for a lightning-flash moment. She tried to take each tread as silently as possible, but her clothes remained determined to rustle loudly.

So she continued her climb.

Adrien scanned the hall, a well-pleased smile growing on his face at the incredible happiness around him. 'Twas good to see families reunited. Aye, the villagers weren't overly happy to share this day with Norman soldiers, but they set aside the animosity for one evening. Eudo's few men were well-behaved, and the sergeant was wise enough to see the need for good relations. All was pleasant.

Only Ediva's absence marred the occasion. She'd said she was tired and that the day had been too much for her. Mayhap she didn't find anything worth celebrating.

Why would she? The missive Eudo sent had carried bad news. Even he found himself regretting that he would have to go to Ely. Hereward the Wake's return to fight for his country was inevitable, so therefore was the battle at Ely. But at the same time, Ediva's concern touched him deeply.

Adrien stood. The soldiers, catching their baron rising, also rose, as did the villagers. "Enjoy your night," he called out to them and headed for the door.

He turned for one last look at the revelry. The dais was empty. Where was the chaplain? Had he slipped out during Ediva's more obvious exit? Mayhap he'd also grown tired as he was no longer a young man.

Spying Ediva's maid, he motioned to her. She'd been chatting with several maidens but now hurried over. "You followed your mistress upstairs, didn't you?"

"Aye, my lord." She paused before adding, "But she dismissed me so I could return."

"Are they relatives, the ones you were speaking with?"

"Nay, these women are good friends." She shook her head. "I have no family here. My sisters serve in Lady Ediva's family home."

With a frown, Adrien left the hall. The festivities weren't the same without Ediva, but unlike Margaret, he found he could not celebrate without his family. Namely, his wife.

* * *

The top of the tower had long since collapsed, taking the ceiling of the upper floor with it. Now exposed, the second floor filled the task of look off. Ediva picked her way over the rubble toward the edge, hoping to see her attacker before he arrived. A soft breeze rustled some tall weeds growing within the mess around her. Moonlight washed the floor in a pale yellow, except where the wall had only partially collapsed. She waited. But no one came. Was he already near, waiting for her?

Her patience eroded, she stepped further away from the stairs with careful movements, half afraid the old floor would give way. But it seemed sturdy enough. With a deep breath, she called out, "This is Lady Ediva. I want to talk to you. Show yourself. I know you're here."

A bat darted by, startling her. With her breath still tight in her lungs, she held herself rigid.

When she could stand still no longer, she set down the sack and sheathed the knife she'd gripped so tightly that it hurt her hand. She stepped into the center of the exposed room.

"You shouldn't have bothered bringing your treasures, my lady. I have no need of them."

Not yet ready to retire, Adrien headed for the parapet. He faced the south, staring down at the bailey. One guard patrolled the battlement, his form clear in the bright moonlight. Another, merely a shadow now, stood sentry at the gate.

To his left, the village lay quiet. Only a few had retired from the feast, mostly those with young children who would be impossible tomorrow if they had their sleep disrupted.

Adrien leaned forward, his attention caught by some-thing.

A slight figure skulked about the midwife's house.

Who was it? Eudo had added a postscript to his dis-concerting letter, the one that mentioned he had found a young woman with birthing knowledge and planned to send her. Geoffrey had no claim to his mother's house, as it was leased from the king. The new midwife could have it. It should be empty.

So who was that down there now? He peered hard, but the hut sat in the keep's shadow, and the figure had long disappeared around the far side. He considered investi-gating for himself, but the urge to see his wife right away won out.

Adrien turned and reentered the keep, pausing at the long corridor that led to Ediva's solar. He needed to talk to her. He took a single step down the corridor but stopped. What would he say? That he didn't really want to fight now? Nay, but being here, being close to Ediva, was be-coming a lure like no other.

He wanted to tell her how much he cared, but hadn't he already proved he was an idiot when it came to speaking? Hadn't he already called her old like some battered pot and told her to prepare to be pruned like a bramble bush?

Nay, first he needed to sort out his feelings before he stumbled over words trying to express them. He headed back the way he came. And while weighing and measur-ing his thoughts, he would use the time to confront who-ever it was sneaking about the midwife's house.

The voice had come from behind. Ediva spun. Stand-ing in the shadow of the only remaining wall was a man.

He stepped forward and picked up the sack she'd set

down. "Do you think that I came here seeking jewels and fine cloth?" His voice bore a familiar hitch.

"Nay. But what you have demanded, I cannot give. I want you gone from my estates. This would ease your passage."

"*Your* estates?" his cracking voice mocked her. "The land is now King William's, not yours."

She slowly reached across her body to the scabbard.

"Nay!"

She stilled her hand. The voice, not as sharp and tight as she remembered, was faintly familiar. Yet different. As was the movement of this man. Had the darkness of the stairwell painted a different picture of him in her mind?

She swallowed. Her assailant stood there, ready...but for what? Some sign of acknowledgment or recognition?

The scent carried to her by the soft wind was more familiar than his shape. *The sharp, pungent odor her assailant wore.*

Stripped of other smells, the air carried the scent freely.

She knew that odor well, from more than just her attacks. 'Twas the scent near the midwife's house. But 'twere other times she'd smelled it. Why could she not recall those instances?

"Drop your blade, Ediva. Slowly." Her Christian name carried easily on his tongue, similar to when he'd spoken it in a hoarse voice. But it was so curiously familiar.

She stayed still, her hands remaining at her sides. "Nay, I will not drop it."

The screech of unsheathing sword rent the night air. A Saxon blade reached into the space between them.

Her assailant stepped closer, forcing her to retreat. The wooden floor beneath her gave slightly like a wet fen. Dirt had accumulated, capturing seeds that had sprouted to hold more water and rot the wood planks further.

A creak of protest rose from the floor, and she froze. She didn't dare move backward any more.

"Do as I command, Ediva."

That voice! Who was it? Ediva ducked to the left, but the floor there had softened further. The man ahead of her shook his head. The cowl was thrust too far forward for her to glimpse his face. The moon had reached its peak and shone down from atop, casting the man into shadow.

"Look in the sack. I'm offering you all my riches," she suggested.

"You think you can buy me off?"

Aye, she thought. She'd been willing to relinquish it all for the chance to save Adrien and begin a proper, loving marriage with him. "Aye. And you'd be a fool to let it go without looking at what's there."

"I know what you have, woman! And I know what I want. I want Lord Adrien dead!"

He jerked closer with a groan. His gait was labored.

She stepped to the other side. The floor remained firm beneath her feet, but there was nowhere to go. Ediva feared the wood at the edge had rotted more.

She glanced up at her assailant as he took another awkward, limping step. His voice sounded labored and cracking.

She couldn't think, but felt realization lay just outside her grasp.

It didn't matter right now.

Lord, protect me. I know I'm not worthy of Your protection, but I need it now. Show me what to do.

She stood straight. "Who are you? Do you want Adrien dead only because he's a Norman? Why are you so interested in our lives? We are a small keep in the middle of nowhere!"

"You're valuable to me, Ediva. That's why I haven't killed you yet."

The Saxon accent chilled her very core. And the words sounded frighteningly familiar, too.

She gasped as realization washed over her. Only one person spoke like that.

But she'd buried Ganute. She'd put his dead body in the cold ground nearly ten months ago.

How could this be?

Chapter Twenty-Two

Adrien ordered the gate opened, drawing his sword as he bolted through it. His steps slowed as he approached the village. He heard movement and, oddly, a soft humming.

His blade high, he stepped around the corner of the midwife's hut. The slight form gasped before opting to take flight.

Adrien acted fast. He caught the dark, baggy clothing with his sword's tip and lunged forward to imprison his hostage against the daubed wall.

The creature cried out, wiggling so much he nearly ripped his captured shirt. Adrien yanked back his sword. At the same time, he grabbed the youth to shove him against the wall. Dried daub showered down on them.

Adrien turned his hostage into the moonlight.

Rypan! "Hold still, boy!" he ordered, "or you'll hurt yourself!"

Rypan stilled, though his limbs shook. Adrien's grip remained tight. "What are you doing here?"

A coarse howl let loose from the boy's lungs. Impatient, Adrien leaned close to tell him to stop his caterwauling.

Then he sniffed. And sniffed again. What was that smell?

"What do I smell on you?"

Rypan shook with fear. Immediately, Adrien eased up on his grip. What was the use? His English wasn't good enough for the youth to understand it fully.

Still, he sniffed again, then held the youth back. *He stank like the wool covering he'd found in the stairwell.*

Tightening his grip on the youth, Adrien dragged him into the bailey and up to the kitchen. He called out for a cook, who was standing in the corridor watching the festivities. The woman was Rypan's aunt—she would know how to get him his answers. Spying them, she hurried over.

"My lord, has Rypan been bothering you?"

"I found him at the midwife's house. Ask him what he was doing there."

Instead, the cook leaned forward to sniff him. She grimaced. "'Twould do no good, milord. He's been into the midwife's herbs. He won't be able to speak for a while."

"'Tis impossible. Geoffrey brought all the herbs here."

"Not that one. I won't have it in my kitchen. It stinks too much. The midwife grew it in her garden but kept it separate."

"What did she use it for?"

"For the boy." The cook took the boy's wrist, allowing Adrien to release his hold on him. With her free hand, she smoothed down Rypan's clothing and hair, all the while shaking her head. "He's always been a bit stupid, so his mother had asked the midwife for some herbs to make him smart. The midwife would give him that herb each week."

"Did it make him smarter?"

The cook shrugged. "It made him mute. I didn't like that, but it never affected him for too long. Rypan must have taken some, thinking 'twas time for his dose." She asked her nephew if he took his weekly dose. The boy nodded.

She grimaced. "There you go, my lord. I dare say he misses the midwife. She would feed him right after she dosed him. When that muteness wears off, he'll be able to talk." The cook shrugged. "He's a bit smarter, but his mind still wanders."

"What causes the smell?"

"'Tis the juice, really. The juice dries up like a ball of dung and smells about the same. The midwife called it stink gum." She kept on smoothing her nephew's clothes, all the while looking sadly grim.

"I've not heard of it before."

"Count yourself blessed, then, milord. The midwife said it came from the Far East, grown by Romans ages ago, like it was something better than what we have here."

"And it makes the boy mute?"

"Aye. Not as bad as when he was younger. He would be mute for several days when he was small, but as he got older, he could talk a bit and sounded normal much sooner. I expect he's just scared of you. Watch."

She released the youth and he let out a squall and dashed off. "See?" the cook said with another shrug. "He can speak now, though he will be hoarse. As he gets older, the herb will just change his voice for a short time." She sniffed the air, and shook her head. "'Twill take all night to clear this air."

Adrien frowned. "'Twill just change his voice when he's older?"

"Aye, my lord. 'Tis the effect it has on adults."

"How does it taste?"

"The midwife claimed it went sweet when fried but I won't try it. It's to ease stomach troubles also, so mayhap if we don't get a midwife, I'll have to try it out when someone gets sick."

Adrien pulled a face. The herb would not be used as a poison if 'twere used for stomach troubles.

The cook flapped the front of her apron to force the foul smell out the open door. "I should burn something fatty in the fire."

With the cook bustling off, Adrien stepped outside. Had Rypan gone to the midwife's house to get his weekly dose? Although the boy was slightly addled, surely he wouldn't go in the midst of this reunion, when good food was being offered? The boy liked to eat. Such illogic sat cold and hard in his belly.

The answer lay with Rypan, and Adrien set off to find him, heading first for the stables. The boy was more comfortable with animals than people.

The stables were dark, but outside, attached to the wall, a spark box, left by the chandler, held glowing embers. Adrien lit a tallow lamp and took it inside.

"Rypan? Where are you, boy? I'm not mad at you. I want to talk to you."

No one moved. His courser and the gift mare were side by side and both snorted at him. He walked down the line of stalls until the roof dipped low. The stalls in the back were reserved for smaller ponies. A quiet rustling alerted Adrien, and he peeked over the half wall with the lamp.

Huddled low, Rypan stared up at him, eyes wide.

Adrien opened the stall door, determined not to frighten him further. "Come out, boy," he said in his quietest, most gentle English. "I won't hurt you. I just need to talk to you."

When the boy didn't move, Adrien hung the lamp on a nearby hook and crouched down beside him. "Are you hungry?"

When the boy nodded, Adrien grimaced. He should have brought some sweetmeat to tempt the youth. "I'll give you a fine meal if you answer my questions. Would you do that for me?"

The boy nodded again.

"Can you speak?"

There was a short squawking noise, but Adrien could hear the "a bit" in it. "Did you take your dose of herbs tonight?"

Again, there was another short bob of the head.

"Where did you get them?"

"Garden." The answer was more like a rusty hinge than a spoken word, but Adrien understood it.

"Who else knew of this herb?"

The boy drew up his knees and set his head into them.

Adrien sighed and shifted to sit and lean against the stall door's jamb. He closed his eyes. Not the most appropriate place for the lord of the keep, but he needed Rypan to trust him.

He opened his eyes and stared at the empty stall, trying to decide what else to ask the boy that wouldn't close him off any more than he already had. But he was distracted by a sudden realization.

The stall was empty. No mounts were needed tonight; the stables had been full to capacity earlier. Indeed some mounts had been doubled up as the soldiers who'd escorted the tenants home stabled them for the night. So why was this stall empty?

He stood. The nag Ediva had used was gone, as was another pony. He looked at Rypan. "Where are the ponies?"

Rypan looked into the stall and then at Adrien before mumbling something.

"Say it again, boy. Slowly."

"'Twit milady."

Adrien blinked. Had he heard right? "With Lady Ediva?"

The boy nodded. Adrien stared at him, feeling his mouth drop open.

"Both ponies? Why? Where did she go?"

Rypan shrugged. He pointed to the north.

Frustration rising in him, Adrien stood. Ediva had been too tired and retired early. She couldn't have left. "*Quand?*" he barked at the boy, demanding to know "when" in harsh French.

The boy looked confused. Adrien reached for him, but Rypan ripped past to disappear into the night.

Adrien grabbed the lamp and hurried out, but the bailey was empty. With a growl, he tore into the keep, pushing past several villagers who were exiting the hall and thrusting the lamp at one of the guards.

He took the stairs two at a time as he raced to Ediva's solar.

He threw open the door and startled the maid who was now lying on her pallet. His first glance was to Ediva's empty bed. "Where's your mistress?"

Sitting up, the woman pulled up on her blanket, and gaped at him. She'd added coals to the brazier, and it offered only the thinnest of light to the room.

"Are all the people in this keep addled?" he thundered. "Woman, tell me where Ediva has gone, or I will have you cleaning the stables all winter!"

"I don't know, milord! She wouldn't tell me. I think she went to buy off her attacker. The man who wants to start a rebellion!"

"When did she leave?"

"Shortly after she came up here, milord. She talked to Geoffrey about meeting the man at a tower on the road to the abbey."

"Geoffrey let her go by herself?" But as soon as he

spoke, he guessed who the other pony was for. Geoffrey had accompanied her.

Adrien strode out, slammed the door and stormed down the stairs. In his chamber, he lit a lamp and pulled out the map from his trunk.

After spreading on the table, he smacked his forefinger onto the vellum. There, to the north! The main road, where it forked. The symbol of a tower.

Grabbing the map, Adrien rushed into the corridor. Harry was nowhere to be found, so he stalked down to the nearly empty hall. Many of the men who'd returned had left for their huts. Only a few soldiers still enjoyed the evening.

Adrien spied his sergeant. He motioned to him and the young man hurried over.

"Saddle my courser. Take a horse for yourself and one other. Choose your most sober man who is good with a bow. I want you both armed and ready to leave immediately."

"Has there been an attack, my lord?"

"Lady Ediva has ridden off to confront the man who attacked her."

The sergeant's brows shot up in horror as he pivoted sharply to shout at another man. Blood pounded in Adrien's head as he watched the man leave. He could only hope that Ediva and Geoffrey had just left.

What had they been thinking, going off like a pair of children on a lark?

Adrien did not like the answer forming in his head. Ediva was determined that he not die. So much so, she'd risk her own life.

Chapter Twenty-Three

❦

"Nay, you cannot be Ganute!"

The man peeled off his cowl, and Ediva gasped in absolute fury. "Olin! How dare you!"

"How dare I?" He took another limping step forward. "You're the one who allowed that Norman dog to beat me! I should be the master of Dunmow Keep, not him!"

"You're addled. I'm the mistress, and Saxon law allows me to keep my estate if my husband had no issue."

His lip curled. "And wasn't it convenient that Ganute fathered no children?"

"'Twas the Lord's will."

He snorted. "It had far more to do with you fighting your place with Ganute than your 'pious' prayers."

Ediva refused to answer. How dare Olin bring up the horror that was her marriage to Ganute? She drew in her breath to calm herself. "My marriage was not your business, fool."

"You will not address the master of Dunmow in that manner!"

"You're not the master of Dunmow!" She quickly chose a different tactic. "Olin, I'm offering you riches that nearly match that of the keep. Just look in the sack I've brought."

"I don't care for them! I want the keep!"

"But the Normans have taken everything! We Saxons have nothing."

"Idiot woman." He waved his short sword. "I'll collect more taxes and give only what I see fit to the king."

"The records will show what is given."

Olin laughed. "Have you never heard of lying? And no one will believe the stupid villagers should they complain."

Ediva bit her lip. "The king will find out!"

"Our keep is one of thousands. 'Tis too expensive to scrutinize all of England. What's one small keep with a loyal Saxon there? I have already made myself known in London as one who can be trusted."

She nearly laughed aloud at his boast. The Normans were hardly stupid. And the king, whilst cruel, was no fool. And only a fool would trust Olin. Besides, if anything were to happen to the Norman knight to whom he'd entrusted the keep, William would burn it to the ground before he'd put it in the hands of a Saxon. Olin was deluding himself if he thought otherwise.

Ediva glanced around. What she needed to do was get away. The ground was down too far for her to jump, but she could manage the steps better than the limping Olin.

Limping? Why? His whipping wouldn't have hurt his legs.

She took a step forward, her mind spinning swiftly. The attack on Adrien? Hadn't Adrien said that he'd injured the man?

Nay, Olin could never have attacked her, being so injured. He was working with someone—but who? "You are addled, Olin. You blame me for not giving an heir to Ganute, but had it been so, you'd have no claim on Dunmow Keep. What will you do now? Do you plan to kill me?"

Olin laughed heartily. She shivered, recalling to her

mind how Ganute would sometimes laugh when she cried for mercy. 'Twas the same sound and she hated it.

"I have no intention of killing you. But my plans needed changing after I realized you wouldn't kill your husband. You're what will draw him here. I'll take something special of yours and have it delivered with a note to Adrien. When he comes, I'll kill him and blame you. And since you have so kindly offered me your jewelry, I'll have even more money."

"Your plan will fail."

"Nay, Adrien will come for his wife."

"He cares little for me. I'm only part of the property given to him."

"But as his property, he won't give you away. He'll come if only to take back what is his and punish you for your willfulness."

She grit her teeth. "Nay, he will not!" Adrien's kindness and respect, and his love for the Lord told her 'twould not be so. And the words he quoted from the Scriptures: *A man is to love his wife as Jesus loves the church.*

A jot of peace settled into her and blossomed within her very soul at her certainty in her marriage. Ganute held no more power over her—and neither did Olin. She would not let him use her. Which meant that she needed to get away.

At the moment, Ediva took a step forward. "You think you've planned this all out, Olin, but look at what I have brought first. 'Twould surprise you, I believe, and you can still walk away a very rich man. All you need to do is look into the sack."

His greed greater than his desire to berate her, Olin turned. Now was her time to move.

In the bailey, Adrien found several men mounted, with Harry gripping his courser's reins firmly, a look of worry haunting his face. Several of the men carried torches. He swelled with pride when he saw both Norman and Saxon faces in the crowd of rescuers.

"Leave all but one torch here," he told the men. "'Tis best if we don't give ourselves away."

The torches were relinquished and the remaining one was extinguished. A young squire fetched a spark box to ignite it later.

Continuing, Adrien said, "The road forks at the tower. We'll close in from two sides."

"Aye, my lord. I have learned the layout from several men," the sergeant added. "If we're quiet, we'll be able to slip past the tower to the west and surround it, but there are brambles to the north that choke off that side. I suggest we also stay at the fork, for it is closest to the east side entrance."

"Excellent," Adrien finished, liking the plan. "Keep near the woods so the moon doesn't catch you. I'll take half the men up the abbey road and call like a bird." He demonstrated, so the men would know the sound. "When you hear that, begin your attack on the west side. Keep your archer far enough for him to see the top of the tower. A sentry may be there. I will enter the tower to retrieve Lady Ediva."

"Several villagers warn the floor is rotting and trees have already begun to sprout through it," the sergeant cautioned him. "Be careful, my lord, where you stand, and beware of the winding stairs on the right, for they may hide our attacker."

With a nod, Adrien mounted his stallion and turned it to face his sergeant. "You have devised a good plan, sergeant."

"'Twas formed by these Saxons, my lord, not me."

With a curt nod, he ordered the gate opened and they charged out. The moon had passed its zenith, now casting longer shadows on the road ahead. Adrien allowed his mount to gallop as long as he dared. When the trees parted ahead and he spied a misshapen tower, he slowed the group to a walk. His courser nickered with complaint. With the night being far calmer than he expected, the sound echoed loudly.

"We dismount here," he ordered, not wanting the horses to give away their position. A few minutes later, on foot, they reached the fork in the road. He indicated for the sergeant and his men to move to the west, as he took the other half to follow the abbey road.

The tower was silent, and two ponies stood by the wall. Ediva's nag lifted her head and sniffed the night air, smelling their approach.

Please, Lord, keep her silenced.

She snorted once, but after months of dealing with the soldiers, she was used to their smell and returned to her attempt to reach the tall grasses growing up the side of the short wall. A quick, stealthy walk beside the wall, and Adrien found the entry gate. He could see the broken door at the rear of the tower, now bathed in moonlight. Beyond lay a thicket of brambles.

Adrien stilled his men and listened carefully.

"Stay still, woman!"

The words cut clearly through the night, followed by a cry. 'Twas Ediva's cry, followed by the sickening scrape of wood and stone giving way underfoot.

He prayed swiftly for Ediva's safety. As he plunged forward, a sharp scream rent the air. Immediately after, he caught the cold gleam of moonlight on steel directly in front of him and he swung out his sword.

Olin grabbed for Ediva as he ordered her to stay still, but she ducked and lunged for the stairs.

'Twas no good. Olin was faster, despite his limp. With a grunt, he caught her arm and swung her around.

"I will have the keep and all your goods before long, woman!"

Ediva struggled against him, all too aware that the dew-slickened wood would not hold their combined weights much longer. Below her, the sharp clank of steel on steel reached her. Who was down there? Who was Geoffrey fighting?

Olin's grip tightened as he dragged her down the stairs to be free of the tower. But the ground floor only revealed a more dangerous predicament. Two men were battling at the entrance to the tower.

Olin hauled Ediva closer to him, as she gaped at the men. "Adrien!"

He turned and, at that moment, his attacker stepped back to readjust his swing. Moonlight bled down on that man, exposing his identity.

Geoffrey! He was fighting Adrien!

Olin clamped his filthy hand over her mouth and hauled her back up the stairs. She lost sight of Adrien and could only pray he turned in time to defend himself.

At the top again, Olin threw her into the center of the floor. It groaned under her weight and sagged downward. On her knees, she stilled, daring not to move lest it give way.

Olin slunk into the shadows, hidden in a safer section. Then he pointed the tip of his sword into her arm. She dared not move away from the blade's reach for fear she'd fall through the floor. "One word and I will run you through."

She could barely breathe. Below them, the fighting stilled with a cry of pain and the thump of a body.

A man pounded up the stairs to them. She bit her lip when moonlight hit him.

Adrien!

He stopped when she gave him the barest shake of her head. Ediva knew he couldn't see Olin. And there was only one way she could expose the evil man.

"Adrien, to your left!" As she called in French, she rolled further away from Olin, whose raging anger spewed as he burst from the shadows.

He lifted up his sword in fury. Adrien met the weapon and thrust it away with the murderous clang of steel on steel.

Below her, Ediva felt the floor creak further and reached out to grab the rubble scattered ages ago. Her fingers closed over a hunk of rock and she tightened her grip.

Adrien shifted and let out a shrill whistle. Confused, Olin stalled his actions. Ediva heard the hiss of something fly over her head. She gasped when she saw Olin.

An arrow had pierced his chest, and with a look of shock, he slumped forward to fall at her side.

But the sudden weight was too much for the rotting floor and it relented. She grappled about, but her hands slipped, and with a scream, she plunged deep into the bowels of the tower.

Chapter Twenty-Four

"Nay!" Adrien lunged forward. The tower had swallowed Ediva like a hungry beast.

He dropped to his knees and peered down. "Ediva? Can you hear me?"

There was no answer, so he raced down the stairs to the ground floor. "The torch!" he called to the men. "Bring it here!"

It took far too long to light the torch, but once lit, it sent the darkness scurrying. Ediva, in a heap amid the rubble that was the ground floor.

Adrien stormed to her side. She lifted her head as he rolled Olin's body aside. "Adrien, you're safe. I heard a hiss and feared that arrow was for you."

"Nay, I called for the archer to shoot Olin." He lifted her head and shoulders carefully. "Do you hurt much?"

"Aye, all over."

"'Tis a good sign then. If the injury was great, you would feel naught but numbness. I thank God you fell only a short distance."

"I hung onto the wood up there for a moment, and fell onto Olin. But I may have twisted my ankle." She gripped

Adrien as she struggled to sit up. "Were you fighting Geoffrey?"

"'Tis strange, but I was. I had not thought him disloyal to you, but his dislike of Normans was obvious. Mayhap he attacked you? With his mother's herbs he discovered a way to alter his voice."

"I think both men attacked me. I knew something was different in the second attack. I think it was Geoffrey." She gasped. "Of course! The herb she would give Rypan! 'Tis foul and would render the boy mute at first, then change his voice for a few hours. Geoffrey must have used it."

When she tried to stand, he held her down. "Not yet, my love." He paused and the moment filled with promise. "Please. I don't want you to make your injuries worse."

With that, he eased up on his grip and slid his arms closer. She immediately obliged, snuggling into him. "But why Geoffrey?"

"We'll never know for sure. He's dead. I'd wager it was Olin who had convinced him of some evil plan."

"Olin wanted—"

"Not another word, my wife," Adrien interrupted. "Save your strength for the journey home. Shall I order a cart here for you?"

She pushed away and allowed Adrien to help her up. She leaned against him. "A cart is worse punishment than a horse."

"Then I'll carry you." Without another word, he scooped her up and carried her down the road to where the horses now stood. He set her up on his courser and mounted easily. With an order to have the ponies bring the two bodies to the keep, Adrien gently led the way home.

Sunrise glowed in the east as they finally reached the bailey. Adrien dismounted first before lifting her off the horse and carrying her up to her solar where Margaret waited anxiously. Ediva wanted to talk, as he expected, but he promised he'd return after she rested.

Ediva awoke to discover she ached worse than when she fell down the stairs. With a wince, she turned. Immediately, her maid was at her side. The woman fussed and doted until Ediva could stand it no more and ordered her away. The sun shone high, indicating 'twas nearly noon. A moment later, the door opened and Adrien entered with a tray in his hand. "Are all the servants too busy?" she asked, smiling.

"I promised you I would return and here I am."

He set down the tray and sent the maid away. Refusing help, Ediva hobbled to the table and began to set out the meal. Roast venison, vegetables, rich broth and sweet cheese pastries. And a large tankard of cold juice to wash it all down.

After giving thanks, they sat and ate for a moment, but Ediva could stand Adrien's calmness no longer.

"Olin wanted the keep," she blurted out. "He planned to kill you and offer to buy the title after I'd been executed for your death. He said he planned to tax the villagers further and only give the king a portion of it."

"'Tis not unheard of to collect one amount and write another in the ledger. Though William would have found out."

"Olin employed Geoffrey for his scheme."

Adrien nodded. "Aye. Geoffrey attacked you the second time in the keep. Olin would have been too sore from both the flogging and the attack on me. Geoffrey also took foodstuff from your larder to him as he hid in that tower, I've learned from Rypan, who would watch him. The steward didn't want a Norman here, so he tried several times to poison me. But Geoffrey didn't know that I dislike spicy food. I think Geoffrey's mother supplied the herbs and poison."

"And Olin killed her. How could Geoffrey continue helping him after that?"

Adrien paused and set down his knife. His expression was grim. "Nay, Ediva. Geoffrey killed his mother. I'm sure of it."

She gasped. Adrien went on, "We've examined the men's bodies. Olin had long feet, and the footprints we found in the midwife's hut were much smaller. Her son's size. Neighbors claim he was there early that day. Olin was never there."

Her stomach dismissing food now, she sat back. "But why would Geoffrey kill his own mother?"

"He'd warned you that he'd kill a villager if you didn't kill me. I'd say that he chose his mother because she knew he'd stolen the herbs to poison the food. I think the midwife feared repercussions. Geoffrey must have felt threatened by her. She likely knew of other crimes of his, for I believe he was the one who pocketed the coins Eudo left in the strongbox and then marked it down in the ledger as if Eudo had taken them."

Ediva nodded. "Aye, the coins I found in his laundry. I returned them to his mother, thinking them payment for eggs, so she certainly knew of them. 'Twould make sense, in an evil way. But why wasn't I killed by those herbs when he tried to poison you?"

"Margaret told me you vomited up all the food before it had a chance to work in your stomach. And she went to the midwife for some herbs to help you. That must have been when the woman realized what her son had done."

"No one would suspect he'd kill his own mother. And having died, she was no longer a risk to him."

As if trying to shield her from the awfulness of what

had happened, Adrien pulled her onto his lap. He drew her head down to snuggle in the crook of his neck and held her in silence for a moment, then said, "Ediva, 'twas foolish to think you could buy Olin off."

"I know." Without looking up, she continued, "I had to try. I was willing to offer him everything to save you. For a chance to be with you properly, as your wife should be with you."

His eyes warmed. "Why?"

"Because I love you." Her eyes watered over and his smiling face swam in unshed tears. "I've fallen in love with you. But…" She trailed off, uncertain if she could, or should, continue.

"Finish," he urged gently. "But what?"

"But you'll go to Ely, and I'm afraid you'll die there. You love soldiering more than anything."

"Ediva, I love you. And I have realized that I certainly love you more than I love fighting. When we married, I thought only of the battlefield. 'Twas safer for me than to expose my heart to anyone. But I was wrong. I fell in love with you and began to reconsider my life. I was only running away to protect my heart. But when I fight now, it won't be with a careless attitude. Now, I have something to fight for. My home here. My wife here. 'Tis more potent that any elixir to spur on survival."

He pulled in an uneven breath. "When I learned you refused to go to chapel, I didn't want to care for you and couldn't understand why God brought us together."

"To teach me how much He loves us."

"And to teach me not to tempt Him by my foolish ways. He needed to teach me to love even myself." He paused a moment.

Ediva brushed away the tear that had begun to trace a line down her cheek. She knew he'd go to Ely if the king ordered it, but with the love they were sharing and the many prayers they'd say, she knew he'd also return safely home.

Their new home.

Epilogue

Adrien puffed with pride as his wife, heavy with child, waddled like a duck out of the keep. Naturally, he didn't dare say those words, but he smiled nonetheless. A duck Ediva may resemble right now, but she was the most beautiful duck he'd ever seen.

The bailey gate opened and into the mud and mire of that wet, spring day rode three people on horseback. The first rider, Adrien's sergeant, carried Eudo's new banner as Baron of Colchester; the second was a woman and the third a guard.

Eudo's promise of a midwife had come to fruition. And just in time, Adrien thought, considering his wife's size.

There would soon be new life in this estate, he mused. 'Twas good.

Ediva finally stopped beside her husband. "The midwife?"

"Aye. And none too early, I would say. You'll deliver soon."

"Nay, I need a few more weeks. The babe has not yet dropped. But 'tis good to have her here. She'll be needed in the village sooner than I'll need her."

Though Adrien had been exempted from fighting in Northumberland, tensions were ever ripe to the north and they both knew the time may come when he'd be called to Ely. Hereward the Wake had settled in there, at the center of the fens that surrounded the estate, and was fully prepared to fight. But William's troops outnumbered his. The man whose fight was personal, the talk claimed, would soon lose.

Enough of that, Adrien told himself. He would enjoy his wife and, God willing, he'd see his first child grow strong.

The midwife, a young woman with dark red hair, accepted a hand from the sergeant as she dismounted, then closed the distance between them. After her courtesies, she asked to examine Ediva. The two women walked slowly into the keep.

Adrien turned to his sergeant. "What news have you brought with you?"

"You brother has taken a wife, my lord, and she is expecting their first child. All the stone has been gathered for the castle in Colchester, and that midwife has given me a headache."

Adrien laughed. "How so?"

"She has a will of her own and can outride most men. She comes with good knowledge, I'm told, though I wouldn't want to be ministered to by her."

"Mayhap she shall open a riding school between birthing children."

"I won't take lessons from her, my lord. She's already corrected me several times on my equestrian skills."

Chuckling, Adrien watched his wife turn at the door and smile at him. 'Twas good to see his wife have proper care and, realizing that, he offered up a prayer for all the blessings he'd received.

Of home and family. Of love and faith. Blessings from God Himself.

* * * * *

Dear Reader,

Almost 20 years ago, my daughter and I traveled to England to visit my sister and her family. She lived in Colchester, and I fell in love with the town. Its castle was fascinating. And atop of the town hall's roof were figures from the town's history. One of them, a tall slender man, stylized in typical Victorian fashion, was Eudes de Ries, or Eudo, as he was called. He was the first Constable of Colchester.

My fertile imagination took wings and flew. Having always been fascinated with medieval life, I could easily picture this man, a Norman, steward to William the Conqueror, having an abundant life. This led to a fictitious brother, Adrien, and eventually to the story you have just finished reading.

The story is more than real life and fictitious characters. The story is about love. God's love. Just as the father in the story of the prodigal son spotted his son from afar and hurried to him, God sees us coming slowly toward him from our own far away land of distrust and hurt and pain. He comes to us with open arms. This was something my heroine, Ediva, had to learn the hard way.

It's scary to relinquish the hold we have on ourselves and to trust God. And faith doesn't always start in a "Road to Damascus" moment. That's why we have the story of the mustard seed. So while the story is about love, it's also a story of encouragement, to keep going, to take those baby steps of trust and faith and remember the father that waits for you at the end of the road.

I invite you to email me at barbarap@eastlink.ca or drop me a note via the publisher with any comments you may have, and please pass on this book to a friend. I always enjoy reading and answering letters.

God bless,

Barbara Chinney

Questions for Discussion

1. What attracted you to this book? What kept you reading it?

2. To you, Adrien symbolized what Biblical figure?

3. Adrien tries to tell the story of the vine, but regrets it later. Have you ever told a Bible story, then thought it was not quite the right one to tell?

4. Did Ediva ring true to you? She lived in a different time and couldn't escape her first marriage. What would you have done in her place?

5. The chaplain would have received respect by virtue of his position. Considering the animosity between him and Ediva, how could he have done things differently?

6. Did Adrien appeal to you? How so?

7. "God is Love" is the theme of this story. Was it adequately portrayed here? Who best portrayed it in this story?

8. Have you ever wondered if God was out to get you for your sins? If so, what did you do?

9. Harry, who plays comic relief in this story, is similar to Eudo. What did you think of this boy's character? Did he ring true to you?

10. Eudo de Ries was a real person and well-liked in Colchester. Did you like his character? Why or why not?

11. Any author looks for emotional impact in a story. What scene provided the most emotional impact for you?

12. Ediva's return to God is slow and unsure, and she doesn't immediately feel anything wonderful, just feels a little peace. If you have given your life to God, how was your conversion?

COMING NEXT MONTH
from Love Inspired® Historical
AVAILABLE APRIL 2, 2013

SECOND CHANCE PROPOSAL
Amish Brides of Celery Fields
Anna Schmidt
John Amman never forgot Lydia Goodloe when he left to make his fortune in the outside world. But when the prodigal son returns to his Amish community will his first love welcome him with open arms?

FAMILY LESSONS
Orphan Train
Allie Pleiter
Plain Jane school teacher Holly Sanders thinks no man will ever love her. But a catastrophe in her small Nebraska town leaves her wondering if she should take a risk with brooding sheriff Mason Wright.

HIS MOUNTAIN MISS
Smoky Mountain Matches
Karen Kirst
Lucian Beaumont is a jaded aristocrat, and Megan O'Malley is a simple farmer's daughter. The terms of his grandfather's will brought them together—and now she's challenging his plans and his heart.

THE BRIDE WORE SPURS
Janet Dean
Self-sufficient tomboy Hannah Parrish will do anything to save her ranch and give her dying father peace of mind, even if it means marrying a widowed rancher determined to protect his heart.

Look for these and other Love Inspired books wherever books are sold, including most bookstores, supermarkets, discount stores and drugstores.

LIHCNM0313

REQUEST YOUR FREE BOOKS!

2 FREE INSPIRATIONAL NOVELS
PLUS 2
FREE
MYSTERY GIFTS

Love Inspired.
HISTORICAL
INSPIRATIONAL HISTORICAL ROMANCE

YES! Please send me 2 FREE Love Inspired® Historical novels and my 2 FREE mystery gifts (gifts are worth about $10). After receiving them, if I don't wish to receive any more books, I can return the shipping statement marked "cancel." If I don't cancel, I will receive 4 brand-new novels every month and be billed just $4.49 per book in the U.S. or $4.99 per book in Canada. That's a saving of at least 22% off the cover price. It's quite a bargain! Shipping and handling is just 50¢ per book in the U.S. and 75¢ per book in Canada.* I understand that accepting the 2 free books and gifts places me under no obligation to buy anything. I can always return a shipment and cancel at any time. Even if I never buy another book, the two free books and gifts are mine to keep forever.

102/302 IDN FVXK

Name	(PLEASE PRINT)	

Address		Apt. #

City	State/Prov.	Zip/Postal Code

Signature (if under 18, a parent or guardian must sign)

Mail to the Harlequin® Reader Service:
IN U.S.A.: P.O. Box 1867, Buffalo, NY 14240-1867
IN CANADA: P.O. Box 609, Fort Erie, Ontario L2A 5X3

Want to try two free books from another series?
Call 1-800-873-8635 or visit www.ReaderService.com.

* Terms and prices subject to change without notice. Prices do not include applicable taxes. Sales tax applicable in N.Y. Canadian residents will be charged applicable taxes. Offer not valid in Quebec. This offer is limited to one order per household. Not valid for current subscribers to Love Inspired Historical books. All orders subject to credit approval. Credit or debit balances in a customer's account(s) may be offset by any other outstanding balance owed by or to the customer. Please allow 4 to 6 weeks for delivery. Offer available while quantities last.

Your Privacy—The Harlequin® Reader Service is committed to protecting your privacy. Our Privacy Policy is available online at www.ReaderService.com or upon request from the Harlequin Reader Service.

We make a portion of our mailing list available to reputable third parties that offer products we believe may interest you. If you prefer that we not exchange your name with third parties, or if you wish to clarify or modify your communication preferences, please visit us at www.ReaderService.com/consumerschoice or write to us at Harlequin Reader Service Preference Service, P.O. Box 9062, Buffalo, NY 14269. Include your complete name and address.

LIH13

SPECIAL EXCERPT FROM

Love Inspired HISTORICAL

*When a tragedy brings a group of orphans to a small
Nebraska town, shy schoolteacher Holly Sanders is
determined to find the children homes...and soften dour
sheriff Mason Wright's heart, along the way!
Read on for a sneak preview of*

FAMILY LESSONS by Allie Pleiter,
the first in the ORPHAN TRAIN series.

"You saved us," Holly said, as she moved toward
Sheriff Wright.

He looked at her, his blue eyes brittle and hollow. She so
rarely viewed those eyes—downcast as they often were or
hidden in the shadow of his hat brim. "No."

"But it is true." Mason Wright was the kind of man who
would take Arlington's loss as a personal failure, ignoring
all the lives—including hers—he had just saved, and she
hated that. Hated that she'd fail in this attempt just as she
failed in *every* attempt to make him see his worth.

He held her gaze just then. "No," he repeated, but only a
little softer. Then his attention spread out beyond her to take
in the larger crisis at hand.

"Is she the other agent?" He nodded toward Rebecca
Sterling and the upset children, now surrounded by the few
other railcar passengers. "Liam mentioned a Miss..."

"Sterling, yes, that's her. Liam!" Holly suddenly remembered the brave orphan boy who'd run off to get help. "Is
Liam all right?"

"Shaken, but fine. Clever boy."

"I was so worried, sending him off."

He looked at her again, this time with something she could almost fool herself into thinking was admiration. "It was quick and clever. If anyone saved the day here, it was you."

Holly blinked. From Mason Wright, that was akin to a complimentary gush. "It was the only thing I could think of to do."

A child's cry turned them both toward the bedlam surrounding Miss Sterling. The children were understandably out of control with fear and shock, and Miss Sterling didn't seem to be in any shape to take things in hand. Who would be in such a situation?

She would, that's who. Holly was an excellent teacher with a full bag of tricks at her disposal to wrangle unruly children. With one more deep breath, she strode off to save the day a second time.

Don't miss FAMILY LESSONS
by Allie Pleiter, available April 2013
from Love Inspired Historical.

Copyright © 2013 by Harlequin Books, S.A.

LIEXP0313

Love Inspired HISTORICAL

In the fan-favorite miniseries
Amish Brides of Celery Fields

ANNA SCHMIDT

presents

Second Chance Proposal

The sweetest homecoming.
He came home…for her.
A love rekindled.

Lydia Goodloe hasn't forgotten a single thing about John Amman—
including the way he broke her heart eight years ago. Since John
left Celery Fields to make his fortune, Lydia has devoted herself
to teaching. John risked becoming an outcast to give Lydia
everything she deserved. He couldn't see that what she really
wanted was a simple life—with him. Lydia is no longer the girl
he knew. Now she's the woman who can help him reclaim their
long-ago dream of home and family…if he can only win her
trust once more.

Amish Brides

CELERY FIELDS

Love awaits these Amish women.

www.LoveInspiredBooks.com
LIH82959